RW 5

DEATH AT THE VET'S

Her watch read two minutes to eight. Stan glanced down the hall where the exam rooms waited. Somewhere in the clinic she heard a door quietly close. Maybe Carole had gone out back and was returning. She should let her know she was here.

Stan took a few steps, listened. Quiet. "Hello?"

Nothing. The first door on the left was closed. The one next to it was a bathroom, its door open, the room empty. Across the hall, another exam room, but this door stood ajar. Stan walked over, pushed it wider and peeked in.

"Carole? Nutty and I are he—"

Stan stopped. On the floor, just visible behind the exam table, was a Merrell clog. With a foot inside it. Stan took another tentative step and saw a leg. Horizontal.

"Oh my gosh, Carole! Did you fall?"

She rushed around the table and gasped, recoiling, slamming her hip in her haste to get away, a horrified scream working its way up her throat.

The vet lay on the floor, unseeing eyes staring up at the ceiling. A needle protruded from her neck, her still body and long white hair covered in kibble . . .

KNEADING TO DIE

LIZ MUGAVERO

KENSINGTON PUBLISHING CORP.
http://www.kensingtonbooks.com

KENSINGTON BOOKS are published by

Kensington Publishing Corp.
119 West 40th Street
New York, NY 10018

All Kensington Titles, Imprints, and Distributed Lines are available at special quantity discounts for bulk purchases for sales promotions, premiums, fund-raising, and educational or institutional use. Special book excerpts or customized printings can also be created to fit specific needs. For details, write or phone the office of the Kensington special sales manager: Kensington Publishing Corp., 119 West 40th Street, New York, NY 10018, attn: Special Sales Department, Phone: 1-800-221-2647.

Kensington and the K logo Reg. U.S. Pat & TM Off.

ISBN-13: 978-0-7582-8478-5
ISBN-10: 0-7582-8478-0

First Mass Market Printing: May 2013

10 9 8 7 6 5 4 3 2 1

Printed in the United States of America

For my Gramp. Wish you were here to read this.

Acknowledgments

This book would never have happened without the Sisters in Crime New England chapter under Sheila Connolly's leadership, and my agent John Talbot who was looking for writers in all the right places. Thank you, Sheila, for presenting this opportunity for me to realize my dream. And thank you, John, for recognizing the need for gourmet pet food in the world.

Sherry Harris, my dear friend and crack editor, made the book a million times better with her amazing eye for detail before I handed it over to John Scognamiglio, my editor at Kensington, who gave it his expert eye.

Dr. Alexis Soutter of the Manchester Veterinary Clinic in Manchester, Conn., generously gave her time and expertise to explain my choice of weapons at a vet hospital. Also, thanks to Dr. Martha Lindsay of Alternative Veterinary Services in North Andover, Mass., who is a champion of homeopathy and nutrition for animals. She has educated me since the day I met her, and has been a hero to animals for many years.

Eric Walsh, owner of The Big Biscuit in Franklin, Mass., deserves props for sharing his nutritional (and bakery) secrets. Eric invited me to spend time in his store, explaining everything from business plans to dried cow tracheas. His input has been invaluable and I look forward to learning more tricks of the trade as the series continues.

My writing mentors: Seascape Writers Retreat teachers Hallie Ephron, Roberta Isleib, Susan Hubbard and Hank Phillippi Ryan; Jenny Siler; my fellow Sisters in Crime and Guppy members; and the Wingate Writers Group, where it all began for me—thank you all for your contributions to my career, and happy publishing to all of you.

A special thanks to my companions on this amazing publishing journey: Edith Maxwell/Tace Baker, Jessie Crockett and Barbara Ross for their support, critiques and insightful ways of looking at plots and characters. To many more fabulous York beach house retreats! And to Christine Hillman Keyes for her never-ending support and friendship.

Thank you to my animal rescue friends and all the amazing groups I've been lucky enough to be affiliated with over the years, but especially Journey Ewell from Friends of Manchester Animal Shelter and Geraldine Tom of Animal Rescue Fund. What you do for animals is truly awesome. So many other groups including CT Votes for Animals, Our Companions, Salem Animal Rescue League, Friends of Feral Cheshire (Conn.) Cats, Merrimack River Feline Rescue Society, The Pat Brody Shelter, Brooklyn Bridge Animal Welfare Coalition and Throwaway Pups also deserve major kudos for helping our furry friends.

Cynthia and Doug Fleck—who says families have to be blood relations? Thanks for always being there. And Kim Fleck, I wouldn't be where I am today without you to believe in me and teach me what truly matters. For all the patience, love, support and extra scooping, thank you. You inspire me every day. Love you!

And to the furries—Tuffy, who wandered into the yard one day and never left, and Shaggy, rescue dog from South Carolina, the models for Nutty and Scruffy. And the rest of the crew (also all rescues), who teach me unconditional love daily. Life wouldn't be complete without you.

Chapter 1

"You, missy, are a two-bit hack."

The harsh words, shouted from next door, broke the stillness of the small-town Saturday and startled Stan Connor enough that she dropped her last moving box. The one full of things she didn't trust the movers or Richard to handle. Miraculously, Richard leaped over and saved it, right before it almost hit the pavement in her new driveway.

"And I'll make sure everyone in town knows it." The shouting continued, creeping closer.

Stan and Richard turned to see a woman with long white hair storm down the driveway to their left, jabbing a finger at someone they couldn't see.

"Oh, try it," another voice yelled back. "Everyone will see who's really the hack. You're not the star you think you are around here!"

The white-haired woman said something else Stan couldn't hear and stormed over to a green SUV. She got in, revved the engine and roared down the road. A thirtyish woman, with a golden retriever by her side, appeared. She watched the truck disappear. When she realized she had on-lookers she turned abruptly, called the dog and vanished into the house.

Stan glanced over at Richard, who watched the scene with interest.

"So much for peace, love and harmony in a small town," Richard said with a smirk. "You sure you don't want to rethink the condo in the city?"

Stan shook her head. "Not a chance. See? You thought I'd be bored, but now I have front-row seats for the neighborhood brawls. They were too proper for that in West Hartford." Stan closed the car door. "I wonder what that was about."

Richard precariously balanced his last two boxes, hefting them higher into his arms. "Who knows? Maybe she didn't milk the cow right."

"I don't see cows in the yard. But there's a dairy farm two houses down."

"Yeah, I can smell it."

"Oh, hush." Stan held the heavy oak front door, with the beveled glass sidelights, open for him, forgetting all about the argument as she stepped into her new home. Victorian. Bright. Happy. And all hers.

"Can you put those on the kitchen table? Care-fully? My Vitamix is in that box."

He grunted at her as he moved inside, trying not to trip with his cargo. Stan stood on her new porch and surveyed her surroundings. Her yard. Her driveway. Her town green—didn't it belong to everyone, after all?—directly across from her house, its grass lush and inviting in the summer sun. Her neighbors. Cows, arguments and all.

She loved Frog Ledge already.

She followed Richard into her new tangerine-colored kitchen, wincing as he dropped the box on the table. She heard a clatter from within the heavy cardboard and sighed.

"Have you seen Nutty?" Her Maine coon cat didn't like upheaval and hadn't been thrilled with the move. He'd been hiding since she'd let him out of his carrier.

Richard opened the box and began pulling out kitchen paraphernalia. "The Vitamix looks fine," he said, pulling out the beloved machine she used for everything from soup to smoothies to frozen drinks. "And no, I haven't seen the cat."

"I hope he didn't sneak out in the last-box frenzy." Stan hip-checked Richard out of the way and finished unpacking the box herself. "You can unpack dishes. Or better yet, how about basement stuff?" She turned, waiting for his response, and caught him glancing at his watch.

"What? Oh. Sure. I have a little more time. I told Carl I'd meet him for drinks tonight. You're welcome to join us."

"For drinks. With Carl. Gee, that sounds great, but I'll have to pass. Got a little bit of work to do." *Work that my boyfriend should volunteer to help with.*

"Oh. Well, next time," Richard said, completely missing her sarcasm. "Unless you find really cool things to do around here. In Frog Ledge." His tone suggested she would be more likely to find a rainbow with a pot of gold at the end of it during her morning run.

"Is it necessary to be so derogatory? This town is beautiful. This house is beautiful." Stan swept an arm around her colorful, empty kitchen, already imagining what treasures she could find to make it her own. "Just because it isn't the city doesn't mean you have to shoot it down."

He was raining on her parade, and she didn't have many parades these days. But today she'd woken up excited about the move—so excited, in fact, that she'd chosen a theme song for the day. Something she hadn't done since "The Elimination." And even though it was the cheesy eighties song "I'm So Excited," heck, it was still a theme song.

She was getting back on track.

"Come on, Stan. You're angry about your position being eliminated. I get it." Richard took the empty box out of her hand, collapsed it for recycling. "I wish you'd thought more about it before up and moving out here. I mean, who even comes to this side of Connecticut? Except to go to the casinos. And who lives in a town called Frog Ledge? We could've figured something else out."

Nutty chose that moment to slink around the corner. Stan ran her hand down his back to the tip of his tail as he proceeded cautiously by her to investigate the unpacking. And probably look for his homemade treats, which she was running low on.

"Who's 'we'? Like you pointed out, I'm the one who lost my job." She yanked open a drawer and threw utensils in it. "You're still Richard Ruse, vice president, fancy-pants sales guy. Your life didn't change much, aside from having to drive a half hour to my house instead of ten minutes."

Richard still worked at Warner Insurance, the financial giant where Stan had ruled the media spotlight. Until two months ago. Losing her beloved public relations job—and corresponding expense account—gave her the right to be a little cranky, didn't it? She was trying to make the best of having her professional life and most of her social life yanked away. Not dwell on the past, and all that. And moving had seemed the most appropriate way to do that.

"Of course this changes things for me," Richard said patiently. "We were a great power couple in the company."

Her face must have said it all. He had the decency to flush. "You know what I mean. Look, all I'm saying, Stan, is you didn't have to move to the other side of nowhere. And financially, staying in the condo would've been better. Smarter."

She turned, eyes narrowed. "Don't play that card with me. We both know I'm in better financial shape unemployed than most people are working. I paid for this house in cash. I'm good with investments, to put it mildly. And I'm getting severance for almost two years. Money is not the driver here. Changing my scenery was. Now, can we not argue? I'd like to unpack and enjoy my new house. And I wish you would enjoy it with me." She hefted the next box onto the counter and began pulling out dishes, piling them in cabinets.

"I am enjoying it with you," he said, his voice soothing. "Want me to hang some of your pictures in here? I brought my tools." He picked one up from the pile the movers had leaned against the wall. It was a depiction of a Paris café, only the backs of the patrons visible as they faced the city street.

"Sure. I think there." She pointed above her two-seater bistro table.

Richard picked up his tool bag and pulled out a level, hammer and nails. He held the picture against the wall. "Tell me where."

"A little higher. Over to the left." Stan stood back, cocked her head to determine if the picture was straight. "That's good."

She watched as he marked the wall and banged in the nails. Handsome, no doubt about it, with wavy brown hair and big blue eyes. Tall too. She could always wear whatever size heels she wanted when they went out. And such a smooth talker. What else would you expect from a salesman?

She turned abruptly and went back to the dishes.

"Listen," he said, intent on his task, "I talked to Mick Harvey yesterday, and he thinks he can talk to the New York folks about finding you something in a different division. You could probably still be based in Hartford. It wouldn't be exactly like your old job, but—"

"Enough." Stan slammed the cabinet shut so hard, the contents inside rattled. "I don't want to talk about Warner anymore. I don't want to work at Warner anymore. And I don't want you talking to Warner people about me. End of story, Richard."

He finished with the picture and stepped back to admire his work, unfazed by her reaction. "You won't be happy without a job. We both know that. May as well see what they have to offer."

"I wouldn't be happy going back there, either. They didn't want me anymore. They made that clear. Frankly, I don't need them. I certainly don't need to beg anyone for a job, thank you very much. When I want one, I'll find one with no problem." She hoped.

"Come on, Stan. What did you think would happen? McAllister was in a bad spot." Richard moved up behind her and placed his hands on her shoulders, rubbing at the tension there. Waiting for her to see his point. People usually saw Richard's point. That was how he pulled in six figures in commissions last year. "He had to place blame somewhere. You know the game. Jeez, you're a top player."

"Are you defending McAllister?" Stan heard her voice rising, but she couldn't rein it back in. She moved out of his reach. "The president of the company gets caught screwing the competitor president's wife, and it's my fault the media picked up the story? My fault the statement didn't sound better? You really have been drinking the Kool-Aid. There was nothing I could have done to spin that. *Nothing.* Not to mention, by the time I got called, it was too late. And by the way," she said, kicking an empty box across the room, sending Nutty running, "no one really gives a damn what that pompous ass is doing. They were just curious about how he scored a decent-looking mistress."

Richard's blue eyes turned icy, as if she'd insulted him personally. He opened his mouth to respond, but the doorbell rang, shutting them both up.

"Who's that?" he asked.

"No idea." She turned her back on him and headed for the front door. He trailed behind, his footsteps on the hardwood floors sending echoes throughout the empty house.

Stan pulled open the front door. Her mouth dropped in surprise. An unlikely trio stood on her porch. Two women and a man. The older of the women held hands with the man. At first glance they were an odd match. She had short, flame-colored hair teased up off her head and sprayed into place. Despite the heat of the July day, she wore a long-sleeved pink-and-orange paisley dress, which made her generous frame appear even larger. Platform flip-flops had her towering over her partner. Glittery silver eye shadow caked over each eye reminded Stan of her nightclubbing, dancing-until-dawn days. By contrast, her companion, a fiftyish or sixtyish man with a beard and kind eyes, was skinny enough that his jeans were held up by checkered suspenders. He wore a straw hat and looked like he'd just left the farm. Which, around here, he probably had.

The younger woman could be a fashion model. Or a basketball player, given her height. Stan had to look up to see her. Eyes covered by Jackie O sunglasses, long black hair weaved into hundreds of braids. She wore skinny capri jeans, a tank top and purple flip-flops. With one hand, she held on to two leashes, one attached to a boxer and the other to a poodle. In the other she carried a huge basket wrapped in pink cellophane.

The group broke into a cheerful chorus of

"Welcome to the neighborhood!" The poodle woofed. The boxer wagged his tail.

"Oh, my goodness! How nice! I'm Stan Connor." Stan stepped out on the porch and held out her hand.

The man reached over and shook first. His grip was hearty and strong. "Ray Mackey. This is my wife, Char," he said. "We run Alpaca Haven, the bed-and-breakfast–slash–alpaca farm down the way a bit. And that's Izzy," he said, pulling the model/basketball player up next to him. "Isabella Sweet, of the infamous sweetshop, also down the way, but thataway." He pointed in the other direction.

"A pleasure," Izzy said, a slight British accent lilting her voice. She lifted one hand in a wave. A ring in the shape of a gigantic purple daisy almost hit Ray in the face. Brilliant red nails with glittered tips stood out against her caramel-colored skin.

"Honey, did you say 'Stan'?" Char interrupted, knocking her husband out of the way to clasp Stan's hand.

"I did," she said, smiling. "It's short for—"

"I think it's delightful!" Char exclaimed. "I love unique names. I don't even want to know what it stands for."

That surprised Stan. People were always curious when they heard her name. Most agreed it was the most unique nickname for Kristan they'd ever heard. Char, apparently, wasn't most people. She leaned forward and bussed Stan's cheek, noticing Richard lurking in the hall when she did so.

"And who's this?"

"That's Richard." Stan motioned to him to come

out. She shot him a sideways glance that said, *Have some manners.*

Richard stepped forward; his smile was more of a grimace, his handshake formal and proper. "Richard Ruse. Nice to meet you."

"Would you like to come in? For, um, tea?" Stan asked her guests, trying to remember if she'd unpacked her teapot yet.

"Oh, honey, we saw the movers leave just a while ago. You're in no shape to entertain," Char said, but she craned her neck to see around Richard into the house until Ray poked her arm. "We just wanted to drop off something small to welcome y'all to the neighborhood. Izzy?" She motioned to her. Izzy stepped forward and presented Stan with the basket.

"Some treats Char and I put together," she said. "Enjoy."

Stan accepted the generous basket, which looked like it had enough gourmet coffee and goodies to tide her over for the rest of the year. How exciting, to have the owner of the sweetshop on her porch! She'd driven by the shop twice now, but she hadn't yet made it inside. Simply seeing it had been a relief. She'd never tell Richard, but she had been worried about the seeming lack of good coffee in the area. Izzy's shop would take care of that.

"Izzy Sweet's Sweets! I'm dying to get there. And these dogs are treasures. Can they have a treat?" She crouched down to pet them. The boxer nudged his face into Stan's hand. The poodle hung back.

"You can give it a whirl," Izzy said. "Elvira is very

choosy." She nodded to the poodle. "But Baxter will eat anything." The boxer waved his tail in agreement.

"Hang on," Stan said. She went into the kitchen, deposited her basket on the table and took two treats out of Nutty's fish-shaped treat jar. She saw him watching her from around the corner. Was it her imagination, or was he chastising her with those brilliant green eyes?

"Come on, Nutty. We have to be nice to the neighbors," she said. "Don't want to get off on the wrong foot. I'm baking more soon. Okay?"

Nutty turned and stalked away, his fluffy tail standing tall like a proud plume. Or like his own version of a middle finger. Stan went back to the crowd on her porch. Richard wasn't entertaining. He stood there like he'd landed on another planet and didn't anticipate knowing the language. Stan crouched again in front of the dogs and held the treats. Baxter wolfed his down. Elvira came forward and sniffed delicately.

"I'm sorry," Izzy began; then her eyes widened in amazement as the dog plucked the treat daintily from Stan's hand and devoured it. "Well, that's a switch," she said. "What kind of treat was that?"

"Homemade," Stan said proudly. "I bake them for my cat. They're peanut butter and bran."

"Really!" Izzy reached down and scratched Elvira's ears. "I may have to hire you to bake some for me. She's a hard dog to feed sometimes."

"I'd be happy to," Stan said. "I have a bunch of recipes just begging to be made. As soon as I put the house in order, that is. For now, I'll be making the basics. Cheddar cheese treats are on the list next, once I get unpacked. If you want to stop by in a day or two, I'll save you some."

"We just might," Izzy said. Elvira woofed her agreement.

"Well, we'll leave you to it," Ray said, his grip firmly on Char's arm as she edged closer to the door to take another look inside. "Call us if you need anything. I'm the handyman around town, too. I can fix anything. And help you move things."

"Yes, honey, that's right. My Ray can do anything. And I can bring over a bottle of wine and we can have a few sips and watch him work." She winked at Stan and tugged Ray's hand. "We'll leave you to get unpacked. Come over soon and meet the alpacas!"

Stan grinned. She already liked her new neighbors. "Thank you all. I'll see you soon!"

"Come down to the shop when you're settled," Izzy said. "We'll have coffee and I'll tell you all the gossip. Let's go, dogs." She tugged at the leashes. Baxter trotted after her. Elvira continued to stare at Stan. Waiting for another treat, apparently.

"Wait." Stan ran back inside, dumped the remainder of the treats into a bag and prayed Nutty would still speak to her. She returned to the door and brandished the bag. "Take these for her."

"Are you sure?"

"Positive. Nutty eats too much, anyway."

"Say thanks, baby doll," Izzy urged Elvira. Stan fed the dog one more treat, then handed the bag over. Elvira trotted away, only after she saw the goods change hands.

Stan watched them walk down the driveway,

then closed her front door. "Well, wasn't that sweet," she said.

"They seemed a little . . . odd."

"Odd, how? They were nice. And did you see that basket? I need to find my coffeemaker. Did you see what box it ended up in?"

Richard followed her back to the kitchen. "You don't think this scene will wear on your last nerve?"

"Any more than you are right now?" She smiled sweetly to take the sting out of her words. "I don't. I think it will be fun. I never had my neighbors as friends before."

"They'll be all up in your business in no time. You'll hate it. And then you'll beg me to let you move into my place. And, of course, I'll let you." He grinned.

"Gee, thanks. So, do you want to go to the co-op? I'm dying to check it out. I'll get some fresh veggies and make us a late lunch. Or do you want to hang more pictures?"

Richard hesitated. "I should probably get going. I told Carl I'd meet him around five, and I need to shower." He glanced down at his spotless khakis and golf shirt.

Stan pasted an agreeable smile on her face. "Sure. Can you at least leave your level so I can hang some things?"

"I can come back and do it, babe. I'm only in Chicago until Wednesday."

"Oh, that's right. You're leaving tomorrow." For the big sales conference she, too, had attended every year that she worked at Warner.

"I am." He watched her, his face a mixture of

pity and smugness that said, *I told you so.* "See, you will miss it. Do you want me to call Mick?"

"No," she snapped. "Enjoy your trip. Leave the tools. I'm perfectly capable of hanging pictures." Theme song: Sinatra. "*My Way.*" Or maybe Billy Joel's "*My Life*"? Maybe she'd get crazy and not even use the level.

He held up his hands in surrender. "Okay. I'm sorry. I hate leaving right now."

Sure you do. "Thanks for helping. And it's fine. It'll give me a chance to put the house in order." She thought of Ray's offer. "Maybe I can get some of my new neighbors to help."

The quiet could either kill her or save her. Stan wasn't sure which. Not that she could admit that to Richard.

After he left, she'd gone to the town co-op and selected her favorite organic vegetables—mushrooms, zucchini, red peppers, onions, carrots and tomatoes—and made roasted veggies and goat cheese for dinner. Then she opened the bottle of wine she'd picked up so she and Richard could celebrate her new home, poured a glass and decided to take advantage of her new back deck. She opened the French doors to the sunroom, which overlooked her fenced-in backyard, surrounded by full, lush trees and the faint outline of hills in the distance. She stood at the screen door and breathed it all in.

How could Richard not see the beauty of this place? The view was amazing. The air smelled cleaner than any air she'd smelled in a long time.

Well, aside from the manure. And the sense of town camaraderie was apparent in just one afternoon.

Not to mention her new house. What a treasure! It made her smile from the outside in. The happy mint green color brightened up the whole street, which alternated between farmhouses, historical buildings, town offices and some older, gently worn homes. It even outshone the new construction, in her opinion. The dusty rose trim, the inviting front porch accented with latticework, the dollhouse feel. The pointed roof on the south side. The two-car garage set off the driveway, which she had big plans for. She wasn't sure yet what the plans would be, but she'd figure it out.

The house had been a chance finding while accompanying her best friend on a rescue dog delivery. Nikki ran a transport group called Pets' Last Chance, saving dogs from high-kill shelters down south and placing them with families all over the East Coast.

On that particular day Nikki had dragged her along for the ride after swearing she wouldn't let Stan sit around moping about her job for one more day. As Stan stared morosely out the van window, thinking about all the ways her life had turned to crap, the house suddenly appeared, bold and bright and happy. Fate. Once the dog, a beagle named Seamus, had been delivered to his new home, the Realtor had taken them through. Peering around every corner into a new room had given her that delicious feeling of anticipation she hadn't experienced in a long time.

And the rest of the house hadn't disappointed, from the ceiling-to-floor bookshelves in the study to the narrow hallways and shining woodwork, to the large sunroom that begged for a person to curl up with a cup of coffee and a good book. Or the rounded cubby with a window seat on the top floor looking out to the east, over the rolling farmlands. Stan fell in love and knew that minute she had to move here, even though she'd never heard of Frog Ledge before that day.

"Impulsive," her mother had always called her. Richard did, too. She agreed with them, to a point. Some things took her forever to decide on, like the perfect color to paint a room. Others, like buying this house, were intuitive.

Even the name was charming. The Realtor told her this area was highly committed to frogs because of their role in the Revolutionary War, and that she'd have to go read about it sometime at the historical society.

She would, once she unpacked. On her first night, though, the quiet seemed almost ominous. No traffic. No loud music. Somewhere around her the faint sound of children, but brief. She shrugged it off. She was letting Richard's scorn for small towns influence her. Quiet was good. She'd have plenty of time to think.

Her iPhone buzzed from her back pocket. She pulled it out. Nikki Manning, the screen announced. Of course it was. She and her best friend of twenty-plus years practically shared a brain.

"How'd the move go? All unpacked?" Nikki sounded like she was standing in a wind tunnel. Probably in the middle of some Southern town, with twenty dogs in her van.

"It went fine. Only two things broken so far.

Although one of them was a mirror, so I'm worried. And no, not unpacked yet."

"I'm really sorry I couldn't help. If I didn't pick up the dogs today, they weren't getting another twenty-four hours."

"Don't be silly. Saving puppies is way more important."

"Is Richard there?"

"No, he left a while ago," she said, anticipating Nikki's reaction. Nikki and Richard's love-hate relationship began when Stan started dating him four years ago, and the feelings were still going strong. Nikki didn't hate him, exactly. She just had strong opinions on whether or not he was good enough for Stan. "He had to get ready for Chicago. The sales conference."

"Ah. You'll miss going this year."

Stan shrugged, although Nikki couldn't see her. She moved over to the reclining lounger, her one new piece of furniture so far, and sank onto it. So comfy. Perfect for this room, and it reminded her of the one her grandmother had on their porch when Stan was a kid. "I guess."

"I know you will. You've been going every year and now it feels like it's going on without you. I get it."

"It is going on without me." Stan sighed. It did feel, well, bad. "But you know what? There's nothing I can do. It's fine, Nik."

"It is fine," Nikki agreed. "You always told me the food wasn't that great, anyway."

"True." Stan could hear dogs barking in the background. "Where are you?"

"Still in South Carolina. My pickups got pushed

back. I should've been home hours ago, but I'm going to be delayed until Monday."

"Why did they get pushed back?"

"Same old. They closed the facility to rescues because someone had a fight with someone, and the animals ended up paying for it. I just told them I would park myself outside until they opened the doors, because I had people waiting for these dogs."

"And it worked?"

Stan could hear her friend grin over the phone. "Guess they were sick of seeing my face. That, and the call I threatened to put in to the local news about how they stonewall rescues. So they're opening tomorrow."

"Always making friends, aren't you?"

"Someone's gotta do it. Pets' Last Chance doesn't mess around." The rescue had been Nikki's dream since college. Today her operation saved about five thousand dogs each year. "I'll be over to help you as soon as I'm home. Stopping at the vet on the way, but I'll call you."

"Thanks, Nik. Hey, I met some of my neighbors."

"Oh yeah? How are they?"

Stan thought of Richard's reaction and chuckled. "They seem cool. Quirky, but I wouldn't expect anything less. Oh, and the woman who runs the sweetshop came. They brought me a basket of goodies. Definitely relationships I want to cultivate."

"Amen, sistah." The chorus of barking rose in volume and Nikki sighed. "Okay, I'm gonna sign off. These guys are too loud for me to hear myself think. Enjoy your first night in the new house!"

Stan promised she would and ended the call. Then she listened to the silence around her, broken only by crickets chirping outside her door. She locked up and headed back to the kitchen. At least if she busied herself baking Nutty's treats, she'd feel more at home.

Chapter 2

Somewhere nearby, a rooster *cock-a-doodle-dooed.* Groggy, Stan forced herself out of the dream. The sound continued. After a moment of utter confusion, she realized it wasn't a dream. She lived in Frog Ledge now, and roosters lived in her neighborhood. How funny was that!

If she didn't let it be funny, it would scare the heck out of her.

Her next thought: She'd survived her first night. That, in itself, was cause for celebration.

"We did it, Nutty," she told the cat, who sat on alert in the window. He was looking for roosters or watching a squirrel. And planning his escape so he could chase either of them. She joined him.

The Frog Ledge town green stretched across the lazy summer morning. Its grass was lush and dewy and inviting; its gravel path cut through the sheer greenness. Stan opened her window wider and leaned forward, trying to catch that heady summer scent before the heat of the day baked it away.

Before she could stop herself, she was humming

the melody to *"What a Wonderful World."* Tacky, but so what?

"I guess that's the theme song for the day," she said. Nutty seemed unimpressed. He liked contemporary music much better.

"You'll have to pick your own, then. I've gotta go with the first one that pops into my head." When her former coworker had educated her on theme songs, that was her main advice: Let it pick you. You'll know what you need to get through the day. And that's how it was in corporate America—a whole lot of getting through the day. Maybe here she could find better uses for her theme songs.

Still humming, she dressed in her new Under Armour running gear before she even went downstairs for coffee. Over the last year her work schedule had been so demanding she had slacked off on working out. Now she was going to run. And ride the bike she'd bought last year and never used. Maybe she'd even train for a triathlon, or one of those crazy races where the participants crawled through the mud under barbed wire. Something to add to her bucket list. The one she'd never had time to create.

In her new master bathroom she washed her face and twisted her long blond hair into a ponytail. Laced up her pink Pumas and jogged downstairs. She threw veggies, fruit, juice, protein powder and ice into the Vitamix and made her morning smoothie, chugging it down as fast as she could without suffering brain freeze. Deciding to wait on her coffee until she came back, she grabbed her water bottle and iPod and went out the front door.

Frog Ledge got moving early, even on a Sunday. Walkers and runners had already hit the trail, and a maintenance worker rode an enormous lawn mower around the gazebo. His blades cleared the view for the cluster of signs announcing a special town referendum meeting, a spaghetti dinner, story time at the library and a "Meet Our Town" evening with local vendors.

Stan crossed the street and began to jog, fitting her earbuds into her ears. She cranked up the volume on her favorite running playlist and focused on breathing so she didn't get a cramp. It had been ages since she'd allowed time for a morning run. It felt awesome.

The path was wide enough for two people to pass comfortably. She exchanged waves with other runners. Everyone was so friendly. Completely different than running in her old neighborhood. Between avoiding traffic, construction spilling over onto the sidewalks and snobby shoppers crowding downtown, she'd stopped bothering.

A Rollerblader whizzed by, artfully dodging walkers and runners. A double stroller followed, a tiny woman jogging behind it. The contraption was so wide that Stan had to dodge into the grass to avoid her as she passed.

"Sorry!" the woman called, waving apologetically.

Stan waved back in a gesture that meant *It's fine.* In the process she almost tripped over another woman, meditating on a blanket. The woman's eyes flew open at the disturbance. Stan slowed and yanked her right earbud out.

"I'm so sorry. I almost got run over, too."

The meditator waved her off. "It's no problem. All these exercisers are very serious out here. A good thing, I guess."

"It is a good thing. I'm Stan. I just moved in . . . there." She pointed at her adorable little house.

"Oh! We're neighbors. I live there." The woman fluttered her hand at the house right next to Stan's.

Stan realized it was the woman next door, the one with the golden retriever. She had been having the screaming match with the white-haired lady yesterday.

"I'm Amara Leonard." Amara rose gracefully to her feet, reminding Stan of a dancer. Short, though. Her shiny brown hair, cut in a chin-length bob, swung around her face. She wore funky pink glasses that made her eyes look cat-shaped. "I'm the one everyone thinks is crazy. I'm sure you'll hear about it, if you haven't already."

Stan laughed. "Crazy? I hadn't heard. I'm Stan Connor. And are you crazy?"

"A little," Amara admitted. "But not for the reasons everyone thinks. I practice Reiki and homeopathy. Some people around here think it's just a fancy way to say I'm a voodoo princess who's plotting the demise of the town. Especially when I come out here to meditate."

"You'd have to have something better than that for me to think you're crazy," Stan said. "I could use a good Reiki session. And my cat and I could both use a new homeopath."

"Really? I do animal homeopathy only, and I would love to help your cat. Is he ill?"

"He's got some irritable bowel issues. I got him

as a stray. He wandered into my condo complex a few years ago, after he'd been hurt. I took him to the vet, and he ended up staying." Stan smiled. "He didn't really want to, at first. I had to bribe him with homemade treats. That was the first night he didn't scream at the door."

Amara laughed. "Cats are so ungrateful sometimes, aren't they? So how do you treat his IBS?"

"I make all his food. My grandmother taught me as a kid how to bake for animals, and I've expanded into cooking him actual meals. It's helped."

"That's phenomenal," Amara said, clapping her hands. "Oh, I would love to work with you. I don't want to interrupt your run. Please call me for an appointment." She reached for her pockets, then seemed to realized she had none in her yoga pants. "Shoot. No cards on me. Just come by. You know where to find me."

"I will," Stan said. "Great to meet you."

"You too! So exciting. I love people who get it." Amara clapped her hands again, then plopped back down on her blanket, crossed her legs and began her Zen thing again.

That was luck. Stan wasn't sure what she "got," but a homeopath next door was a good thing. Could she really meditate out here? Probably, Stan figured. She seemed way more enlightened. Amara was likely one of those spiritual-but-not-religious types who volunteered at soup kitchens and children's cancer wards, played chants while she read self-help books and went to other countries to find herself or engage in some martyr-type activity to find a purpose. She also had a temper, which was obvious from her shouting match the day before. But everyone had a dark side.

Stan jumped back on the path and picked up her jog. She noticed a woman on a bench watching her. She lifted her hand in a wave, then realized it was the white-haired woman. The other screamer. She looked straight at Stan, but she didn't wave back. Shrugging it off, Stan turned her attention back in front of her a second too late. An enormous Weimaraner bounded into her path. She halted, feinting to the right to avoid being knocked over.

If her reflexes had been slower, she would've ended up sprawled in the grass, or worse. She yanked her earbuds out, automatically reaching up to pat the overly friendly dog who was now standing on his hind legs trying to lick her to death.

"Duncan! For Christ's sake." A man jogged across the grass. He wore a Yankees baseball cap backward, over longish, dirty blond hair, and a tank top, which definitely proved he had muscles. Tan, unshaven, dark glasses. From what she could see, he was very cute. Although she didn't like people who couldn't control their dogs. And she wasn't wild about Yankees fans.

He reached her, panting slightly, and tugged the dog's collar to make him sit. "Bad dog, Duncan. You don't run off like that. I'm very sorry," he said, casting an appraising glance over her. Stan suddenly felt very self-conscious. And sweaty. "Are you okay?"

"I'm fine," she said, reaching up to adjust her

ponytail. "No problem. He's very sweet, aren't you, Duncan?"

Duncan immediately pounced on her again, and this time she did lose her balance. His owner grabbed her arm to steady her. The dog seemed to weigh twice what she did.

"Duncan! I said, 'Sit,'" he commanded. When the dog obliged, tongue lolling, he rolled his eyes. "Sorry again. I'm Jake McGee." He still held her arm.

"Stan Connor," she said, with a pointed look at his hand. He grinned and let her go, lifting his sunglasses up to rest on the brim of his cap. He had cool eyes, too. Catlike, with brown and gold and green all vying for dominance. Stan uncapped her water bottle and took a swig. She ordered herself to stop admiring. Not appropriate.

"Stan, huh?" he said. "You don't look like a Stan. The last Stan I knew was fifty-eight, bald and fat."

She almost spit her water trying not to laugh. "Well, maybe this will change your mental image of all future Stans. It was nice meeting you." With one last pet for Duncan, Stan turned and started to jog again.

A minute later, Jake McGee fell into step beside her; Duncan obediently ran after them both. "Do you live around here, Stan?" he asked, drawing her name out on his tongue.

Stan glanced at him and kept the slow jog pace. "I just moved in yesterday," she said.

"Ah. The green house." Jake snapped his fingers. "I saw you with the moving truck, but you look different."

"You mean sweaty."

Jake laughed. "I didn't mean that. I think it's the hair. It was down and now it's in a ponytail."

"Easier to run with," she said. Why was he noticing her hair?

"Are you gonna keep this pace up?" Jake asked.

"I hope not. I am out for a run, after all."

"I thought so," he said, sighing. "I'm going to have to leave you to it. It was nice meeting you, Stan."

Something about the way he said her name gave her a warm feeling in her belly. She kicked up her speed. "You both, too." She plugged her music back into her ears. After she'd gotten halfway around the circle, she turned back once. Jake and Duncan were no longer in sight.

It took her a half hour to do a three-mile run. Not a bad pace, considering she couldn't remember when she'd actually run last. She showered and was on her way to the back porch with an iced coffee, preparing to plot out the rest of her day, when her doorbell rang.

She reversed direction and headed to the front door. Maybe it was someone with more sweets.

It wasn't. The woman with the long white hair stood on her porch, a straw hat like Ray Mackey's perched on top of her head. Still not smiling. Piercing gray eyes studied Stan and the space behind her. Intense eyes. She reminded Stan of the depictions of Salem witches painted in honor of Halloween every year; the same white hair loose under a hat, only their hats were black and pointy. And they had warts on their noses. Her visitor had no warts, and she wore scrubs with smiling Scooby-Doo images plastered all over them. A happy scene in direct contrast with her aura. She had good shoes, though. Fun Merrell clogs that Stan had admired but never bought because they weren't corporate America shoes. She pasted a polite smile on her face.

"Yes?"

"Hello. I'm Carole Morganwick," the woman said. "I'm the vet in town."

"Hi there. Stan Connor. It's very nice to meet you." Stan extended her hand.

Carole observed it like one would a dirty child reaching for a hug. Instead of shaking, she handed her a thin newspaper. "Your paper was on your lawn. Welcome to town," she added. Her skin was cancer-tan, and hundreds of tiny wrinkles clustered around the corners of her eyes. From the expression Carole wore now, Stan guessed they were not laugh lines.

"Thanks." Stan took the paper and unfolded it. "Although I haven't subscribed to a newspaper." The *Frog Ledge Holler.* Thin. If there were more than four pages to it, she'd be surprised.

Carole waved her off. "It's free. Cyril drives everyone crazy with it."

Cyril? Stan had no idea what person she was talking about. "Oh. Well, would you, uh, like to come in?" Stan glanced behind her and envisioned where the unpacked boxes were stacked. How empty it still looked.

Too late. Carole was already halfway through the door, looking around as if she were at a museum exhibit. "Thank you. I heard you have a cat."

"I do," Stan said, closing the door. "A Maine coon. Nutty. Where did you hear that?"

Carole ignored the question. "Who's your vet?"

"Well . . ." Stan thought about the best way to answer that. She hadn't been to Nutty's "traditional" vet in over a year, nor had she seen his homeopath in a while. And she'd just met Amara, so that didn't count.

Carole turned abruptly at her hesitation. Those intense eyes drilled into Stan's. "You need a local vet, my dear, if you love your cat. And I don't mean those funny people who call themselves 'vets,' but don't do any kind of veterinary work at all. Did I mention I'm the town vet?"

"Of course I love my cat," Stan said, bristling at both the insult and the thinly veiled dig at homeopathic vets. Carole must have seen her talking to Amara this morning and decided to establish some territory. "I treat Nutty like a king. Especially with his condition. And yes, you mentioned you're the vet."

"My practice is next to the town hall. Frog Ledge Veterinary Services. What condition?"

"He has irritable bowel syndrome. Mild."

"What he's taking for it?"

"'Taking for it'?" *This woman fires questions like she's part of the Inquisition!* "Do you mean medicine?"

"Of course I mean medicine." Carole lifted the lid off Nutty's treat jar and peered inside. "What are these?"

"Treats. Freshly baked last night. And Nutty is not on traditional medicine."

"What the devil do you mean, 'not on traditional medicine'? How do you expect him to maintain?"

As if he were on cue, Nutty strolled into the room, his plume of a tail standing tall, his usual posture when he investigated new goings-on. He looked from Stan to Carole, recognized the treat jar in her hand and promptly rubbed against her leg.

Carole observed him. She reached down, pulled his ear back and peered inside. Nutty batted her with his paw. "Looks like mites," she said. "So what did you say you're doing for his disease?"

Stan slapped the newspaper on the counter. "Nutty does not have ear mites. He's on a strict diet of organic food. When he's not feeling good, I use natural medicine," she said. "He's doing extremely well. What can I help you with, Dr. Morganwick?"

Carole sighed heavily and set the lid down on the treats. Nutty gave her a look that said, *I can't believe you were in my treat jar and didn't bother to give me any;* then he beat it down the hall to avoid getting his other ear pulled.

"I thought you might be one of those *organics,*" Carole said, drawing out the last word in distaste, as if Stan had told her she was a serial killer. "Nutty really should have traditional care. And a nutrition consult. I'll tell you what. Bring him down tomorrow and I'll give you a half-price visit this first time. That way he'll be in the system if you need me in a pinch. And we can talk about his treatment then."

Stan was rarely speechless, but she'd never had an experience quite like this before. This woman must be crazy. And she'd let her in—well, she'd had no choice, really—and now the so-called doc was standing in her kitchen near her freshly sharpened set of knives.

"I suppose that's reasonable," Stan said finally, at a loss for any other reply.

"Lovely! We'll see you at eight tomorrow. Please be prompt. I'll sneak you in before my first appointment. I do love new clients." She smiled, finally, then walked out the door.

"These alpacas are adorable." Stan stood in the backyard of the Mackeys' B and B, petting one. The soft brown animal nudged Stan's hand as her movement slowed; she was clearly asking for more.

"Aren't they great? This is Mittens."

"Mittens?"

"Yes. One of our first. We got her when I was still getting used to the cold. Fifteen years after I got here." Char laughed at her own joke. "So how are you liking town? Meeting a lot of people?"

"Some. I met Amara Leonard." She wondered if she should mention Carole's odd visit.

"She's a lovely lady, isn't she? Let's go inside and you can sample some of the gazpacho I'm making for our guests. I do hope you start meeting more people. It's quite a social little town."

Stan followed her in. "I met the vet, too."

"Carole?" Char turned and observed Stan's face. "Where did you meet her?"

Well, now that she'd opened the door. Stan told her about the encounter earlier that day. "It was bizarre."

Char's bright orange sundress lit up the kitchen like a fluorescent bulb. Orange seemed to be her favorite color. She accented the look with chunky red jewelry and matching four-inch platform flip-flops, which were one shade darker than her hair. Her eye shadow today was a warm, glittery gold. The whole outfit reminded Stan of a fancy bowl of ripe fruit. Generous-sized fruit. But in an inviting bowl.

"Carole is an interesting woman," Char said, choosing a knife and then attacking fresh tomatoes, their juice oozing over the wine bottle–shaped cutting board. "She's very passionate about her work. And her town."

"How long has she been a vet?"

Char stopped cutting, knife in midair, to think about that. Tomato juice and seeds dripped red from her blade and splattered on the cutting board. "I'm not entirely sure, but Ray says her family's been doing this forever. Her daddy owned that practice." She lowered the blade again with the confidence of a guillotine operator, slicing the tomato neatly in half. "Put Doc Stevens in the driver's seat when Carole left town. But then she came back.

"I think she's feeling threatened by all the choices people have these days." Char lowered her voice. "Like Doc Amara. I think she's a doc. Are those kinds of people docs?"

"You mean homeopaths? Yes, of course they're doctors. I mean, the legit ones. She was meditating on the green this morning. I almost stepped on her. Carole saw us talking." Stan thought about the way Carole had stared at them. "I think that's why she came over. Marking her territory. There must be some not-so-friendly competition between those two. They were yelling at each other in the street Saturday when I was moving in."

"Yelling? Really?" Char abandoned her tomatoes at the promise of gossip. "What were they yelling about? I can't picture that little thing yelling."

"I didn't hear much. Something about Amara being a 'two-bit hack.' And Amara did her fair share of yelling back."

Char laughed and turned back to her veggies. "Sounds like something Carole would say. I have to admit, honey, I don't know much about that natural stuff. But I do know Carole is very set in her ways. I presume she would think it's all hogwash."

"Then why would Carole be upset? If she thinks there's no validity?"

Char thought about that, the *snap, snap, snap* of her knife against the cutting board the only sound in the room for a moment. "Well, I don't know," she said finally. "I guess that's a good question. I know she made fun of that odd thing Amara does with her hands. What's it called? Raking, or some such thing?"

"You mean Reiki?" Stan chuckled. "You really aren't into natural healing, are you?"

"Honey, I have my natural healers right over there." Char nodded to the far wall of the kitchen. Not a wall but a wine rack. Bottles filled every slot. "I haven't been to a doc in years and I'm a hundred and ten percent."

At Stan's chuckle, Char waved the knife at her. "I'm not kidding. Everybody gets crazy about health and exercise and doctors and food, but they're usually pill-popping, miserable people. No offense, honey. I know you're into that exercise stuff. But where I come from, we don't worry about all that. We have a few drinks. We eat good food. We laugh. That's all."

Stan raised her iced tea in a toast. "Amen to that. Where did you come from, anyway? Maybe I'll move there next."

"Louisiana, baby doll. Right outside N'awleans. We know how to move slow there, let me tell you." Char pushed her diced tomatoes aside and attacked a green pepper. "And we have drive-through daiquiri stands. It's heaven."

"I should have guessed." She could see it now, in the plantation-style furniture, the gargoyle accents all over the kitchen. There were even Mardi Gras beads dangling from various spots—a chili pepper–themed string on a hook near the refrigerator, a coffee-and-beignets string near the breakfast nook. The gas fireplace in the kitchen would make this the favorite room in winter. The long table and benches invited everyone to sit together and enjoy a delicious meal. The mint green walls made Stan think of juleps, although she wouldn't know a julep if she tripped over it.

"So what do I do about Carole? I'm sure small-town politics would suggest I go and play nice. But I'm not in the market for a vet. Especially one who barges into my kitchen and commands me to show up. And I do believe in homeopathy and I don't feel like arguing with someone about it." Stan got up and wandered to the glass doors at the back of the kitchen. Outside, Ray swept the patio, decorated with a few tables and lounge chairs for the guests. Stan could see a cozy wooden porch swing at the far end. Beyond, on the grass, the alpacas milled around behind their fence.

Char sighed and threw her cucumbers into the bowl. "I know. Carole is her own worst enemy these days. She's campaigning for her own business, but she's overdoing it a tad. She's really bordering on obsessive. And Betty isn't helping, either. She's angry and can't resist telling everyone about it."

"Who's Betty?"

"Betty Meany. She's the town librarian. A bit nosy. You'll see."

That Char called someone "nosy" with a straight face made Stan smile.

"She lost her best friend a couple of weeks ago—Snickers, her cat." Char shook her head sadly, measured out two teaspoons of olive oil and added salt. "She's convinced the lymphoma came from all the vaccines over the years. Told Carole to stop, but Carole insisted Snickers needed them."

"My goodness, that's awful," Stan said. "I'd be upset, too. Maybe I should just call her and cancel. Nutty's doing fine right now."

"Well, you know, I'm not sure Snickers' dying was Carole's fault. People can't see reality when they're that upset. I don't know, honey." Char added lemon juice and some other seasonings, which Stan lost track of in the blur of her hands, then threw the whole concoction into the food processor and turned it on. "Y'all should keep the appointment," Char shouted over the roar of the machine. "What's the harm?"

"'What's the harm?' she asks. It's the hours of mea culpa and baking that I'm going to have to do to get you to talk to me again," Stan said to Nutty the next morning. They were having their usual cat carrier standoff in the bathroom. It was seven-forty. Stan knew she would eventually win, but she'd lose a few battles first. And some skin. And probably be late. Why had she let this woman badger her into an appointment, anyway?

Theme song: "*Mission: Impossible.*" Nutty waited behind the toilet, watching her every move, tail flicking in displeasure like a possessed dust mop. Stan crouched down, attempting to talk sense into him. "Come on, Nutty. Let's do it the easy way."

Nutty never saw the value in the easy way. After a session of fake-outs, scratches and some hissing, Stan scruffed him and dropped him into the upright carrier.

Nutty gave her a dirty look as she locked him in. "Hey," she said. "I warned you."

She carried him outside to the garage and loaded him into her Audi. They drove the mile and a quarter down the road. Past the green, across from the library, next to the town hall. As promised, a small house-turned-business with a hand-carved wooden sign in the shape of a cat and dog, tails entwined, came into view as she rounded the corner. A frog sat about the FROG LEDGE piece of the name. The cheery yellow color of the building seemed out of character for the serious vet. And the sign was amazing. Stan knew next to nothing about woodworking, but even from the street she could tell the detail was painstaking.

Stan parked on the street in front of the clinic. The same green SUV that had roared away from Amara's house the other night was parked in the tiny lot.

Inside the carrier, Nutty had resigned himself to the trip and was curled in a ball. "It'll be short, I promise," she said. "No shots. No meds. Pinky swear." He ignored her. She glanced at her watch. *Five to eight. I might as well get it over with.*

She got out and hefted the carrier. They walked up to the front door. It stood slightly ajar. Stan pushed it open and called out, "Hello? Carole?"

No answer. The lights were on, so Stan stepped in. The waiting room felt comfy. A sign tacked up to the counter read: PETS WELCOME. Chairs were set up in twos and threes around the room, next to coffee tables stacked with piles of *Dog Fancy* and *Cat Fancy*. A computer hummed on a desk behind the counter. No receptionist or tech in sight. The room was cold, like someone had cranked the air-conditioning before the heat set in.

Stan set Nutty down on a chair and strolled around the room, checking out posters on the wall for packaged dog and cat food, a schedule of pet-friendly events in town, a bulletin board with ads offering pet-sitting services and showcasing lost pets. The lost pet ads always made her sad, but she felt compelled to look in case she ran into the missing animal somewhere.

Her watch read two minutes to eight. Stan glanced down the hall where the exam rooms waited. Somewhere in the clinic she heard a door quietly close. Maybe Carole had gone out back and was returning. She should let her know she was here.

Stan took a few steps, listened. Quiet. "Hello?"

Nothing. The first door on the left was closed. The one next to it was a bathroom, its door open, the room empty. Across the hall, another exam room, but this door stood ajar. Stan walked over, pushed it wider and peeked in.

"Carole? Nutty and I are he—" And stopped. On the floor, just visible behind the exam table, was a Merrell clog. With a foot inside it. Stan took another tentative step and saw a leg. Horizontal. "Oh, my gosh, Carole! Did you fall?" She rushed around the table and gasped, recoiling, slamming her hip in her haste to get away. A horrified scream worked its way up her throat.

The vet lay on the floor, unseeing eyes staring up at the ceiling. A needle protruded from her neck, her still body and long white hair covered in kibble.

Chapter 3

"I've told you three times already. I had an appointment. A new patient appointment for Nutty. My cat." Stan pointed to the carrier, where Nutty frantically rubbed against the wire door. "I got here and found her on the floor." Stan swallowed, remembering how Carole Morganwick looked, still and unmoving, covered in kibble. Once the police had gotten photos and collected their evidence, they'd taken her body away, but Stan figured she'd see it in her mind for the next few years.

"You're right. That's what you told me three times already." The resident state trooper leaned against Carole's reception counter, intense green eyes drilling a hole through Stan's head. "But what I want you to tell me is what you were really doing here."

Stan had a few choice words about what she was doing here right now, but she didn't think it wise to opine. Especially to a state trooper. Stan had learned during this morning's course of events that a trooper was the responding officer in towns of this size with no local police force, something she still could barely comprehend. No police. At all. Except for this woman, who looked like she was barely out of her twenties and didn't need makeup, both of which counted against her in Stan's mind. She knew it made her an awful person—a stereotypical, awful person—but she'd been expecting a middle-aged, donut-eating male, not this redhead with the perfect skin and thick hair. Not one of those pale, pasty-looking redheads, either, or an orangey redhead like Char. The cop had some good genes. Or her coppery hair was straight from a bottle.

And this whole concept of resident state troopers who kept office hours in town was crazy to a city girl. On a better day she would be curious about how that worked, but it was not a better day. Stan had a blazing headache; it was freezing in this office; the vet was dead. And not by natural causes. Maybe she'd committed suicide and stabbed herself with some drug, but Stan figured that was unlikely. This cop—TROOPER PASQUALE, according to her badge—apparently felt the same way.

"I'm not sure what you mean," Stan said, rubbing her shoulders to try to chase the goose bumps away.

"There was nothing in her appointment book with your name on it. And the practice doesn't open until eight-thirty."

Stan sat up straighter. The trooper's insinuation was not lost on her. Theme song: "The *Twilight Zone.*" She mentally prepped herself, as she would one of her executives before they faced a difficult question from the media. Just the facts. "Dr. Morganwick came over yesterday to introduce herself. She was eager to take my cat on as a patient and told me to come in today before her first appointment."

"Then why isn't it in her appointment book?"

"I have no idea why. She probably forgot to write it in. We spoke in my kitchen. I didn't call and talk to a receptionist or anything. But I did talk to Char Mackey about it. Whether or not I should come. You can ask her."

"What's wrong with your cat?"

"Nothing's wrong with him." Stan glanced inside the carrier. Nutty had been clawing frantically at the wire door until a few minutes ago. He'd since given up and gone to sleep.

"Nothing's wrong with your cat, but you came in before Dr. Morganwick's regular appointments." Pasquale's dry delivery had Stan's hackles rising.

"She asked if I had a vet. Being new in town, I don't. She insisted I bring Nutty in to see her. Said it was an introductory visit so she could meet him in case there was an emergency. I thought it was weird, but I didn't want to make her mad or anything. Being new and all."

"Ah, yes. You're new in town." Pasquale's tone indicated being new was right up there with having genital herpes. "Where are you from?"

"I just moved here from West Hartford."

"What do you do for work?"

She met Pasquale's gaze steadily. "I'm in between jobs right now."

"What do you do when you're not in between jobs?"

"Public relations."

Pasquale did not look impressed. "Did you see or hear anything odd when you got here?"

"Just the back door closing."

Pasquale's eyes narrowed at that. "Walk me through what happened."

"The door was open, so I walked in. I put Nutty's carrier on that chair." Stan pointed to where he sat now. "No one was around. I thought I heard a door close out back, so I figured the doctor had gone outside for something and hadn't heard me come in. When no one came out, I called for her. Then I walked out back." She shivered, more from the memory now than the cold. "I saw her and thought she had fallen, but when I went around the table, I realized she . . . I ran out and called for help."

Pasquale opened her mouth again, but the door banged open and another trooper came in. Male, also young, a little pudgy, eager-looking. TROOPER STURGIS, his badge said. He glanced at Stan, curious, then turned his attention to his counterpart. "Jessie, I canvassed the area, but it was pretty early. No one saw anything. Not even Oliver, and he's always out riding that bike around." He had a patch of hair on his chin, which he kept rubbing, clearly proud of it. Probably his first.

"Where was he today?" Pasquale asked.

"He'd gone out to your brother's place last night. Had a few too many. Slept in."

Pasquale didn't like that. Stan could tell by her pursed lips and the way her eyes shifted away from Trooper Sturgis. She wondered who her brother was and what kind of place he had. And what he was serving. She might need some.

"You hit everyone?" Pasquale asked.

"Everyone nearby." He smirked a little. "Didn't bother asking the Hoffmans' cows. They usually mind their own business."

Pasquale turned the death stare on him and his smile faltered. "You check around out back, Lou?"

Lou hadn't. He left pretty quickly. Stan thought it was about time to do the same. She got up, picked up Nutty's carrier. He opened one eye and glared at her. "Are we done, Trooper Pasquale? I'd like to get my cat home."

Pasquale looked like she was not done, but she didn't have a good reason to detain her. She flipped through her notebook one more time. "You're out by the green. In the Victorian."

Stan nodded, and Pasquale read off Stan's cell number to confirm. "If I have any other questions, I'll follow up with you," she said. "In the meantime, be careful. There's a murderer out there."

Chapter 4

News traveled fast in small towns. When Stan exited the vet clinic carrying Nutty, Pasquale hovering behind her, half the town had gathered across the street behind the newly positioned police barriers.

A man with thick white hair and an old yellow Lab stood at the front of one of the barriers. He looked like one of those people the newspaper always honed in on after a tragedy—a shocked onlooker with no idea he was being photographed for posterity.

"But I have an appointment," Stan heard him say, and Lou leaned over and said something in a low voice. She couldn't see the older man's face, but she could tell from the hunch of his shoulders he was upset.

Stan could hear the buzz of conversation, speculation, in the larger crowd. A white van marked FROG LEDGE ANIMAL CONTROL was parked haphazardly outside the clinic. A woman leaned against it, one hand shielding her eyes from the sun, the other covering her face. Stan hurried past her. Frantically pushing her unlock button as she approached her car, she finally heard the locks release. She loaded Nutty into the passenger seat and went around to the driver's side. Jammed the key into the ignition, missing a few times, and willed her hands to stop shaking so she could drive without running anyone over.

She kept it together until she pulled out of the parking lot, away from the crowd of eyes staring at her as she drove away, wondering what the new chick had to do with whatever was going on. God, she hated being speculated about.

When she reached her driveway, she lost it. She jammed her car into park in front of the garage. Overcome with an insane urge to sob, she closed her eyes and bit down hard on her bottom lip until she tasted blood. The pain helped her force the tears back, and she folded her arms and laid her head down on the steering wheel. Even more than she hated being speculated about, Stan hated to cry.

But holy crap, she'd just seen a dead person. Her first un–funeral-homed dead person. And even more disturbing than that, it was a mur-dered dead person. Because that needle didn't just fall out of a cabinet into Carole's neck.

She had almost been in the same room as a murderer. She checked to see if her car doors were locked. It seemed ridiculous on this bright sunny day in a town where cows outnumbered people. And why was she sitting in her car, anyway? She should go inside. Or back to West Hartford. Call Richard. But he was in Chicago.

Who else could she call? Her mother? No. Death was too scandalous for her mother's sensitive disposition. Nikki. She should call Nikki. But Nikki hated getting phone calls during a transport. Understandable, when she had a van full of barking dogs, trying to listen to a GPS navigate her home.

Was there really no one to call? That was pathetic. As a fresh bout of tears threatened to overwhelm her, she realized that's the way it was. She had spent so much time at work, where people pretended to be friends but didn't trust each other, and hadn't spent enough time cultivating other relationships. If not for Nikki, she'd be friendless right now.

It was a crappy feeling, but not the time to tackle that, too. *Get a grip, get out of the car and go inside.*

Really, she wanted her dad. More than she'd allowed herself to want him since he died nine years ago. He'd know exactly what to say right now to make her feel better, to help her keep a good perspective. But she couldn't talk to him, so it was a moot point. Maybe she'd try some of her all-natural stress reliever. If Nikki were here, she would tell her to take a damn Xanax, then dig one out of her purse.

Stan sucked some air into her lungs and pushed her car door open. The heat slammed into her, like hitting a brick wall. Grabbing Nutty's carrier, she hurried inside and locked the door behind her.

She took Nutty's chicken and rice out of the refrigerator and spooned some into a bowl. She was so frazzled that she forgot to heat it up, but he immediately attacked it. Already feeling sick to her stomach, Stan turned away from the food. She poured a glass of iced water and headed for the stairs. A long, hot bath would make her feel better. Then she could figure out what to do. She hoped the police found clues. She shivered. They would move fast on this. It was a small town. They wouldn't want a murder hanging over their heads—unless they had no idea how to solve it.

Her doorbell rang before she made it to the bathroom. Maybe this was what Richard meant about her getting sick of the small-town scene. She would give anything to be left alone right now.

Leaving her glass on the hall table, she went back downstairs and peeked out the hall window. There was no mistaking Char's flaming hair. No sooner had Stan opened the door, she found herself wrapped in a huge bear hug, her face pressed against Char's generous bosom, ensconced today in a bright yellow sundress.

"Oh, baby doll, are you all right?" Char exclaimed. "I heard all about what happened—you poor thing! We're all so torn up about it, but you—my goodness, finding her like that. Raymond, bring that soup in here right now."

As Char released her grip, Stan could see the other woman's red-rimmed eyes were slightly puffy, despite the silver eye shadow that remained still firmly in place. Ray stood behind his wife, looking equally somber, and holding a Crock-Pot.

"You are both too sweet, but that's really not necessary," Stan began, but Char pooh-poohed

her and stepped inside, dragging Stan by the wrist.
Her yellow wedge sandals had to be at least four
inches high.

"Come sit down and tell me all about what happened. What a terrible, terrible tragedy! Y'all
need a good old-fashioned Southern meal to heal
this trauma." Char dragged Stan to the kitchen
and nearly shoved her into a chair, waiting for Ray
to set the soup down.

"Char, really, I'm not hungry," Stan said, but
Char wouldn't hear it.

"Where are your bowls, honey? Ray, find the
bowls." Char lifted the lid off the soup and inhaled deeply. "This is just what you need. Gumbo.
My specialty." She turned and winked, fanning
herself with her hand. "My goodness, it's hot in
here."

"I can turn the air-conditioning up."

"I'll fix myself a drink. I needed one, anyway. I
think we all do, after today. I just can't believe—"
Char broke off, sniffling, and turned away, reaching for her ginormous purse. Fishing inside, she
came up with a bottle of vodka.

"How you holding up, Stan?" Ray said, bending
down to buss her cheek.

"I'm fine, really, and the bowls are right there."
Stan pointed to the cabinet. Ray nodded, snapped
his suspenders and went to work on the soup.

With steaming bowls of gumbo and rice in front
of them, and a martini for Char, mixed in a water
glass, since Stan hadn't finished unpacking the
kitchen, they dug in. Well, Char and Ray dug in.
Apparently, they were still able to eat, despite their
grief over Carole. Stan pushed the soup around

with her spoon, wishing she were hungry—it did smell awfully good—but still feeling sick. She wanted her bath. Or to go back in time to this morning so she could change her mind about going to the vet.

"So what in the world happened today? I heard just the bare facts. Poor Carole. Beaten with a bag of kibble!" Char shuddered.

"'Beaten with a bag of kibble'?" Stan repeated.

"No?" Char leaned forward, her bracelets clanking together. "Well, we all know how these stories go, the more they're passed around. So how did she die?"

"Char, the poor girl doesn't want to relive that," Ray chided his wife. "Eat your gumbo, Stan, and don't think about it anymore."

"You're absolutely right, love. I'm a terrible friend. I'm so sorry, honey." Char turned apologetic, puppy dog eyes to Stan. "Forgive me?"

"There's nothing to forgive. I have no idea how she died. The police have to do an autopsy."

"But was there kibble involved?" Char couldn't help herself. She set her chin in her hand, waiting expectantly.

Stan remembered the kibble scattered atop the dead woman and tried to chase the image from her mind. "How did you hear about this so fast?"

"Diane told me," Char said.

"Diane?"

"Kirschbaum. The animal control officer. And, of course, Gene was there, too. He had an appointment with Junior, his dog. He was in shock, Diane said."

"Who's Gene?"

"He's the town's sign maker. A woodworker. Amazing talent. He's very gifted. He makes other things, too. Decorations, lawn pieces. We have a lovely whiskey barrel for flowers Gene made us. I'll show you next time. And he grew up in town, so naturally he knew Carole from years ago."

The man with the white hair and the Lab. Stan remembered the look of disbelief on his face and felt sorry for him. "What about Diane? Was she friendly with Carole?"

Ray and Char exchanged a look. "I think they'd done business a few times. You know, it would be hard not to," Char said.

"But they weren't friends?" Stan asked. "She looked pretty upset. I saw her outside this morning, after . . ."

"'Reluctant colleagues' might be a better term," Ray said. "They had differing opinions about animals."

Sounded like Carole had differing opinions with people about a lot of things. "Word gets around quickly here," she said, instead.

Ray nodded. "You don't live in the city anymore, my dear. This is a small town, and everyone knows everything. Trust me." He leaned forward conspiratorially. "Just like everyone knows that Hal Hoffman was in a bar brawl last night at Jake's place and almost got his behind kicked. If it weren't for Jake, that college kid would've taken him right down."

Stan shook her head. "Who's Hal Hoffman? And why does anyone care?"

Both Char and Ray stared at her.

"What?" Stan asked. "Why would I care that

some guy named Hal Hoffman got in a fight like a teenager? Is he a teenager?"

"Well, he may as well be," Char muttered, earning a dirty look from her husband. "Hal is your neighbor, honey. The Happy Cow Dairy Farm. He and his wife, Emmalee, run it. I'm sure you've seen him outside on the tractor. And Jake runs the bar in town. Irish pub. A classy place. He hates when there are upsets."

"And like I said, you live in a small town now," Ray reminded her. "You have to care."

Yikes. Apparently, there was a lot she had to learn about small-town life. Stan wasn't sure how she felt about that. She had enough going on without worrying about who was getting in bar brawls. "Is this Jake McGee?" she asked.

"The very same. Have you met him?"

"I did. When I was out running."

Char smirked a little. "I'm not surprised."

"Why?"

"Ah, honey. You're an attractive woman. Jake likes the ladies."

Stan flushed.

"Have you been to McSwigg's yet?" Ray asked.

"That's the name of his bar?"

"Most certainly is," Ray said. "You would like it."

"As long as Hal Hoffman isn't brawling."

"Righto," Ray agreed.

Then it dawned on Stan. "Is that the only place around here people drink at? Like people who live in town?"

"Mostly. Some of them go to the next town. The fancy microbrewery. But most of us locals, we patronize Jake."

"Does some guy who rides a bike or something go there, too?" She racked her brain for the name Trooper Lou had used. "Oliver?"

"He sure does," Ray said. "You haven't seen Oliver's bike yet?"

"No. No, I haven't." Stan slumped back in her chair, her stomach feeling sicker than before. Jake McGee was Trooper Pasquale's brother. Had to be. *"He'd gone out to your brother's place last night. Had a few too many. Slept in."*

Char and Ray were watching her, probably wondering why discussing Oliver's bike had had such an adverse affect on her.

"So Jessie Pasquale is Jake's sister?" she said.

"Sure is," Ray said. "Kept her ex's last name. Probably for their daughter's sake."

Stan digested that info as best she could and turned the conversation back to Carole.

"Does Carole's family live nearby? I can't imagine how they must feel."

"I don't know much about her family, at least what's left. Do you, Ray?" Char asked.

Ray thought about it. "Well, now, I can't be sure. The Morganwicks were a big name around here years ago. Big part of the town's history. But the last few generations . . ." He shrugged. "Carole's parents passed, and no one's seen her brother in decades. Carole herself left for a while. Married, divorced. I really can't say if there's anyone. She kept to herself, mostly. Oh, but wait. Where did her boy end up living?"

"My goodness, sweetie, you're right. I forgot all about him! What was his name?" Char tapped her huge ring against the table as she thought. "Alexander, Adrian . . ."

Ray snapped his fingers. "Adam. Must've gone off on his own. He'd be old enough."

"Or maybe with his dad. He never returned with Carole."

Stan listened with interest. "Carole had a son?"

"Yes, just one. I don't think they were close. She was very much absorbed in her work."

"Did Carole take care of your alpacas?"

Char and Ray exchanged another odd glance. Not just odd. Guilty.

"Yes. Yes, she did," Char said, but not convincingly.

"I've known Carole since we were toddlers," Ray said. "We went to school together. Like I said, she grew up in these parts."

"So how long did she take care of the animals for you? What will you do now?"

Char got up and began clearing plates. "Why, I have no idea. It's too soon to think about that. Anyone want more? How about a martini, Stan?"

"No, thank you. She must be leaving you with big shoes to fill. She was good at caring for the alpacas?"

Silence. Then, "Tremendous," Char declared, downing the rest of her drink and setting the glass on the kitchen table with a snap. "Carole was very devoted. This is a terrible thing for our town, just terrible." She fanned her face as her eyes filled with tears again. Ray rose and went to her, rubbing her back.

"Why do you ask, Stan?" he asked in that quiet way he had.

"Just curious. Char told me Betty wasn't happy with her care and that people were having second thoughts about her."

Char pursed her lips and looked at the ceiling, still dabbing at her eyes with a napkin. "I shouldn't have made it sound like that. Betty is Betty. You know how people get when something sticks in their head. I'm not sure what other people think. Oh, my goodness! What a lovely kitty! Is that the little man in question? Come here, sweet pea," she crooned as Nutty entered the room, playing shy.

"We did use Carole for the alpacas. For some things," Ray said, returning to the table. "We also used an outside vet. But you can't tell anyone."

"Why would I tell anyone?" Stan shook her head, bewildered. "But why can't you just use the vet you want to use?"

"You can, of course." Ray wiped his mouth with his napkin, balled it up and tossed it from hand to hand. "But it's polite to buy locally."

"Polite. Okay. But again, what if you—oh, never mind." Stan was getting a headache. So was Nutty, by the looks of it. Char had him cradled in her arms like a baby, singing to him. He looked horrified. Stan stifled a giggle. "Here, give him a treat." Stan got up and fished one out of his jar, handing it to her.

Char sniffed it. "This smells almost good enough to eat myself. What kind is it?"

"Cheese and spelt. I make them. I make all Nutty's food, actually. He has stomach problems."

"Really? So does Savannah. Our dog that watches the alpacas. Carole couldn't ever figure out what was wrong. Our other vet had some ideas, but I hate all those medicines. Do you think we could try some of the food you give Nutty? We'll pay you, of course."

"Oh, don't be silly. You don't have to pay me. And I'd be happy to look into some dog recipe ideas. I've never cooked for a dog before."

"Aren't you wonderful. Ray, isn't she wonderful?"

"She sure is," Ray said. "Now we need to get back to the B and B and explain this to our guests. We can't possibly do afternoon tea while all this is going on."

"Afternoon tea?" Stan asked.

"We have some guests of English descent. They requested it." Ray looked unhappy about disappointing anyone. "I can't possibly expect Char to bake scones when she's so distraught, and Lord knows I'm no good at it. The gumbo was already made when we heard the news."

Stan had a feeling the vodka martinis were more of an inhibitor for Char than grief, but she kept her mouth shut. "Thank you for coming," she said.

"Oh, honey, don't think anything of it. We all stick together around here. Ready, darling?" Char asked Ray.

"Ready. You take care now, Stan, okay? And call if you need anything."

Stan promised she would and saw them to the door. She closed and locked it behind them before returning to the kitchen to clean up. Nutty peeked out from the cabinet he'd wedged himself into.

"Coast is clear," Stan told him. She swore he

emitted a sigh of relief as he jumped out and went in search of his next napping spot. She felt the same way. That conversation had been tiring.

The walls might be closing in on her. Stan had wanted to be left alone, but after Ray and Char left, she had no idea what to do with herself. She'd texted Richard, but he hadn't responded. And when she called, his phone went right to voice mail.

She floated from room to room, unpacking half a box here, a few things there. She mopped the downstairs bathroom floor and hung one picture; then she took it down because it didn't look right. The old Blue Öyster Cult song *"(Don't Fear) The Reaper"* played in a continuous loop in her head until she thought she might go crazy—when theme songs go bad. She went in search of a calming jazz CD and turned it up.

The whole time she tried to force the dead vet out of her head.

"Want treats?" she finally asked Nutty, who was hanging around the kitchen watching her manic movements with interest.

He meowed.

Stan rummaged around the cupboard. "They'll have to be pumpkin. I can't go out right now to get other ingredients."

Nutty blinked, indifferent. Stan turned the oven on, pulled out her mixing bowl and added spelt flour, canned pumpkin, eggs, peanut butter, some water and ground cinnamon. She used her favorite wooden spoon to mix it all together, working the ingredients into a smooth batter.

"I knew I shouldn't have gone to that appointment," she told Nutty as she worked. "I really didn't need to find a dead person. That was definitely not on my bucket list."

Nutty yawned and dropped to the floor, resting his head on his paw.

"I hope they find out who did it soon. And why they threw kibble on her. Do you think it was someone mad about food? Maybe someone like this Betty person, who thought Carole didn't do things right?"

She glanced at Nutty. He didn't have the answers and wasn't shy about letting her know that. He'd fallen asleep. Stan sighed. It stank having no one to talk to when you were trying to solve a murder.

Chapter 5

For a one-man show, the *Frog Ledge Holler* worked fast. A "special edition" was out first thing Tuesday. Front page above the fold, naturally, was all about the murder. The paper was two pages thin. She winced as she read the headline: LOCAL VET FOUND DEAD AT CLINIC, FOUL PLAY SUSPECTED. She took it to the kitchen and read it, standing up.

Frog Ledge—Carole Morganwick, local veterinarian and daughter of town scion Henry Morganwick, was found dead Monday at her veterinary clinic on Main Street.

Resident state trooper Jessica Pasquale responded to a 911 call from a client, who found the body around 8 A.M. While the cause of death has not been determined, foul play is suspected. No suspects have yet been identified, but state police are following a number of leads.

Morganwick, who was 61 at the time of her death, has run the Frog Ledge Veterinary Clinic since 2007, reclaiming ownership after the death of Dr. Randolph Stevens. The clinic originally belonged to Morganwick's father, Henry, who placed it under Stevens's management in 2002. Henry Morganwick died in 2003, leaving instructions that the clinic be returned to any of his remaining family's management upon his and Stevens's death. Carole returned to Frog Ledge after Stevens's death to continue her family's legacy of caring for local animals and helping the community.

Carole Morganwick is survived by her brother, Henry Junior, and a son, Adam Cross. Memorial services have not been planned at this time.

There was no mention of the kibble, at least.

"Murdered? Jeez, Stan. That's a helluva way to get welcomed to town." Nikki sounded out of breath on the other end of the phone. In Nikki's world it was a normal morning—as normal as you can get taking care of fifteen dogs and a few cats. But it wasn't a normal morning in Stan's world at all. She had woken up with *"Highway to Hell"* pounding in her head. If anyone could make her feel better, however, it was Nikki.

"What happened? And who was it again?" Nikki asked.

"The town vet."

"Was Nutty sick?"

"No."

"Okay, I'm confused. Hang on." Stan heard a blast of static, some rustling like Nikki was shuffling cards in her ear, then a bang and finally quiet. She came back on the line a second later. "Back. Had to finish dealing with one of the new dogs. He had an accident all over his kennel."

"Sounds like fun."

"More fun than a dead vet. So why were you there? Help me with this."

Stan sighed. "The vet came to my door." She relayed Carole's visit.

"And you went? What the heck's happening to you out there in the middle of nowhere?"

"I'm trying to play nice in the sandbox. Apparently, we're supposed to care about each other around here. And buy locally."

"Hard to care about someone you don't even know, who shows up at your door like that. And I'm all about buying locally, but not when someone's stalking me to do it. But you always were good at that political crap. Okay, so you went. And she was just dead? How do you know she was murdered?"

"Because she had a needle sticking out of her neck!"

"Huh." Nikki was silent for a moment, thinking about this. "You know, aside from the tragedy of it, it's pretty funny. Like *funny ironic,* not actually *funny.* But all those years in Hartford, you never came across a dead body, and that's where it wouldn't seem so bizarre."

"Well, there was the time we got shot at." She, Richard and another coworker had been at a red light shortly after leaving the office when someone had come running out of a house and started shooting at the car in front of them.

"They weren't shooting at you."

"They could've missed. And they didn't hit the person they wanted to hit, either."

"True. Do they know who killed this vet?"

"No." Stan didn't mention the long questioning session that she endured.

"Are you doing okay?"

"I'm okay."

"No, you're not. Want me to come over? I'm doing a couple of drop-offs today, but my schedule isn't too crazy. I can stop by later tonight."

She really didn't want to see anybody. "Maybe tomorrow? I have a bunch of work to do here, and, honestly, I don't feel good."

"Okay. Try to relax. And all kidding aside, be careful. Just because it's a small town doesn't mean everything's wine and roses. This woman got herself killed."

Frog Ledge seemed to have its share of hypocrites. Stan had gotten the loner vibe from Carole. And the flat-out disliked vibe from a number of people, too. But as dusk covered the town the day after the vet's death, people flocked to the green with candles and stuffed animals and photos. She heard them through her open bedroom window. She'd hidden herself up there for most of the day, trying to sleep but not succeeding. Or sitting on the bathroom floor, waiting to get sick. Stan tried to ignore the murmur of voices first; then as the volume grew she gave up and dragged herself to the window. Holy crap. Was she supposed to make an appearance at this?

Stan fought back tears for the millionth time that day. First in line to find a dead body. Now she had to put on her game face, get dressed and go pretend she was torn up about Carole's death. Well, she was torn up, but she didn't think it had to do with Carole personally. She couldn't be. She'd had one conversation with the woman—if you could even call it a conversation.

Then she saw Char and Ray joining the crowd. Char had traded in her brilliant colors for a billowy black dress. And was that . . . ? Stan leaned forward. Yes, it was. Amara Leonard had joined the flow of people heading to the green.

If Amara put in an appearance after that screaming match she'd had with Carole, Stan knew she had no choice. She heard Ray's voice in her ear: *You live in a small town now. You have to care.* Groaning, she forced herself to get up and dressed in a pair of black shorts, a light sweater and comfy flats. Tromping unenthusiastically downstairs, she ate a few Saltine crackers to settle her stomach and called Nutty. He didn't respond or come running, so she figured he was sleeping.

"I'll be back," she called to him, in case he cared. No response. Apparently, he didn't. She shut the door behind her and twisted the handle to make sure it had locked. Slinking to the edge of the green, Stan followed the crowd up to the other end, near the library and the congregational church, where the crowd gathered. She wondered what religion, if any, Carole Morganwick practiced and where her funeral service would be held. If this was any indication, it would be well attended.

She'd lost sight of Ray and Char, and Amara was small enough that Stan might never find her in the crowd. She hung back near a flowering dogwood tree, watching everyone around her. No one cried, but there were a lot of solemn expressions and whispering. Up front, two teenaged boys were setting up a makeshift podium on the pavement behind the library, where a group of three women and two men stood. A circle of Carole's friends? Stan inched closer for a better view and felt someone grab her arm. She turned and almost bumped into Izzy Sweet. Baxter and Elvira immediately crowded around her, sniffing excitedly.

"Oh, hello," Stan said, bending down to pet them. "I'm sorry, I don't have anything for you."

The dogs both sat and stared at her, as if encouraging her to change her mind.

"How are you?" Izzy asked, a twinge of sympathy in her voice. "I heard what happened."

"Who didn't?" Stan muttered.

Izzy threw back her head and laughed, drawing the attention of the people closest to them. She didn't seem to care, or even notice. "Welcome to small-town America. I'm just sorry you were . . . involved. Was it terrible?"

"It wasn't pleasant," Stan said. "And I feel weird being here. I didn't know her."

"It's appropriate to pay your respects. And

quite noticed when you don't." Izzy smiled wryly. "Let's move up to the front."

Stan followed Izzy as she weaved through the crowd, noting how people parted to let her through. She scanned faces as she went. It could be her imagination, but people's words faded as she passed, and they moved farther away. Up front, more people had joined the teens. A man tested a microphone, which kept screeching feedback into the crowd, while a short woman with gray hair oversaw the whole operation, one foot tapping impatiently.

Izzy stopped in front of an old-looking yellow Lab. He looked familiar. Then Stan realized his owner was the man outside the clinic yesterday. The woodworker.

"How're you doing, Gene?" Izzy squeezed his arm sympathetically and petted the dog's head. "Hi, Junior."

Junior wagged. Gene shrugged. His face seemed to sag with the weight of misery. "Okay. Just can't believe it."

"No one can," Izzy said. "Do you know Stan?"

Gene focused on her; his eyes were bleary. He shook her hand. "No. Gene Holdcroft." Despite the hair, Stan could tell by his face he wasn't as old as she'd first guessed. He stepped forward, more of a shuffle, really, with one leg dragging slightly. He shook her hand.

"Hi. Stan Connor."

Gene squinted at her, still holding on. "You were there. Monday. I saw ya come out. You're the young lady who—"

"Gene, with Stan being new to town and all, I

don't think she's seen your work yet," Izzy broke in. "Well, other than the signs around town. Maybe I can bring her by the shop and we can get her something for her new house?"

"Sure, sure."

"Good. We'll see you soon." Izzy took Stan's arm and pulled her ahead. "Poor guy. His wife passed away a while ago, and I think he was sweet on Carole. He's taking it pretty hard."

"I hope he wasn't going to say I was the young lady who did it," Stan said.

Izzy shook her head. "He's a nice guy. Lived here his whole life. One of those small towners who knows where all the bodies are buried. No pun intended," she added hastily.

Stan wasn't even in the frame of mind to laugh at that. Then she saw Jake. He talked with a guy wearing a SAM'S ELECTRIC hat. Jake saw them at the same time Stan's gaze locked on his. A slow, lazy smile settled on his lips. Izzy grunted beside her. Jake's companion said something and walked away.

Jake ignored Izzy's less than thrilled acknowledgment of him. "Good evening, ladies. Somber occasion, but lovely to see you, anyway."

Stan started to say hello, but Izzy had other ideas. "Oh, save it, McGee," she said.

Stan's mouth dropped. She stepped in, attempting to salvage the situation. "Hey there. How's it going?" Stupid question for a memorial service.

He winked at her. "Going fine. And don't mind Izzy. She treats me like this every time she's forced into my presence."

Izzy's face darkened and she opened her mouth,

presumably to let loose a firestorm of insults. But before she could get going, a woman dressed straight out of the American Revolution pages of a history book hurried over and grasped Jake's wrist.

"Thank goodness you're here! We need you up front immediately," she said, pulling him with her before he could even respond. "There's something wrong with the microphone. The boys just can't get it to work."

Jake gave Stan an apologetic wave and let the woman drag him to the parking lot. Izzy turned blazing eyes on Stan.

"I really hope you have better taste than that," she said. "Please don't tell me you're interested in that beast."

Wow. There was being protective toward a new friend, and then there was going overboard. "Hold on. One, I have a boyfriend. Two, I met Jake and his dog out running. There's nothing wrong with being friendly in my new town, is there?"

"He's a disgusting womanizer," Izzy said.

A shrill voice next to Stan diverted her attention before she could ask how Izzy knew that.

"Betty Meany's here? She must be making sure the library doesn't get vandalized during the service," the woman said loudly to her friend, and they both sneered.

Betty Meany. The one Char told her about, who had lost her cat allegedly at Carole's hands. Stan turned to Izzy. "Which one's Betty?"

Izzy pointed to the gray-haired foot tapper watching the setup activities. "I'm afraid the catty one's right, in this case," she said with a nod to the woman who had made the comment. "Betty despised Carole. She probably thinks there'll be riots after the memorial and will want to keep the library safe."

Stan's response was overwhelmed by the roar of a little blue convertible speeding up the street. It careened to a stop, half on the grass next to the church. A young woman with brown-and-blond–striped hair stepped out of the driver's seat. She wore skinny jeans and sandals with heels that would give even Char pause. An oversized T-shirt slid down over small arms, tank top straps visible on her shoulders. The outfit reminded Stan of something Madonna would have worn in her heyday—minus the shoes. The girl moved with a strut that declared, *I own the world.* She headed over uneven ground to the makeshift podium, embracing one of the women waiting in the circle. Stan almost didn't notice the boy slouching out of the convertible's passenger seat, forgotten by the driver. He did not move with an I-own-the-world strut, but rather hunched over into himself, hands jammed in his pockets, shaggy hair and sunglasses covering most of his face. He was skinny enough that his jeans were falling down, but not in the trendy way that was all the rage these days.

Izzy followed Stan's gaze. "Whatcha watching? Oh, the Galvestons." She rolled her eyes.

"Who are they?"

"Big shots around here. Old money, own half the town, et cetera. Mona is the mayor. She's probably speaking. The rest of the town council will stand by and nod solemnly. That's her daughter, Perri." She pointed at convertible girl. "And the boy is Paul. Her twin. They live up there." She pointed to the east. Stan followed her finger past the sky streaked with the beginnings of night and just saw the outline of a house, seemingly miles away, lit up against the hills behind it. It looked grand.

Stan wondered where Carole had lived. "Were they close to Carole, or is this just what they do around here if someone dies?"

"Mona and Carole used to be close. Heard she was like an aunt to Perri and her twin for a while. Perri took to her because when she was a kid, Perri wanted to be a vet. But not so much anymore. I think they're getting started. That's Mona." Izzy nodded toward the podium as a hush fell over the crowd. Around them Stan could smell lighters as they brought the candles to life.

The crowd fell silent as Mona Galveston walked behind the podium. She looked very mayorly, with her tidy, short haircut, simple yet somber dress and a hint of red lipstick. She tapped the mic. The crackle blared through the night, silencing the last of the talkers.

"Good evening," she said in a crisp, clear voice that easily commanded attention. "Thank you all for coming. Tonight we are a town reeling from the tragedy and horror of losing one of our own. A friend, a neighbor, a woman with a rich history here. Carole Morganwick." She bowed her head slightly as she said Carole's name and waited a beat to ensure the crowd did the same.

The rest of the group stood around her, heads bowed in solemn remembrance of their friend and neighbor as Mona offered up the perfect mixture of praise, reminiscence and sorrow. By the time Mona was done, Carole sounded a lot more appealing than she had seemed in person.

Then, another familiar face on the fringes of the crowd. Trooper Jessie Pasquale. Shouldn't she be off duty? Still in uniform, she scanned the crowd with her flat eyes. Looking for the murderer, no doubt.

The murderer. Was he or she here? Stan suddenly felt chilled in her thin sweater, even though it was still in the seventies. And was Pasquale staring at her? Or was it her imagination?

"Are you okay?" Izzy nudged her.

"Yeah, why?"

"You look like you're about to faint or something."

"I don't faint." Stan forced herself to breathe. That tall man standing by himself, looming over the bench. He looked evil. Was it him? Or Betty Meany, arms crossed, all one hundred pounds of her guarding the library door? Could a little old woman do that? Then again, Betty wasn't all that old, when you got right down to it. She was probably in her early sixties. You didn't have to be a spring chicken to stab someone where it counted with a needle. Especially if the other person wasn't expecting it.

Mona Galveston finished her speech and the councilmen and councilwomen joined her at the podium. They all held hands and led the group in a moment of silence. Then Mona asked everyone to join her for the short walk up to the veterinary clinic, where they could leave their trinkets as a tribute in front of Carole's favorite place.

Stan felt what little food she'd choked down

today churn in her gut at the thought of going anywhere near the clinic. "I'm going home," she told Izzy. Before the other woman could reply, she stepped out of the crush of the crowd, which was moving forward with their candles, teddy bears and stuffed dogs and cats. Izzy was swept along, so all she managed was a wave and a look of sympathy.

Stan stood off to the side for a few minutes, breathing deeply, willing herself not to throw up in front of the whole town. When she felt a little steadier, she walked toward her house. The air had turned cooler now, and she scrubbed at the goose bumps popping up along her arms. She turned back once to find Trooper Pasquale lingering, too. And watching her. Stan deliberately turned away, but she felt the cop's eyes all the way to her front door.

Chapter 6

Stan tossed and turned all night. Dreams of people chasing her with needles woke her every hour. She finally fell asleep around four. When her cell phone rang next to her head, it felt like mere minutes later. She reached for it, squinting at the clock. *Nine-thirty! How can that be?* She didn't recognize the number, but forced herself to sound awake.

"This is Stan."

"Kristan Connor?" A woman's voice, it sounded clipped and efficient.

"Yes. Who's calling?" She sat up, throwing the pillow aside.

"This is Bernadette Macguire. I'm a recruiter for Infinity Financial. I've seen your credentials, and I'd like you to come in and speak with us about a vice president, media relations position. When are you available?"

Infinity. One of her old company's biggest competitors. Glee surged through her, but she tried to play it cool. Infinity only wanted the best people, and their recruiting efforts were pickier than most. "I . . . Can you tell me a bit more about the position?"

"Of course." Bernadette shuffled some pages on her end and reeled off the particulars of a job that sounded almost identical to the one Stan had lost. "Basically, the position is responsible for the media presence of the company. And we'd love to talk with you about it. Shall we set up an interview?"

"Please."

"What day works for you?" Bernadette clicked keys on her end of the line.

"Can we do next Tuesday?" Maybe Bernadette would think she was interviewing the rest of the week and not see her as desperate. And maybe at that point the police would have apprehended Carole's killer and she could focus on other things.

"Terrific. I have a ten and a two."

Stan chose the two and hung up. "What do you think of that, Nutty? Warner can go pound sand!"

He ignored her and went back to sleep. Stan wanted to do the same, but she knew it would be impossible. She leaned back against the pillows and thought about having a job again. An expense account. A place to wear her fancy shoes and nice suits. She had another chance. A new world to rule. "*I Will Survive*" began playing in her head.

Interestingly, the prospect didn't excite her as much as she thought it would. Maybe with some coffee. Before she could get out of bed to make it, her iPhone rang again. Her mother.

Stay positive. "Good morning," she nearly sang, grimacing at herself. God, she sounded fake.

"Did I interrupt anything?" Patricia asked in a tone suggesting she wasn't overconcerned if she had.

"No, just getting ready to go for a bike ride." Yes, that's what she would do today. Get the bike out and explore her new town. "How are you, Mom?" She forced herself out of bed and went downstairs.

"A bike ride? Don't you have a job interview?"

Stan forced the smile to remain in her voice as she got the coffeepot ready and pressed the button to grind the beans. "No, Mom, I don't." Had her mother tapped her phone?

"Kristan, you can't be serious. What are you *doing* with your time? Especially in that godforsaken place you moved to. Richard told me all about it."

"Richard did? When did you talk to him?" She moved to the refrigerator and grabbed smoothie ingredients while the coffee brewed.

"Oh, the other day," Patricia said dismissively. "The point is, you're in a funk. You need to get back into the land of the living."

Stan laughed. "Because I don't have a job? That's funny, Mom. When was the last time you worked?"

"Kristan! That was uncalled for. I do other things with my time. You're well aware of all the volunteer work. The fund-raisers. The contributions I make to the local community."

In other words, the luncheons she hosted and the vodka-and-tonic cocktails she drank. Stan threw a handful of berries on top of her carrot and apple slices. Dumped in protein powder and spinach leaves. "I know, Mom. Just saying." She turned the Vitamix on and walked away so she could still hear.

"Well, I'll chalk your comment up to the obvious distress you've been through. I called to let you know I gave a friend of mine your number. His name is Randolph Simon."

"The senator?"

"The very same. He's going to be looking for a new chief of staff. A division of time between Rhode Island and Washington. I told him you'd be perfect for the job."

Her mother never ceased to amaze her, even after thirty-five years. Stan had been seven years old the first time she asked if she had been adopted. To this day she wasn't completely convinced there hadn't been a swap at the hospital. Only problem was, she resembled her mother to a tee.

"Mom, I don't want to be a chief of staff for a senator. And I'll take care of my own job search, if and when I'm ready. Okay? I appreciate the thought, but please don't worry about it." She switched off the machine and poured the contents into a glass. Poured a side of coffee.

"You don't have to be ungrateful." Patricia's voice ticked up a couple of octaves. "I'm only trying to help you get back on your feet."

"Thanks, Mom. I appreciate it," she lied. "But I'm fine. And I need to get going. I still have a lot of unpacking. You should come see—"

"Never mind," Patricia cut her off. "I'll stop bothering you." And she disconnected.

Stan stared at the silent phone for a few seconds;

then she shook her head. Their conversations always seemed to go down this path. She wondered why she bothered, but then she remembered she hadn't. Her mother had called her.

Dropping the phone, she wandered into the sunroom with both her cups, alternating between a swig of coffee and a slurp of healthy. Observed her backyard. The grass was long. She needed to find someone to mow it. Char would know who.

Finishing her beverages, she changed her clothes, gathered her key, phone and water bottle and went out the front door. She almost slammed into a man wearing a trench coat standing on her porch. Stan gasped, startled, feeling her heartbeat kick up to high. Carole's lifeless body flashed through her brain again.

The strange-looking man snapped to attention when he saw her and stuck out his hand.

"Kristan Connor?"

The second time someone had asked her that today, and it was barely ten. Stan eyed him suspiciously. She did not offer her hand. What was up with the outfit in this heat? Jeans peeked out from the bottom of the coat. Sandals topped the look. He had a full head of unruly curls. Big glasses made his face seem slightly out of proportion. He carried a notebook and pen.

"Who's asking?"

The sandy-haired man bared his badly discolored teeth in an attempted smile. He dropped his hand and uncapped his pen. "Cyril Pierce from the *Frog Ledge Holler.* I understand you found Carole Morganwick's body?"

Oh no! Only then did she notice the press pass clipped to his jacket. It looked handmade. She remembered Carole's remark about the free paper—how Cyril drove everyone crazy with it.

She wanted to go back inside, lock the door and hide. But she couldn't, so she went to her backup survival skill: spin mode. "Yes, I was the first client with an appointment on Monday," she said. "It was terrible. Such a tragedy. But the police are engaged, and I'm confident they'll find the person responsible quickly."

"The police report said your name wasn't on her schedule. Can you explain?"

"Carole and I spoke about an appointment when she came to my house Sunday afternoon. She told me to come in before her first appointment."

Cyril Pierce scribbled furiously in his reporter's notebook. "Is it true that a bag of kibble was involved in this death?"

"You'd have to ask the police. It's an ongoing investigation." She crossed her arms and waited for him to finish writing so he could leave.

"Did you feel your animal . . . Is it a cat? A dog? A rabbit? Did it get the best care from Dr. Morganwick?"

"I have a cat. This would have been my first appointment, so I can't comment on the care she provides. And I have nothing further to say. If you'll excuse me."

Cyril nodded and closed his notebook. "Thanks for your time, Ms. Connor. And welcome to town," he added. "I hope you enjoy the newspaper." Cyril walked down her front steps and got on an old-fashioned bike with a basket in front. He tucked his notebook into a bag attached to the handlebars and pedaled away, trench coat flapping.

Stan shook her head. At least it wasn't the *Hartford Courant* knocking at her door. That was all she needed. Fired first, murder suspect next. Her former colleagues would have a field day.

Chapter 7

The black bike with the purple stripes stood against the garage wall, spiffy and shiny. Unused. Richard had gotten on a kick last year about how they should be biking through the local state parks. They'd never gone even once after she bought the bike, and Stan had never taken the initiative to go herself.

Well, things were different now. She didn't need anyone to "take" her biking. She was a grown woman and perfectly capable of going on her own excursions. Strapping on her matching purple helmet, she wheeled the bike into the driveway and hopped on. It had been a while, but it was true: You never forgot how to ride a bike. Stan pulled out of her driveway and turned left.

Yes, fresh air would help, whether Cyril Pierce wrote a story about her or not. Now she had to get her mind off this nonsense and start thinking about her life. The police would find the killer, and Frog Ledge would eventually get back to normal. She could get on with whatever she was going to do next.

Stan circled the green and rode through the center of town, mulling over her to-do list. She had to buy paint for her office. Furniture for the guest room. Curtains for the living room. She needed incense, as well as oils for her aromatherapy burner. And a trip to the health food store for organic ingredients. She loved playing with all the delicious, local ingredients available today and making Nutty's treats even healthier. And she'd promised trial meals for Char and Ray's dog, Savannah, and treats for Izzy's dogs, so she had to buy extra supplies.

But it was another beautiful, sunny day, and she needed to be outside. The green was hopping. Children rode bikes and chased dogs; others enjoyed their morning walks. She saw a few remnants from last night's memorial on the grass, but she figured the brunt of that would be at the clinic. She could see a flurry of activity at the library. In front of the War House, the historical home where the American Revolution's masterminds had strategized, volunteers sat out front in their rocking chairs, waiting for someone to wander by so they could talk history. She could see Izzy's shop in the distance and thought about stopping there. But then she'd just eat and would never get her bike ride in.

She turned the other way, instead, although she knew she should avoid going any farther down Main Street. There was no need to drive by the clinic right now—except she needed to see if anything was happening. She drove around the front of the library. Police tape still stretched across the clinic's front entrance. Orange cones blocked the parking lot. The building already had that deserted feel to it, like the house on the block the children avoided because something bad had happened in it. The stuffed animals and candles were gathered in a clump. A wooden cross was propped against the pile, and someone had scrawled, *Rest in Peace,* using sidewalk chalk, in front of the whole memorial.

She rode a bit closer. She stopped her bike and balanced on her toes, inwardly reciting what she hoped would pass for a prayer. It had been a while since she'd done any praying. Putting her feet back on the pedals, she started off down the street as Amara Leonard and a man came around the clinic from the back. Their heads were bent close together as they talked intently, sticking to the side of the building. It was like they didn't want anyone to notice them.

She and Amara locked eyes as Stan cruised by. Stan lifted one hand in a wave. Amara did not wave back. She averted her eyes as if she hadn't seen Stan. Interesting to see Amara by the clinic. The man didn't look familiar. He had a goatee and thin mustache and wore a suit.

Stan took a right and pedaled back down by the green, coasting around the south end nearest her house. A piece of plywood with paint scrawled on it announced a concert this weekend. There was supposed to be a farmers' market today, but some- one had crossed the date out and put Sunday's date, instead. Carole's name and *RIP* was notated next to the change of date. Apparently, she had been mourned enough to postpone even that sacred event.

She hung a left and headed down a lovely street called Pollywog Avenue. They really did have a thing for frogs around here. More old farmhouses lined each side of the street; flowers and other greenery grew over walls and onto the sidewalks. The large old houses were interspersed with newer, smaller homes, much like on Stan's street. Some were kept well; others were run-down. Frog Ledge seemed to be a place of contrasts. It made it more endearing.

Approaching a yard with a large wooden sign on it, Stan slowed to read it: GENE'S WOOD CARVINGS. There was a small silhouette of a man whittling away on some wood while a dog sat next to him. The woodworker's house. By contrast to the beautiful sign, the house fell into the old and run-down category. The white paint was faded and dirty. The porch steps sagged. She could see rotted wood in some spots. The decrepit barn next to the house must be the wood shop. Through the open barn doors, Stan could see a large table cluttered with saws and other equipment. She heard cutting noises and music.

As if the dog were on cue, the old yellow Lab lumbered out on the grass to see who was coming to visit, tail wagging lazily. Stan stopped her bike, holding out her hand. He came over and sniffed.

"Hey there, boy. How're you doing today?"

"That's Junior."

Stan jumped, almost dropping her bike. Gene materialized without a sound from behind a large bush. He smiled when he saw her.

"Sorry. Didn't mean to startle ya."

"It's okay. Stan Connor. We met last night at . . ." Stan's voice trailed off. She didn't want to bring up Carole's memorial.

"I remember ya, of course." He shook her hand. His hands were large and calloused. "Sightseeing?"

"Just getting some exercise." Stan reached into the front pocket of her messenger bag and pulled out her travel stash of treats. "Can Junior have a treat?"

"Well, he don't have a lotta teeth."

"These are soft. See?" Stan demonstrated by bending the cookie. Junior already sat at attention, with his eyes following her every move.

"Don't see why not, then. Go 'head, boy."

Stan leaned over and held the treat for the dog. Junior took it very politely and inhaled it, wagging his tail for more.

"Guess he likes 'em," Gene said, petting his dog. "Now, Junior. One's enough. He don't get out and exercise too much these days. Not like all you young people, running and so forth all over town."

"These are good-for-him treats. I make them myself."

"Whatever they are, he likes 'em. Course he likes lots of food," Gene said.

Stan didn't know if that was an insult or a compliment, so she let it go. Instead, she pointed to a wooden wagon on his front steps, filled with summer blooms. "Did you make that?"

He turned and surveyed the decoration. "I did."

The wood gleamed in the morning sun. Even

from where she sat on her bike, Stan could see the detail of the piece. "I love that. It would be perfect for my porch. I just moved into the green Victorian. Over by the town green."

"Ah." Gene nodded. "That's a nice house."

"It is. Could you make another one?"

He nodded.

"How much?"

He thought about that for a minute. "A hun-nerd fair?"

One hundred dollars sounded like a bargain to Stan. "Sold."

Gene nodded again. "I'll deliver it when I'm done. Take me about a week. Maybe a bit longer. I've got my new apprentice. Russ! Come on out. New customer."

Behind him, in the barn, Stan could now see a boy with black hair covering his face, bent over the table. The boy ignored Gene.

"Oh yeah. The dog's out here. He's afraid of dogs."

The old Lab didn't look like it would run if a bear was chasing it, never mind strike fear in the heart of a young boy. Stan petted Junior's head again and offered him another treat.

"So you're the official sign maker for the town?" she asked.

Gene smiled. "People need a sign, they call me. You need a sign for sumthin'?"

"Me? Not at the moment. Maybe someday. I'd rather have a wagon."

"I did all them signs for the center of town," he said.

"They're lovely. And I think it's such a nice idea

to have everything match." She thought of the sign outside of Carole's place. "I especially noticed the one at the vet clinic, since I was there the other day. With the cat and dog tails curled together."

Gene's face fell. "I made it. Made the other one for Doc Stevens too, when it was his. You prob'ly didn't see that one. But when Carole came back, I felt like she'd need a new one. So it was hers, know what I mean?"

"Of course. Did you know Carole well?"

"Sure did. We lived here together all our lives, 'cept when she left for bigger and better parts. She was friendly with my wife, Celia."

"I'm sorry. It's such a tragedy."

Gene glanced away, eyes blinking furiously. Someone who had liked Carole. It made her feel better.

"I'm sorry. I didn't mean to bring it up."

Gene made a *shrugging* motion. "Ain't nothing we can do about it." He scratched his head. "You want some eggs?"

"Eggs?" The conversation shift threw her off. Did he want to make her breakfast? "I, um, already ate, but thank you."

Gene looked at her like he didn't quite understand her. "Well, now, I don't know you'd want to eat them from the carton, but my chickens just laid a bunch this mornin'."

Stan felt the flush creep up her neck. He wanted to give her fresh eggs, not cook her scrambled eggs. Boy, did she have a lot to learn about country life. "That would be lovely, but I don't have anywhere to carry them."

"I could leave some for you on your porch," he said. "Or do automatic delivery, if ya like 'em."

Automatic delivery. For some reason this struck her as immensely funny and she had to hold back a giggle. This place certainly had its share of characters. "You know, that sounds great, Gene. Just let me know how much and I'll pay you for a week's worth, okay?"

Just then, two chickens ran around from the back of the house, squawking. "New customer!" Gene yelled to them, and they stopped and looked at him as if they understood what he was saying.

Stan waved good-bye and kicked her bike back into action. She wanted to log a few miles. Frog Ledge had a lot of hilly, winding roads. Stan approached the hills aggressively, forcing her legs to work harder for the reward on the other end. Reaching a downslope, she coasted, loving the feel of the hot breeze and sun hitting her face. She'd forgotten the exhilaration of bike riding.

Around the next bend Stan spotted a cemetery shaded by oaks and maples on a rolling hill. Stan braked at the entrance. She liked cemeteries, a quirk that her family and friends didn't quite get. If you thought about it as a bunch of bones rotting in the ground, or a boatload of corpses, sure, it might seem strange. But she loved to look at the names, imagine the stories of the people and the families and the legacies they'd left behind. Cemeteries were hopeful, if you looked at them in a different light. If you believed in coming back again as something or someone else, it was the start of a new life. If you believed in the afterlife, it felt good to think of your loved one there, happy. Peaceful.

It had been a long time since she'd visited one for no reason. The last cemetery she'd been in had hosted her maternal grandfather's funeral, a resting place for society's big names. Pretty but overdone, as most society affairs were. This grave-yard looked simpler. A lot of older stones. She pedaled through the gate and cruised down the main path. The grounds extended a lot farther than she'd thought. The older stones were situ-ated to the right, and continued back as far as she could see. Stones on the left side appeared to be newer. Fancier.

Stan turned her bike right and ventured down the historical path. The old stones appealed to her, both in appearance and possibility of the stories resting with the people beneath. She'd never been a huge history buff, but people of any time period fascinated her. Imagining their lives, their families, their secrets. A fun way to spend a summer morning.

And Cyril Pierce wouldn't look for her here. At least she hoped not. Towering oak trees, strategi-cally placed, provided some shade and dimmed the outside noise. As she moved on down the lines, a name caught her eye: *Elias Morganwick.* An old grave, thin stone, the dates faded by age and weather but still readable. *1817 to 1889.* One of Carole's early relatives? A hearty one. Seventy-plus years couldn't have been common back then. She wondered if Carole would be buried in this ceme-tery when they released her body for a funeral. After they determined what killed her, of course.

She cut across the path, forced herself to focus on the beautiful day instead of the murder. That's when she noticed the blue sedan idling up on the main path. Someone must be looking for a relative's stone. Stan rode on, lost in the sounds of summer. Chirping birds, a lawn mower, dogs barking, kids shouting.

Boy, was it hot. The sun seemed to follow her. Her helmet felt like a hundred pounds on her head, making her swelter inside it. She didn't realize the blue car had moved closer, until she caught a flash of light, the sun glinting off the paint. Uneasiness crept over her. There was no one else in the cemetery. Not even a grounds-keeper. And there *was* a murderer on the loose.

She turned back, casually, and picked up the pace. There had to be another street exit to this place. She didn't want to have to reverse direction and ride by the lurking car. Although she'd love a glimpse of the driver. She couldn't see anything from over here. But getting back to the main road, where there were people, would be the smart thing.

Stan left the path and cut through the head-stones, hoping she wasn't pedaling herself into a corner. She could sense the car coming closer, keeping pace with her, but she didn't turn. It was still far enough back that she wouldn't be able to identify anyone, anyway. Instead, she pedaled faster, ignoring the reality that she was also pedal-ing blindly, urging her screaming legs to pick up the pace. She would pay for this tomorrow. If she made it to tomorrow. Her imagination kicked in and she imagined a *Sopranos*-like scene where the driver of the car pulled out a fancy, silenced gun and popped her off right here. Or grabbed her and drove away to a house of horrors and torture.

Who would feed Nutty?

Under any other circumstance, and without the murdered vet hanging over her head, she'd have found her paranoid thoughts amusing and would have laughed them off. She wasn't part of a hit TV show or a best-selling horror novel.

Not today. Today she felt like she was part of a real-life drama a heck of a lot scarier than a TV show. Stan careened around a huddle of stones, heading for the perimeter. Worst case, she could haul the bike over the stone wall. It wasn't that high. Then she'd be on the street, where at least there might be witnesses to her untimely death. Or she could leave the bike and run.

She risked a glance around. The car gained on her. Her lungs were going to burst and her arms and legs ached. A rock in her path almost tipped her over, and she fought to keep control of the bike and not pitch forward over the handlebars. The blue car sped up and cut left, heading straight for her. Her eyes widened. She envisioned the car plunging over headstones in some desperate attempt to get to her. She was screwed.

And then a red Saab convertible appeared from the other direction. Stan thought about flagging the car down, but she'd look crazy. And the woman driving the car wasn't paying attention, anyway. Her music blared and she sang at the top of her lungs. Apparently, she was either happy to visit her deceased loved one, or really happy they were deceased.

Whatever her reasons, her presence halted the blue car. The Saab passed it. Stan took advantage of the lull, pedaling furiously, keeping close to the wall. She'd hit a slight decline in the terrain and used it, pushing her legs harder. Then she saw huge iron gates. A much larger entrance than the one on the other end. And the gates were wide open. She wanted to sob with relief. What a glorious sight! She flew through, wild with freedom and civilization, as cars whizzed past and the noise level rose a few octaves. She glanced behind her. The blue car wasn't in sight.

She paused to rest for a minute. Now that imminent danger had passed, she felt a little silly. What if she'd imagined the car stalking her? It could have been someone looking for a headstone. Or a funeral director looking for a plot. Or someone else who just liked cemeteries.

The stress of the move and Carole's death was getting to her. She reached for her water and realized she'd lost the bottle during her all-terrain ride. Shoot. It was hot out here and she was suddenly very thirsty.

And she had no idea where she was. She couldn't be that far off track from the road she'd been on when she first found the cemetery. But she sure as heck wasn't going back through it, imagination or not. She'd had enough for one day. She felt around in the small bag she'd brought for her phone. She could use the GPS. But the phone wasn't in there. She vaguely remembered throwing it on the table after speaking with her mother.

She turned left and started pedaling again,

keeping the cemetery next to her. That had to bring her back somewhere near her house. Of course it was all uphill. Stan could feel sweat dripping down her back and wished she could find a pool to jump into.

A honking horn behind her startled her, and her bike jumped the curb. Almost into oncoming traffic. Cursing, she wobbled to a stop and turned. A black pickup truck idled across the street. Jake grinned at her. Duncan pushed his head next to him in the window and howled.

"Sorry 'bout that," Jake said. "Didn't mean to startle you."

Stan waited until the cars had passed; then she crossed the street to them. "Between the two of you, I'm lucky I'm still alive." She reached in and scratched Duncan's ears. "Hi, fella."

"You doing a triathlon or something?" Jake asked. "The only thing I haven't seen you do is swim."

She smiled, thinking of her still-empty bucket list, the athletic event she'd thought about adding to it. Why hadn't she? "No. Just figured I'd check the town out a bit. Found the cemetery." She glanced over her shoulder. Wondered if she should mention the car and figured he would think she was crazy. "By the way, do you, um, know the quickest way back?"

He laughed. "Got yourself lost, did you? You want a ride? It's damn hot out here. And you're a good few miles out."

"I am?" She looked around dubiously. "I came

through the cemetery, but I didn't want to go back that way."

He watched her, then opened the door. "Get in. I'll throw your bike in back. I have cold water in the cooler. You don't want heat stroke."

Stan opened her mouth to protest, but then she remembered her lost bottle of water. Oh, well. She could live with being a wuss if it meant a cold drink. She hopped off and unhooked her helmet. "Thanks."

"No problem." He hefted the bike easily onto the bed of his truck. Stan couldn't help noticing again how cute he was. Which made her remember Richard, who was cute in an uptight sort of way. Jake looked like the laid-back sort. She walked around to the other side of the truck and climbed in. Duncan immediately plopped onto her lap.

"So you went through the cemetery? It's one of the biggest in the county," Jake said, jumping back in and pulling out into traffic. "Nice paths, if you like that sort of thing. Cooler's right there." He nodded at her feet.

"Mmm," Stan said noncommittally, reaching around Duncan and pulling out a blessedly cold bottle. She looked out the window as they drove, noting every blue car that passed. None of them looked like the car in the cemetery. "I hope I'm not taking you out of your way."

Jake glanced at her with a smile. "The whole town isn't but forty miles around. Not much is out of my way around here. Don't chug the water. You're probably overheated. Don't want to shock your system."

Good point. Stan resisted the urge to do just that, but she took a big swig. "Thanks. It's hot out there." She pulled her treats out of her pack and fed one to Duncan. He wagged his tail so hard that he almost shifted the truck into another gear.

"It is. Happens this time of year. What are you feeding that unruly mutt?"

Stan smiled. He looked scruffy today. Unshaven, his hair too long. *It makes him look dangerous. Which he is,* she reminded herself. *Izzy will certainly tell me that.* "Some of my homemade treats. Pumpkin spice."

"You coming to the farmers' market on Sunday?" He made a left and suddenly they were driving by Gene's place. Gene was still outside with his dog and his chickens, hard at work on a piece of wood. Stan wondered if it was for her wagon.

"I just saw the sign this morning. I'm definitely planning on it. I need some goat cheese."

"Well, you'll have plenty to choose from. It's a big event." He jerked a thumb at the back of his truck. "That's why I'm hauling tables around. We won't tell anyone your bike was on top of them. They won't want to put their veggies out."

"Do you eat goat cheese?"

"I do. Sadie Brown's goat cheese is the best, if you want my opinion." He placed his hand over his heart. "You'll be instantly in love. If that's your thing."

"It is," Stan said. "Which farm does Sadie Brown run?"

"The Sandy Beach Goat Farm. It's down the

other way from my place. Hey, you know, they're not formal about who sells stuff there. You should bring some of those treats. With the dog population around here, you'll make some extra cash, guaranteed."

"You really think so? I've never sold my treats. Except at adoption events."

"Heck yes. Your pal Izzy has a table at every farmers' market. Why don't you set up on a corner of it and see what happens?"

"It wouldn't hurt to try, I guess." She was already thinking about how much she should bake and how she would have to add to her grocery list.

"Not at all. Dunc will make me buy some, I'm sure." Jake nodded at the dog nosing her pack and took a hairpin turn onto Stan's street. She could hear her bike skidding along the truck bed. He pulled into her driveway and left the engine running while he fetched her bike out of the back. Duncan remained across her lap, pretending to be asleep.

"Come on, fella. I have to get out," she urged. He didn't budge. Jake came back and hung his arms in the open window. He shook his head.

"Dunc!" The dog lifted his head, blinked lazily at Jake, then dropped again. Stan laughed.

"I know, I know, he's not well behaved," Jake said as Stan hefted him enough to get a leg out of the truck. Then she wriggled the rest of the way out from under his death grip.

"It's okay. He's cute. Thanks for the ride. And the water." She patted Duncan's head. He gave her a woeful glance.

She leaned in and whispered, "I'll come see you soon and bring treats. You don't have to buy any."

He wagged his tail.

"You conspiring with my dog?" Jake asked.

"I conspire with all four-legged creatures," Stan said. "See you at the farmers' market."

"Oh, I'm sure I'll see you before then," Jake said.

Chapter 8

Jake pulled away with a wave, Duncan hanging out the window, tongue lolling. Stan stashed her bike and helmet in the garage and went to the front door. Before she went inside, she turned and scanned the street. The blue sedan hadn't reappeared, but there were a dozen eggs sitting on her porch. Gene's chickens worked fast.

She unlocked her door and heard a *thump* and then running feet across the porch. A black cat with a shock of white on the top of his head trotted over to her, meowing loudly. He tried to squeeze past her inside the house.

"Well, hello," she said, crouching down and holding out her hand. The cat came closer and sniffed her, still mewing. Stan wondered if he was lost. He wore a purple collar with a tag. She flipped it over and read the information: *Houdini*. And a phone number.

"Houdini, eh?" Stan said. "Are you lost? Do you want to come inside and I'll call your mom or dad?"

Houdini responded by slinking into the house. Stan hoped Nutty stayed upstairs. "Come on, then," she told the cat. He followed her obediently down the hall into the kitchen. Stan closed both doors to keep Nutty out, turned and surveyed her new friend.

"Here, have a treat while I call." She bent down, flipped his tag over and pressed the digits into her phone. She fed him his treat with her other hand. He nearly swallowed it whole and rubbed on her leg for another. A woman answered.

"Hello, this is Stan Connor on Town Green Road. I think I have your cat, Houdini, here."

"Oh, my goodness! That little rascal," the woman exclaimed. "I think he snuck out this morning when I came back from my early walk. I'm so glad I got him a tag with my cell number on it. This has happened a few times lately. I'll come right over and get him. Which house are you, dear?"

"The green Victorian," Stan said. "And don't worry. He's inside with me. Having some treats."

"Well, how nice of you," the woman said. "I'm Betty, by the way. I'm just up the street at the library. I hope I'm not holding you up."

"Not at all. If you want me to keep him until you're done at work, that's fine, too."

"Oh, how sweet. But I can grab him in a pinch and drop him off at home."

Stan hung up and fed Houdini another treat. He gobbled that one, too. "Did you miss breakfast this morning, or do you just like my treats?" she asked. "I guess it could be my treats. Lots of animals like them." She gave him another and poured herself a glass of iced tea while she waited. Houdini's owner had to be the infamous Betty Meany. Maybe she could get some information. The thought perked her up a bit. Maybe Houdini had really wanted her to meet his mom and gotten lost on purpose. Cats could be so considerate that way.

Stan left him locked in the kitchen and went looking for Nutty. This house was so large compared to their last place that she felt like she never saw him. He was always finding new corners to explore and sun spots to lounge in. She called him a few times and was about to give up when she noticed him lounging on the window seat at the top of the stairs, half hidden behind one of the pillows.

"Ah. There you are. Just wanted to let you know we have a guest, and I have a lot of treat baking to do. We're going to sell our goods at the farmers' market this weekend."

Nutty didn't look impressed. He blinked lazy eyes at her and swished his tail.

"Well, I have to get appreciation somewhere, don't I?" She went back downstairs, leaving him to it.

It wasn't long before her doorbell rang. She hurried out to greet Betty. It certainly looked like the foot-tapping woman assisting with last night's vigil, but Stan hadn't gotten close enough. Barely five feet tall, Betty reminded Stan of Helen Mirren with her short, spiky gray hair. She also wore fun red glasses with rhinestones, which matched her red blouse.

"Hello, I'm Betty. Betty Meany. So lovely to

meet you. Now where is that fresh little boy? And what did you say your name was, again?"

"I'm Stan. And Houdini's right this way. I put him in the kitchen so he wouldn't fight with my cat if they saw each other." Stan led her down the hallway. "I'm so pleased to meet you. I've heard a lot about you already. Do you live nearby?"

"Two streets over, thataway." Betty waved in the general direction of Stan's backyard. "Houdini used to be an outdoor cat and I rescued him, but he still has a wild side and loves to escape. That's why I call him Houdini. There you are, you silly little boy!" She set her purse down and scooped the cat into her arms, nuzzling her face in his black fur. "What a bad boy!"

And then she burst out crying.

Alarmed, Stan immediately grabbed a box of tissues from the counter and handed it to her. "Don't cry, Betty. He's fine," she said. "And I'm sure he's sorry. Right, Houdini?"

Houdini responded by jumping out of his owner's arms and onto the counter, where he rubbed on her treat jar. "I'm so sorry you're upset, Betty. Please sit." Stan pulled out a chair and motioned to it.

Betty sank into it, pulled off her glasses and dabbed at her eyes with a tissue, still clutching the box. "I'm sorry I'm such a wreck. It's not your fault. I'm glad Houdini turned up. I would have been devastated. I just lost one of my babies. My Snickers."

The name caused her to go off on a fresh bout of tears. Betty blew her nose loudly; then she crumpled the tissues in her hand, still sniffling.

"I'm so sorry," Stan said. "That must be hard."

"It is," Betty agreed with a hiccup. "Especially when they don't have to die. Snickers was fifteen, but she should have lived another ten years. Well, at least five. Cats can live that long, you know. Especially ones who are treated well. And my babies are treated like kings and queens. Would you like to see her picture?"

Without waiting for an answer she pulled her wallet out of her bag and extracted a photo of a pretty calico cat, sunning herself on a cat bed.

"Adorable," Stan said. "What happened to Snickers?"

Betty narrowed her eyes. "That awful woman happened to her. I know you shouldn't speak ill of the dead, but I'm sorry. She killed my cat as surely as if she'd shot her with a gun."

"Who?" Stan asked carefully. She wanted to hear it straight from Betty.

"Dr. Morganwick." Betty nearly spit the words. "And she shouldn't have called herself a doctor. She was nothing but a fraud, who wanted to push her vaccines and her bad food. What kind of treats are those, anyway? I've never seen him so hell-bent on a treat. He doesn't usually like the ones I buy, and I refuse to buy the garbage at the grocery store."

Stan turned to where Houdini was rubbing the jar and purring loudly. "They're homemade. Those are cheese-flavored treats. I also have pumpkin spice. I can give you some to take home, if you'd like." She got up and fed one to the cat.

"How thoughtful," Betty said. "I have another baby at home. A tiger cat. Copperfield."

"I can send some for him, too."

"Snickers loved treats."

"So you were telling me what happened to Snickers." Stan got up to put treats in a plastic bag. She heard scratching on the kitchen door. Nutty, wondering why his mother was packing up his treats for someone else. She was in for it when Betty left.

"I had Snickers since she was a baby. Just a tiny six-week-old kitten." Betty traced a finger over the photo.

Stan had never thought about losing Nutty— why would she, he was only four or five—but now she realized how awful it would be. And especially after fifteen years! She brought the treat bag back to the table.

"She went to Dr. Stevens. He was wonderful. And not just out to make a buck. So many vets, I've heard stories where they would rather let these sweet animals die than put someone on a payment plan. It's shocking. But Dr. Stevens wasn't like that. He would treat a hurt possum, if you brought one in to him. He loved animals.

"Anyway, Dr. Stevens never bothered me about getting all these shots for Snickers. He understood she never went outside. None of my cats do. Unless you count this one, when he sneaks out." She shook her finger at Houdini. He rubbed Stan's leg and meowed. "He knew those vaccines do more harm than good. They're just money-makers. If you don't know that, you should do some research. Because that's what you'll find. Moneymakers." Betty pounded her tiny hand on the table for emphasis.

Stan made a sound of agreement.

"She was doing just fine, Snickers was. And then Dr. Stevens got sick and had to stop practicing. That was terrible. Just terrible. We had no town vet for almost a year. Can you imagine? And then"—Betty paused, and sighed dramatically—"Carole came back to town."

"So you knew her before she left?"

"Knew her! Of course. Her family has been here for years. There's no one left, though, just Carole and her brother, but he lives clear across the country. She was the last one. Well, her boy, but I have no idea what happened to him. They moved away and she came back alone. Her ex probably took him from her. They were always fighting, those two."

Ex-husbands. Angry customers. And Jessie Pasquale had her as a murder suspect? "Sounds like Carole had a rough life."

Betty snorted. "She made her own bed, that one. Her family name provided her with a cushion around here, and she still managed to screw it up. But none of that excuses what she did to Snickers. And probably all these other unsuspecting cats and dogs. I hope your baby wasn't subjected to her!"

"She died before Nutty could see her. So what happened when she came back to town?"

"She took over the practice, like her daddy intended. And, naturally, everyone who loved Dr. Stevens didn't think twice about going to her. Because that's what you do in towns like ours. You support each other. Plus, we already trusted her name. Her father had been a vet here, too.

Horses and farm animals, mostly. He even took care of the Galvestons' racehorses. I brought my babies over to introduce them to Carole, and the first thing she did was insist Snickers—all of them—get those awful rabies shots. Lectured me on how it's the law. Well, *law, schmaw,* in my opinion. It's a way to get money, and everyone knows those shots hurt our pets. But she made it sound so . . . *dire.* Like the health inspector was going to come to town and take them away from me. Such a terrible way to operate, scaring your customers. But I love my kitties, so I did it. And then Snickers started getting lumps, right where the shots were. I told Carole, but she insisted the shots had nothing to do with it. Told me I had to get them, that it was for her own good. I listened to her. When I finally listened to me, it was too late for Snickers." Her eyes filled up again. "She already had cancer. Lymphoma."

"That's terrible." And, boy, was it easy to get information around here! It just walked through your door.

"Anyway. Enough of that stuff. I don't mean to dump all this on you when you were so nice to save Houdini." Betty shoved herself out of the chair, leaving dirty tissues in her wake. "You should come to the library and get your card. I would love it if you signed up."

"I will certainly do that," Stan said. "I love libraries."

Betty beamed. "Excellent. I should let you get back to your day. I'll see you at the circulation desk!" Betty stood up, gathered her purse and picked up Houdini.

"It was my pleasure. Here, don't forget your treats." Stan handed her the bag. "And I'm so sorry about Snickers."

"Thank you, dear." Betty switched her funky red glasses for a pair of enormous sunglasses, hiding her eyes. "Unfortunately, I'm not sorry that awful woman is gone."

Chapter 9

Nikki arrived promptly at seven with her hands full of goodies: two bottles of Stan's favorite Merlot, take-out sushi, cannoli for dessert and a buttercream-scented Yankee Candle.

"Housewarming," she announced, sweeping through the front door. "Wow, it looks great in here! You've been busy."

Nikki had cleaned up after her long day in the kennel. She wore knee-length denim shorts with a sequined T-shirt and her trademark cowboy boots. Her black hair was streaked with candy-apple red, cropped short in the back with longer pieces framing her face in front. Her nails were painted a wicked purple. Stan always wondered how she took care of the dogs without breaking a fingernail. Those suckers were long.

"I hung some pictures. That's about as far as I got." But the long hallway did look great with the framed photos of New York City in various stages of night telling its story all the way to the kitchen. "Where's Justin tonight?"

"Diving conference in California." Nikki's boyfriend, a dive instructor and surfer dude, spent a lot of time on the West Coast. He always tried to bring Nikki, but she resisted leaving the transport for too long. "I have to go look around again, now that it's really yours. Then we can chow."

She dropped her messenger bag on the floor and took off down the hall. Stan followed, anxious to see the rooms again through her friend's eyes. Though very different, each room was cozy and inviting and had so much potential. She loved the glorious orange kitchen, with its tan soapstone counters and matching deep sink to offset the bright walls, an economy-sized stainless-steel dishwasher, and even a hanging rack for pots and pans, poised over the island in the middle of the room.

Dining room, living room, with a gas fireplace, office, den and half bathroom made up the rest of the downstairs. Three bedrooms upstairs. Hers had a master bathroom, and there was another full bathroom down the hall. A huge difference coming from a two-bedroom condo.

"This is so great." Nikki finished her tour back in the kitchen. "I can't wait to see what you do with the place. Come on, let's bust open this wine and eat. Then we can get some work done."

"If we drink too much wine, that might be tough," Stan said. "Honestly, I'm not feeling much like decorating." And after the bike ride and the blue-car incident today, her nerves were even more shot.

"I know," Nikki said sympathetically. "Do people know you found her?"

"I think the better question would be, does anyone *not* know I found her." Sighing, she pulled out plates and wineglasses. "I guess Richard was right about small-town people."

"What does Richard know about small towns?" Nikki's back was to Stan as she unpacked the sushi and arranged it carefully on one of the plates; then she did the same with seaweed salad and edamame. She tried to keep the edge out of her voice, but Stan could hear it, sharp as a sushi chef's knife.

"I don't know. Common knowledge? He just made a comment. Forget it. Come on, let's go sit out there." She motioned to the sunroom, where it had already cooled off from today's eighty-plus temps.

"I just don't want him to make you second-guess yourself. I think coming here will be good for you." Nikki grabbed the plates and chopsticks and went to sit.

"Dead bodies and all?" Stan poured the wine and followed; the candle and lighter were tucked under her arm.

"Well, that's just a fluke." Nikki placed the sushi in front of her with a flourish and handed her a set of chopsticks. "Spicy tuna, avocado, shrimp tempura, and the fancy one you like with eel and tuna and mango."

"You're awesome." Stan popped a spicy tuna into her mouth. "Haven't eaten all day. Or really, since it happened."

"Hear anything new about the murder?"

"No, but I'm sure I will tomorrow. The *Frog Ledge Holler* reporter showed up at my door today."

"Frog Ledge Holler?" Nikki sneered.

"Yeah. It comes out once or twice a week. Or whenever there's news. It's a one-man show, but it's still the press."

"You know how to handle the press. Here, toast. To your new life." Nikki held up her wineglass.

Stan clinked it, trying to keep her smile in place. "Not when I'm the subject of the inquiry."

"What do you mean?"

She sipped her wine, watched her friend wolf down sushi and salad, popping edamame between bites. "They're suspicious of me. Carole never wrote in the appointment. I found the body. At first, I thought the cop was being overly argumentative because it was the murder scene, but she was watching me last night at the vigil."

"I'm sure she was watching everyone. Don't they figure their murderer will show up at stuff like that? It was a candlelight vigil?" At Stan's nod, Nikki waved her chopsticks dismissively. "You're reading too much into it. Cops are supposed to stare at people during events like that."

"I don't know, Nik. It freaked me out, to be honest."

"Don't let them get to you. You didn't do anything wrong. They're just floundering right now. Plus, it's a small town. Anytime people die in small towns—especially if they're offed—people get crazy. Believe me, I've lived in small towns forever, unlike Richard. It's how it works. It'll die down. Oops, sorry."

Despite herself, Stan smiled. "Hopefully."

"It will." Nikki popped her last piece of sushi in

her mouth. "Delish," she pronounced. "Tell me, what do we need to unpack? When you're done, I mean. Take your time." She looked pointedly at Stan's still-full plate. "Keep eating."

Stan took a bite of seaweed salad and forced it down. "I did the clothes in the spare bedroom. Even my poor, sad suits. They're like orphans now. Oh, and I organized my shoes. And wrote grocery lists. Hey, that's what I need to do. Go to the store for ingredients for treats. Want to go? There's a little general store down the street."

"Sure, let's go. We might need another bottle of wine." Nikki drained her glass as if to prove the point. "And you've hardly touched yours."

"I'm working on it. And we're not going to a package store. It's a general store. You know, supplies, cutesy things. Probably lots of spoon rests shaped like cows."

"My idea of a good time."

The general store, like the rest of the buildings in Frog Ledge, had that New England small-town feel. Nothing like the small food markets in her old neighborhood. The general store had one of Gene's signs out front announcing their hours. Plants and flowers cluttered the porch, and an old whiskey barrel had been carved out and crammed full of outdoorsy baubles. A bench completed the welcoming feel. A small group of teenagers putzed around in the near-empty parking lot with their skateboards.

"Wow, they're open until eight. That seems late for around here," Nikki said. "It's late where I live, that's for sure." Nikki's property in nearby Rhode Island, only forty or so minutes away, was perfect for her rescue operation. It was not a metropolis. Her farm-style house had enough room for her own four dogs and five cats to live apart from any inside foster animals. She'd turned the barn out back into separate dog kennels, where her transport rescues lived until adoption, and her land was large enough and far enough away from her neighbors that no one bothered her. The property had been in her family for years, and her parents gave it to her when she started the transport business in earnest. Then they'd hit the road and moved to Florida.

"It must be because they serve coffee, and everything else is closed." Stan pushed the front door open, setting a bell jingling. She could smell still-fresh coffee and pastry in the air, mixed with the faint scent of apples. The woman behind the counter looked up and beamed.

"Good evening! Can I help you find something?" Plump and motherly, her salt-and-pepper hair stood out in frizzy curls around her head. A small fan positioned right at her wasn't keeping up with the beads of sweat on her forehead.

Stan smiled at her. "Hi, I'm just looking for some local honey and rolled oats."

"Right over there." The woman stepped out and pointed down the middle aisle. "I have local bee pollen, too, if you need some."

"Bee pollen?" Nikki repeated.

"Oh, yes, it's wonderful. Great for allergies. We get ours from our local beekeeper right down the road." She smiled. "I'm Abbie, the owner. Holler if you have any questions."

"Do you have organic meats, too?" Stan asked.

"Chicken, beef, turkey and lamb, right in that freezer." Abbie pointed to the back of the store.

The bell dinged and Gene Holdcroft walked in. His overalls were covered in wood dust and his work boots left little puddles of it. He nodded at the three of them.

"Evenin', ladies."

"Hi, Gene!" Abbie lit up. "I have some more of those cakes you like. Just got fresh ones in today. Aisle two."

"Thank ya," Gene said, and headed that way. Abbie watched him adoringly.

"Actually, I do have a question." Stan turned to Abbie. "Do you know anyone who mows lawns?"

Abbie thought about that. "Most folks do their own round here. How much lawn? And how you been getting by so far?"

"Oh, I just moved to town this weekend. The lawn isn't that big."

Abbie's face changed, almost imperceptibly, but Stan could see the flutter of recognition in her eyes, the wariness replacing the warmth. "This weekend, eh? The green Victorian?"

"Yes," Stan said.

Abbie fought to keep the smile in place, obviously thinking about her sale. "Well, that's a lovely house. No one comes to mind for the lawn, but I'll keep an ear out."

The bell over the front door clanged again, breaking the awkward moment. Stan could almost feel Abbie's relief as she turned to greet her new customer.

A young man stumbled in, hair sticking up in what could either be a chic new hairdo or evidence of him rolling out of bed and coming to the store. Despite it being nearly night, he wore dark sunglasses that hid most of his face. He hitched up his falling-down denim shorts and nodded at the three women staring at him.

"'Lo," he muttered, then lurched down the aisle to the far right.

Abbie shook her head.

The bell clanged again and Perri Galveston hurried in, looking like she wanted to take someone's head off. She was much shorter without her ginormous heels.

"Hi, Abbie, sorry, did Paul just barge in here?" She stopped and smiled at Stan and Nikki. "Hello."

Stan realized the skinny boy who couldn't keep his pants up was the same boy who'd gotten out of Perri's convertible yesterday at the vigil. She still hadn't seen his face. He'd been wearing dark glasses then, too. And pants that didn't fit.

"He did," Abbie said, pointing in the direction he'd gone. "He looks like he's having a rough night."

Perri raised her hands, palms up, in a gesture that conveyed, *What can you do?* Then she went off to find her brother. Abbie clucked and muttered something about drugs being terrible; then she busied herself with something behind the counter. Nikki stared in the direction of Perri and Paul. Stan poked her arm.

"Let's get the stuff."

Nikki turned back, distracted. "Huh? Oh, sure. Coming." She followed Stan down the aisle.

"I can use the honey in my peanut butter treats. I'm trying to mix up my recipes." Stan surveyed her honey choices and chose a bottle from Clover Hill Farm. "I hope the dogs like it, although the cats will probably be harsher critics." She turned for Nikki's response to find the aisle empty behind her. Stan grabbed her rolled oats and a small bottle of bee pollen, took some ground turkey out of the freezer and hurried up front.

Nikki was nowhere to be found. Stan checked down the other couple of aisles. Gene was perusing the cakes in aisle two. When he saw her, he beckoned her over.

"Heard you ask 'bout mowing. My apprentice can do it for ya. I'll send him over. Just add it to the egg bill." He smiled.

"Really? That would be wonderful. But I don't have a lawn mower."

"He'd bring mine. Twenty-five bucks."

It sounded like a bargain to Stan. She agreed. Gene promised to have Russ there in the morning. Stan returned to the register, catching a glimpse of Nikki outside the front door. She was engaged in an intense conversation with Perri Galveston.

Nikki knew the mayor's daughter? It didn't look like a conversation of *I just met you. How do you like the local honey?* Abbie steadfastly rang up her purchases, eyes averted. Afraid to make eye contact with the suspected murderess, lest she end up like Carole.

"Thank you so much," Abbie said, fumbling with the receipt tape and finally handing the slip of paper to Stan, eyes focused just over her left shoulder. "And come again!"

Stan grabbed her bag and shoved the front door open. Nikki and Perri had disappeared off the porch, which meant Stan had to search for her and prolong her stay. She gritted her teeth and rushed out the door. In her haste she almost knocked someone off the porch.

"Shoot, sorry," she said. "Not paying atten . . . Oh, hi."

Jake McGee grinned at her. "I probably deserved that for letting my ill-behaved mutt almost knock you over every time he sees you."

"No, I'm much more evil with my payback than that." *Evil? That isn't a good thing to say, especially now.* Then she remembered who his sister was, and cringed even more. Jessie Pasquale had probably sent him to catalogue her purchases in case she planned to poison anyone next. She held the door for him, hoping he'd just go inside.

But he made no move to pass her. "What do you think of our fine supermarket?" he asked.

"I think it's cute." Except the owner hates me already. "Good bee pollen," she added lamely.

"I love good bee pollen." He said it with such a straight face, Stan couldn't tell if he was mocking her or being completely serious.

"Yeah. Well. I have to go find my friend."

Jake followed her gaze to the parking lot, where she could see Nikki and Perri standing next to Perri's car. "Then I'll let you go," he said. "You have a great evening. If you girls aren't doing anything later, stop by McSwigg's. Drinks on the house for first-timers."

Stan laughed. "All of them, or just the females?"

"Wow. Tough crowd," Jake said. "Drinks on the house. End of story."

"Well, I'm still unpacking, so we probably won't, but thank you."

Jake smiled. "The offer's good whenever," he said, and headed inside the store.

Stan watched him greet Abbie and disappear down one of the aisles; then she turned and walked to her car and put her bag in the backseat. Nikki and Perri were still talking. She heard a male voice interrupt, loudly, and turned to see Paul get into the car next to Perri's convertible. He backed up haphazardly, turned and zoomed by her out of the parking lot, nearly taking out Jake's truck in the process.

He drove a blue sedan.

Stan stared after the rapidly fleeing car. She couldn't tell in the dark if it was the same one that had stalked her in the cemetery today. She had to find out about this kid. If what Abbie said was true, he was on drugs. And drug addicts would do just about anything to get a hit. But first she wanted to get out of this parking lot before Jake came back out.

"Nik! You coming?"

"Hang on a second," Nikki's voice drifted distractedly. She didn't seem to be in a hurry to finish her conversation.

Stan blew out a breath, annoyed, and got in the car. Jake still didn't emerge. Finally Nikki hurried over and got in. Perri drove by and beeped. Nikki didn't wave back.

"How do you know her?" Stan pulled out of the parking lot. She kept one eye on the rearview mirror and the other on the lookout for the blue sedan. She didn't want Paul following them home and finding out where she lived. Although the entire town probably already knew that, so it was kind of a moot point.

"What are you looking for?" Nikki asked, instead of answering.

"Nothing. Thought I saw something in the street. So how? Or is it a big secret or something?"

"What do you mean?"

"That was a pretty intense conversation for a casual acquaintance. And it seems like you don't want to talk about it."

"It's really not a big deal. When I used to do transport from New York, she worked with an advocacy group down there."

"Perri Galveston? Really?"

"Yup. I didn't know her well, but a bunch of us were dealing with an awful shelter in Brooklyn, trying to get it closed down. We took all the help we could get. So, are we baking?"

Stan pulled into her driveway, still curious, but Nikki didn't have anything else to say. Stan decided to let it go.

"I'm baking. You drank too much wine." She let them in the front door. Nutty waited. She bent to pet his head.

"And I'm gonna drink more," Nikki said. "Maybe I'll just crash here tonight. And as long as you're baking, can you bake for the adoption event Saturday?"

"Fine with me if you stay. What am I baking? Oh, hang on." Stan dropped her groceries on the table and searched through her purse for her phone, which had begun playing the piano solo that indicated an incoming call. Richard. "Hey," she said. "You back?"

"I am." He sounded tired. "How are you? How's the picture hanging going?"

Behind her, Nikki left the room. Probably to get more wine so she didn't have to hear the conversation. "Pretty good. How come you didn't call me back the other day? I had something to tell you."

"I know, I'm sorry. There were a ton of people around and we left dinner late. But I can't wait to hear your story. Can we talk about it tomorrow? So I can give you my full attention? I need to get some sleep. It was a long few days."

"Oh. Sure. Give me a call tomorrow."

"Thanks, babe. Love you." He disconnected.

"Richard's tired?" Nikki reappeared with the open wine bottle and two glasses.

"Yeah. Those conferences are draining." Stan heard the defensive tone in her voice and forced it back. "Anyway, an adoption event?"

"I'm having one on Saturday. Hoped you might join me. With treats." Nikki turned puppy dog eyes on her. "You know what a hit they are at those things. We always make money off them."

"You should've mentioned it while we were in the store. I would've bought more stuff."

"Sorry, I forgot. It's eleven to three, on Saturday, at that cute store in Jamestown. You know, the one with the handmade sweaters?"

"I remember. Okay, I'll bring a good variety."

Nikki smiled. "You always do."

Chapter 10

Stan's kitchen smelled like a bakery, and it was only eight in the morning. Sleep had eluded her for most of the night. Finally at five, when she heard Nikki get up and leave, she decided to make the most of the time. She'd brewed another lovely pot of Izzy's coffee, made a smoothie and got some treats going. On the menu: peanut butter bran, apple and cheddar and apple cranberry oat. Some new kinds. She wanted to try some of them out on Nutty before baking extra batches for Saturday's adoption event. Once those were in the oven, she started the slow-cooker chicken for Nutty's meals.

She loved cooking and baking. Her grandmother, the original animal whisperer, had passed that love on to her. Humans or animals, her grandma was always feeding something, but her four-legged friends and neighbors had especially appreciated it. Her grandmother had been able to tame the most unruly beast with her cookies. Stan had always wished for the talent.

Now there was no excuse not to cultivate it. And lovely to have the doors and windows open on a beautiful summer day, in her own house, with all the time in the world. The scene would be perfect if she didn't have visions of dead vets dancing in her head and lingering memories of a cemetery stalker.

"*Better take advantage while it lasts,*" that annoying, responsible voice lectured as she offered Nutty a freshly baked and cooled treat. "*You need to get a job. Maybe as soon as next week.*"

Stan pushed the thought away; then she felt immediately guilty. "You need to be excited about this job interview," she told herself out loud, pulling the next batch out of the oven with a gloved hand and setting it on the counter. The morning sun glinted through the windows, bouncing shards of light around the pretty tiled floor where Nutty sprawled, watching her every move, licking his mouth and waiting for more.

"And these aren't for you. These are for the adoption event," she told him. "But I'm making you chicken. With veggies and a little cheese. Do you think this job interview is a good idea?"

Nutty stared at her steadily, his tail swishing across the floor. Clearly, he wasn't about to give her a thoughtful answer without a good meal first.

The sound of an engine roaring to life right outside her window made her jump. She peered through the blinds and saw a black-haired boy pushing a beat-up lawn mower. Gene's apprentice. She'd nearly forgotten. Good thing he hadn't. She went out on the porch and waved. The boy didn't seem to see her. Stan walked over in her flip-flops. The kid paused, but he didn't turn off the machine. Stan couldn't see his face behind that messy hair, but she felt his eyes on her. She wondered if the grass would be even or if he was guessing in which direction he needed to cut.

She waved again. He continued cutting. He must not see her. She stood in the path of the mower. He barely slowed. Stan wondered if she should worry about his ability to do this job. Nah, she had enough to worry about. She waved at Russ once more. Maybe she should get out of the way. But finally he stopped. Let the mower idle. She still couldn't see his eyes, but she assumed he was looking at her.

"Need anything?" she called.

No response. Russ started mowing again.

"Okay, then." Weird kid. She got out of the way and headed back inside to shower. While the slow cooker cooked, she had an errand to run.

Izzy's shop seemed to be the only one in town without a wooden sign by Gene. Hers was a purple-and-white–striped sign. Stan knew it would be politically incorrect to say so since Gene seemed to be the approved sign vendor, but she loved it. Nicely suited to a sweetshop. The large front window offered a tantalizing glimpse of candies, syrups and fudge. A happy, tinkling sound greeted Stan as she pushed the door open. She stepped in and breathed the delectable scents of chocolate, coffee and baked goods, feeling like she'd gone straight to heaven. A few customers were scattered at the café tables, talking over iced drinks and pastries. But the candy counter drew her attention immediately.

It snaked through the middle of the room, a superb S-shaped glass creation filled to bursting with chocolates of all shapes and sizes. Truffles, caramels, cream-filleds, nonpareils, white chocolate seashells, chocolate squares, chocolate fruits. And that was only the first section. Her hand went to her chin, an automatic check to see if she drooled. A smiling face appeared over the counter, looking at her.

"You decided to visit! I'm so glad." Izzy spread her hands to take in the treats. "What do you think?"

Stan laughed. "I think I need to move! If I stay in town, I'm going to be here every day. Everything looks amazing, Izzy. What do you recommend?"

"One of everything." Izzy winked. "Why don't I get us some coffee and we can sit and chat for a while? It's a quiet time of the day for me." She glanced around to make sure her customers were satisfied for the moment; then she pointed at her specials board. "The chocolate chip iced latte is pretty damn good." She leaned forward and gave

Stan a conspiratorial wink. "Or, if you're looking for something more, er, *adult*, I have a Godiva liqueur to die for."

"I think I'll stick with the iced latte for now. Since it's barely past breakfast. But I will definitely take you up on the adult version another time."

"Fair enough." Izzy waved at the seating area. "Pull up a chair. I'll be right with you." She left to take care of a teenager who'd just entered, eyes huge at the candy display. Once she'd armed the girl with a giant peanut butter cup, Izzy went back to the two lattes.

Stan chose a café table in the back, near a shelf filled with brightly colored coffee mugs and coffeemakers. Izzy came over a few minutes later with the two lattes on a tray. She also had a plate with assorted chocolates on it.

"I figured you'd want to try something," she said.

Stan groaned. "I'll have to start planning two runs every day." But she reached over and plucked what looked to be a caramel-filled treat off the plate, taking a generous bite. "Mmm. There was nothing like this in my old neighborhood, and that was considered the height of civilization."

Izzy laughed. "Believe me, I took some crap setting up here. Some days I think I might be better off in civilization."

"What kind of crap? I can't believe anyone wouldn't want a place like this around." And in Stan's opinion, someone who didn't like chocolate or coffee couldn't be human.

"Well, this used to be a diner. Real greasy

spoon–type place. *Eggcellent*, or some kitschy name like that. The owner died. A typical relic here in town. His son put the place up for sale. I was puttering around the area one day and saw it. Decided it would be perfect for my shop. Had the apartment upstairs, so that worked for me. Property was cheap, too, since we're out in the middle of nowhere." Izzy fussed with the napkins on the table, straightening them in their holder. "The regulars were not happy when they realized what I wanted to do with the place."

"So how did you win them over?"

"Short answer, I didn't," Izzy said. "The people who loved the old place haven't set foot in here. I get a lot of college kids. Parents visiting. Cool people from surrounding towns. Don't get me wrong, I have a following. I'm doing okay." She smiled, but Stan could tell it hurt her feelings to feel less than accepted by the people closest to her. "And Char and Ray, of course. They're phenomenal. Char's an outsider, too, so she gets it."

"Huh." Stan sat back. "How can people not love candy and coffee?"

Izzy laughed out loud. "Oh, honey, Frog Ledge isn't the gourmet candy and coffee crowd. So what *are* you doing in this hillbilly town?"

"I think it's adorable," she said. "And I fell in love with the house."

Izzy sipped her drink. "But there's more to that story."

Stan sipped hers. "Delicious. And, yes, there is

more to that story. Maybe we'll have time to talk about it, after you tell me about the neighborhood."

"Ah, the neighborhood." Izzy sat back and propped her leg up on the opposite knee. "It's an interesting one, it is. I've been here about a year, and one thing's for sure. Always something going on."

That made Stan think of Carole, and she sobered. "I hope it's usually something good and this past week isn't the norm."

"Tell me about it." Izzy pushed her cup from hand to hand, observing Stan as she did. "How are you holding up?"

Stan shrugged. "It's crazy. And then yesterday . . ." She trailed off, not sure if she should mention the cemetery incident. She wasn't quite sure which people to trust.

"What?" Izzy demanded when she didn't finish.

"Nothing. I had a weird experience when I was out bike riding."

"What kind of 'weird experience'? Come on, girl. Give it up."

Stan took a long swallow of her drink. "I took a ride through the cemetery and this car dogged me the whole time. Tried to bump me off the path. I lucked out and found the other exit before there was a real problem."

"Holy smoke. Did you call the police?"

"Ha. You're funny. The police are looking for me, not the other way around. By the way, do you know anything about Paul Galveston?"

"That's a change in topic. What do I know

about Paul Galveston? Let's see. Comes in here sometimes and buys his momma some non-pareils. The milk chocolate kind. Oh, and he's a heavy-duty druggie." She lowered her voice. "Momma's paid people off to keep him out of jail, what I've heard."

"And he drives a blue car."

"And he drives a blue car." Izzy nodded. "A Lexus, I think. Why are you . . . Oh." Her eyes widened as it dawned on her. "It was a blue car? Following you?"

Stan nodded.

"You think it was him?"

"I have no idea who it was. I couldn't see the driver. I just saw him driving a blue car and wondered."

"And you really didn't call the police?"

"*Please*. But I bumped into Jake when I was trying to get back. He gave me a ride."

That got Izzy's back up. Stan figured it would. She was curious about why Jake was such a taboo subject for her.

"Jake McGee. He's got his sights on you, has he?" Izzy let out a low whistle, shaking her head. "That boy is a menace. You been to his bar yet?"

"McSwigg's?" Stan chuckled. "No, I haven't. He invited me. Said drinks were free for newcomers." She tried in vain to get another sip out of her cup.

Izzy took pity on her and went behind the counter to make new drinks. "Well, kudos for not falling for that one," she said.

She'd thought about it, but she didn't mention that. "Hey, what do you think of me bringing some treats to the farmers' market to try and sell?"

"I think it's a great idea. Want to share my table? See how it goes?" Izzy carried the drinks over.

"That's so nice of you. I'd love to. That way if people ignore me, it won't be as obvious." She was only partially joking.

Izzy shook her head. "Give yourself some credit, lady." She pushed Stan's new drink over and sat again. "And don't be in a rush to hang out at McGee's bar. The farther away you stay from that one, the better."

"Thank you. And why? He seemed nice enough. A little cocky, sure, but that's an Irish thing." She smiled. "I'm Irish, so, I can say that." She chuckled. "Is his bar a bad place or something?"

"Yeah, well, be careful. The bar is a nice place. No biker dive or anything. But he's a dog. Hits on every woman in town, and then some. Besides, you're tied up, anyway. Right? With that guy who was at your house?" Izzy finally gave in and picked up a chocolate. She nibbled at the corner.

"Oh, I wasn't saying I was interested." Stan felt her cheeks heat up. "I just meant that he didn't seem like a jerk or anything. Except he doesn't have very good control over his dog. And, yes, I am. Well, not tied up. In a relationship. Richard and I have been together for four years."

Izzy couldn't hide her disbelief. "You have? I can't picture that. Sorry," she said, holding up a hand. "I get myself in trouble. Too honest. I guess it's better to be a stinkin' liar. Anyway, I just meant, he didn't seem like your type. Not that McGee does, either."

"You don't know me," Stan pointed out.

"I'm a good judge of people. And a word of warning. McGee isn't anyone's type. He's a charmer, but he's got bad intentions. Period."

"Thanks for the warning. Are you going to tell me what exactly he did to you?"

"Who says he did anything?"

"You wouldn't be so passionate about it, if he didn't."

"I'm observant." Izzy winked. "So, are you gonna tell me how you ended up here?"

Stan hesitated. *Oh, what the heck.* "I lost my job. Decided it was time for a change. I was driving through here with a friend of mine and I saw the house."

"That's it, huh?" Izzy nodded approvingly. "That's the way to do things, girl. I knew I would like you." She glanced up as the bell over her door dinged, signaling a new guest.

Only it wasn't a guest. Stan felt her stomach lurch when she recognized Trooper Pasquale, in full uniform. She knew there was about to be a problem when the other woman didn't even give the chocolate counter a second glance. Pasquale's gaze scanned the patrons, landing on Stan like a homing pigeon on its target. She strolled over and halted at their table.

"Sorry to interrupt," she said, not looking sorry at all. "I need you to come to the station with me, Ms. Connor. I have a few more questions about Carole Morganwick's murder."

Chapter 11

Stan couldn't even think of a theme song suited to this level of humiliation. She knew it was the exact outcome Pasquale wanted, but it still made her want to crawl into a hole. This cop had her sights on Stan and couldn't see farther than her nose. Well, that was fine. She hadn't done anything wrong, and she certainly hadn't killed anyone.

Stan held her head high as she went with Trooper Pasquale out the door. Izzy had even tried reasoning with her, to no avail. The rest of the local coffee drinkers just gaped. The other trooper, Lou from the murder scene, waited outside the front door. In case she got unruly, she guessed. It would have been funny, if it weren't happening to her.

She didn't speak as they drove west out of Frog Ledge. She had no idea where they were going, but she figured to the barracks. Trooper Pasquale's office in the town hall probably wasn't the best place to interrogate people she wanted to intimidate.

Twenty minutes later they pulled into a police barracks parking lot. Pasquale parked and Lou reached in to give her a hand out. She ignored him and climbed out by herself. They went in the back door, down an ugly hall and up a set of stairs. Turned left and entered a small room, which had a table and a few chairs. It looked nothing like what Stan had seen on TV, not that she'd expected it to. More worn-down. Grungy. Tired.

"Have a seat," Pasquale said, motioning to the table.

Stan did. She crossed her legs and folded her hands together. "Well, am I under arrest? Because if not, I have nothing else to say. I have no idea who killed Carole Morganwick, but it certainly wasn't me. If I need to call a lawyer, I'd like to do that."

Pasquale's expression didn't change. She pulled out a notebook, opened to a clean sheet of paper and uncapped her pen. She sat back and tapped the tip of it to her lips. She still wore no makeup, and today her red hair was pulled back in a simple ponytail. Her neutral expression made her look like she was auditioning for a cop show.

"You're not under arrest," she said. "*Yet*. But you'd be doing yourself a favor if you answered one or two questions for me."

"And you couldn't ask me at the café?"

"I wouldn't get too cocky," Pasquale said. "Truth be told, I would arrest you if I had just a smidge more evidence. But I'm giving you a chance to answer me and maybe change my mind."

Stan spread her palms wide. "What are the questions?" Despite her outward cool, she could feel bile rising in her throat. She prayed to whomever was listening that she wouldn't throw up.

"Have you ever worked as a veterinarian, or a vet assistant?"

"No. I was in public relations."

"You never worked in a veterinary clinic?"

"No."

"Do you administer your own medications or vaccines to your cat?"

"Where on earth would I get the vaccines? And I don't even do vaccines for Nutty. He doesn't go outside."

"Have you heard of an organization called Pets' Last Chance?"

Stan's eyes narrowed. Why was she asking about Nikki's animal transport service? "Yes. It's my friend's place."

"Do you work there?"

"No one *works* there. People volunteer. And I've helped out in the past, yes."

"In what capacity?"

"I've done transports with them. Not recently, because I was traveling a lot. I helped at a couple of the spay/neuter clinics. They have them biannually to help with feral cat population and to assist low-income families who need to get their animals fixed."

"And what did you do there?"

"All kinds of things. Laundry, cleaning cages, post-op help."

"Are medications part of post-op work?"

"Some, yes."

"I thought you said you didn't administer medications."

"I said I don't administer medications to my cat, which was what you asked. Have I given a rabies shot or a shot of painkiller at a clinic? Sure. Under a vet's supervision."

"But you had access to medications."

"We had rabies, distemper and pain medication."

"What about euthanasia medicine?"

"There was always some on site, locked up. They occasionally had situations where stray or feral animals came in quite ill, or had undiagnosed conditions that caused cardiac arrest or something from the anesthesia."

"Do you know what medication they used to euthanize?"

"No idea." Her line of questioning finally sank in. Stan wondered what had been in that needle that killed Carole. Of course it made sense that the murderer knew meds and dosages. Her stomach pitched to her knees. It didn't matter that she didn't know those things, as long as Pasquale thought she did.

"When was the last time you attended a clinic?" Pasquale asked.

"A year ago, at least."

Pasquale watched her for what seemed like minutes, drumming her fingertips on the table. Her nails were short, but they were French manicured.

That surprised Stan. She'd pegged Jessie Pasquale for a plain Jane who didn't spend a lot of time on herself.

"How strongly did you feel about the litter of kittens that Dr. Morganwick refused to turn over to your friend's operation?"

Stan forgot about her efforts to remain aloof and confident. She stared at Pasquale. "I have no idea what you're talking about."

"I heard your friend Nikki was pretty pissed off about it."

Nikki knew Carole Morganwick? She hadn't given any indication she recognized the name when Stan mentioned it. Or had she mentioned it? She couldn't remember, but she highly doubted Nikki would kill a vet or anyone else for not turning over a litter of kittens.

"I don't know anything about that. And that seems like an odd reason to kill someone. Have you checked into Dr. Morganwick's personal life? A crazy ex-husband? A stalker? Maybe an old coworker who didn't like her? There have to be other people out there besides me to bother. I told you I didn't even know her."

Pasquale did her silent thing again. Then she said, "Why did you move to Frog Ledge, Ms. Connor?"

"Because I found a house I liked."

"That would make you leave West Hartford? Frog Ledge doesn't have much to offer for city girls."

Stan crossed her arms in front of her. She knew it looked defensive, but she just wanted her hands to stop shaking. "I like it here."

"Did Nikki Manning suggest you move here?"

Stan couldn't keep the disbelief off her face. "Trooper, give me a little credit. I'm a grown woman and I don't need anyone making suggestions about where I live."

"Maybe Carole was making her life hard. Maybe Nikki wanted someone to keep an eye on her."

"You think Nikki asked me to move here as a spy and a hit man? Hit woman?" Hysterical laughter bubbled up in her throat. She coughed to keep it from erupting. If Jake was as crazy as his sister, Izzy had every right to her opinion of him.

"Animal rescue people can be quite . . . What's the word? *Passionate,*" Pasquale said in a tone suggesting she would have chosen a different word. "Once they feel like someone's messing with their cause, they get angry."

Stan's leg wanted to jiggle. She forced it to stop. "Animal rescue people are serious about what they do. And vets technically are animal rescue people also, right?"

Pasquale didn't acknowledge the question. "Where were you before you went to the clinic on Monday?"

"At home. Corralling my cat into the carrier."

"Were you alone?"

"I was."

"Nikki Manning wasn't with you?"

"No. She was on a transport."

"You're certain."

"That I was alone, or that she was on a transport? Both. I was alone, and I talked to her Saturday night. She was delayed in South Carolina. Not home until sometime Monday afternoon."

"And you didn't speak to her on Monday."

"I didn't."

Pasquale made a note on the still-clean sheet of paper in her notebook.

"I'd like to know, Trooper Pasquale, if I should call my lawyer now." She fixed Pasquale with a steely stare and willed herself to hold it in place.

Pasquale looked at her for a long time. "You're free to go," she said finally. "Stick close to home until this is unraveled. Do you want a ride?"

"No, thank you." Stan got up. "I'll call someone."

Nikki's cell phone went to voice mail. Stan cursed and walked out into the parking lot. She'd seen a coffee shop down the street. She'd call Richard to pick her up and go wait for him there. He answered on the third ring.

"Hey, babe. What's up?"

"Are you around? I need a ride."

Silence. She could imagine him calculating the rest of his workday, his gym time, then deciding whether it would be too much of an inconvenience. "From where?"

She glanced up at a beep from a car horn. She saw a little red PT Cruiser parked in the lot. Izzy Sweet waved from behind the wheel.

"Never mind, I'm all set," she told Richard. "Let me call you back." Without waiting for an answer, she disconnected and walked over to the car.

"Taxi?" Izzy asked. Baxter and Elvira crammed their noses out the window. Baxter woofed at her.

"How'd you guess?" Stan slid in and shut the

door. "Hi, guys," she said to the dogs; then she leaned her head back against the seat. "How embarrassing."

"More embarrassing for her when she realizes the real killer is out there laughing." Izzy hit the gas and they whizzed away.

"Cute car." Stan glanced around the spotless interior. "That was sweet of you to come get me. No pun intended."

Izzy grinned. "I'm named for a reason, baby. I figured you wouldn't take them up on a ride back."

"I had no idea they would even offer me a ride back," Stan said.

"They usually do, if they can't find a reason to keep you. They think it makes them look better."

"You sound like you've had experience with this."

Izzy winked. "I have lots of stories. So what was their burning question?"

Stan's stomach twisted again as she remembered the conversation. "I guess my friend's rescue place tried to work with Dr. Morganwick and she turned them down. Or something like that. Nikki never mentioned it to me." And she needed to ask her. ASAP. "They wanted to know if she was at my house the day of the murder. Which she wasn't. She was in South Carolina, for goodness' sake. And it's irrelevant, anyway! I didn't kill Carole, and neither did Nikki."

"Jeez, they're reaching, huh?" Izzy shook her head. "You'd think with a charmer like Carole they wouldn't be so stumped."

"You didn't like her, either."

Izzy made a face. "She wasn't anyone's favorite person—let's just put it that way." They were silent for the rest of the drive. Izzy drove fast, maneuvering her stick shift like it was an extension of her arm. She shortened the twenty-minute drive into fifteen. She pulled up in Stan's driveway with a flourish. "You need anything?"

Stan shook her head. "No. Thanks again, Izzy."

"No thanks necessary. We outsiders have to stick together." With a wink and a beep, Izzy tootled on down the road back to her shop.

Stan went inside, pulling her ringing cell phone out of her pocket. Richard. She'd forgotten all about him.

"Hi," she answered.

"What's going on? I thought you were calling me back."

"I'm sorry. I just got home."

"Is something wrong with your car?"

She had to tell him sooner or later. Later was probably better. "Can we talk about it when I see you? That's tonight, right?"

A pause. "We can, as long as everything's okay."

"Everything's peachy." She let herself into the house. Nutty waited at the door. He arched his back as she stroked the length of him, all the way to the tip of his tail.

"Does this have something to do with what you were going to tell me on the phone last night?"

"It does. But it's fine. It can wait."

"All right, then." He was already distracted by something else, she could tell from his tone of voice. "Can we plan on tomorrow night, instead? I'm looking at a late night catching up here."

Stan swallowed the hurt; she tried to cover it up. There was no law that said a boyfriend had to be engaged in unpacking or providing moral support when his girlfriend was about to be accused of murder. "Sure, that's fine."

"You're the best, babe. I'll see you around seven tomorrow night."

She disconnected and checked her watch. It was only one. Nikki would be starting afternoon rounds in the kennels soon. Good time to catch her for a face-to-face conversation.

Chapter 12

Nikki was outside in the fenced-in part of the yard, playing ball with some puppies. Stan watched from the side of the yard. They made a cute picture. Nikki loved her animals. Did she love them enough to kill for them? And would she let her best friend take the fall?

One of the big dogs saw Stan and barked her arrival. Nikki dropped the ball and turned around. "Hey! What are you doing here? Come to help with the afternoon snack?" She stepped out of the gate, latching it behind her. "You guys can play in here for a while." A little white dog with brown ears chased her to the fence, barking furiously.

"He's cute."

"They all are. A couple of my last-minute grabs over the weekend. So what's going on? Have you had lunch?"

"Nope."

"Come on in, then."

Stan followed Nikki inside through the back door into the kitchen. Dog food cans cluttered the counter, and a calico cat slept next to them, curled in a ball. Neat piles of paperwork were stacked on half the table, probably adoption forms and vet records for the recent arrivals. A whiteboard above the table had schedules and dates scribbled in black. Miscellaneous sticky notes added color. A ceiling fan hummed lazily over the whole scene.

"Have a seat. Don't mind the mess. Is everything okay?" Nikki went to the fridge and pulled out iced green tea. "Tea or coffee?"

"Iced tea is fine. Thanks. Listen, I have to ask you something."

"Okay, shoot." Nikki poured two glasses and placed one in front of Stan.

"Did you know Carole Morganwick?"

"Who?"

"The vet who got killed." Maybe she hadn't mentioned her name. Or maybe Nikki was playing dumb.

"No. At least I don't think so. Should I?" She slid into the chair opposite Stan and tucked her long legs under her.

"Well, the cop who's trying to arrest me thinks you do."

"The cop who *what*? Stan, I have no idea what you're talking about."

No point prolonging this. Stan blurted it out. "I got hauled into the state police barracks to answer a few questions. Apparently, the trooper who thinks I'm guilty of killing Carole said you knew her and had a bad experience. And maybe

I tried to get revenge for you." She recapped the questions Pasquale had asked her.

"And then she finished up with something about you being angry about a litter of kittens, and how rescue people are pretty much crazy." The last part was badly paraphrased, but it was what Pasquale meant.

Nikki stared at her in rapt fascination the whole time. When Stan finished talking, Nikki blew out a breath. "What's the woman's name again? I swear, I don't know who she is."

"Carole Morganwick. Oh, hang on." She pulled her tote bag out from under her chair. She'd stuffed the special edition of the *Frog Ledge Holler* in there the other day, with Carole's grainy picture on the front page. Like in real life, Carole didn't smile. Her eyes stared flatly out of the page, expression indifferent. She handed it to Nikki.

Nikki's eyes widened. "Holy smoke," she said.

"What?"

"Did she get married or something? Or divorced?"

"I think so. *I* didn't know her, remember? That's something everyone seems to forget."

"I do—did—know her." Nikki raised her gaze to meet Stan's. "Haven't seen her in a long time, but her name was Carole Cross then. She ran a clinic in New Jersey. We used to stop there during transports sometimes. It was right on our route. But we lost some animals there."

"Lost how?"

"Died. A dog got a vaccination and two hours later went into cardiac arrest. I don't know if it was a bad vaccine, or if she gave him the wrong thing, but it was awful." Nikki shook her head and handed the newspaper back to Stan. "There were a few other things. I eventually stopped going there, and I recommended against it for any of my transports. But when you do this work, unfortunately, you come into contact with bad vets all the time. If I wanted to pay people to bump off all the morons I've encountered, I'd actually have no money left to save animals."

Trooper Pasquale had to know Carole ran another clinic under a different name. Stan filed this new information away to research later.

"This cop is out of her mind. She thinks I killed this vet, who was also out of her mind." Stan closed her eyes and rested her forehead in her hands. "And she thinks you taught me how to do it. Oh, then she asked me another weird question. She asked if I was alone the morning of Carole's murder, before I went to the clinic. And when I said yes, she asked if I was certain you weren't with me."

Nikki's expression remained neutral this time. "Huh," she said, "weird is right. I'm going to start the doggie dinners. Want to help me deliver?"

"Sure. But why would she ask that?"

"Who the heck knows?" Nikki went to the counter, her back to Stan, and started opening dog food. The calico fluffed her tail at the disturbance, reminding Stan of Nutty. She jumped down and stalked away. "She sounds like she's going out on a limb here. A lot of them, actually."

Nikki measured out dog food. Stan could see the kennels through the window. The dogs were all in the outside part of their runs, engaged in various tasks. They were slurping water, chasing squirrels from their side of the fence or sniffing along the grassy border. The puppies had dropped in an exhausted pile in the middle of their play area.

"That might be true, but that limb has my name written all over it."

"You don't know for sure what she thinks. I mean, she didn't arrest you or anything. She's grasping, Stan."

"Not yet, anyway. But she kept me at the scene forever asking questions, and now she pulls me out of the sweetshop—"

Nikki dropped a can of food at that. "No way."

"Oh yeah, I forgot to mention that's where I was when she tracked me down." Stan nodded. "Marched right in and asked me to come with her. How would she know I helped out at your clinics? How would she even know I knew you?"

"I have no idea. Do you think she saw the van when I was at your house?"

"You didn't have the van yesterday."

"Oh yeah." Nikki paused, spoon in midair, to ponder this. "Well, there's stuff online from our clinics, and your name is all over the place. All she would have to do is Google you, or something. We always put up that stuff. Good publicity. Do you know what was in the needle that actually killed her?"

"No idea," Stan said. "She asked me a lot about what you use at your clinics to euthanize, though."

"Hmm." Nikki thought about that. "Do you think she just got stabbed when you saw her?"

"I don't know. I assumed, because I heard a door closing." She shivered, remembering.

"Well, it might've been potassium. That's something the vets use in fluids, but if you don't dilute it and give someone a good shot of it, that's a death sentence, for sure. Oh, for crying out loud." Nikki raced out of the room in response to a crash and a loud meow, leaving Stan feeling uneasy. Nikki reentered minutes later, carrying a black-and-white cat who looked either crazed or terrified.

"This is Charlie. Charlie's having trouble getting used to the other felines." Nikki deposited Charlie at Stan's feet. "Any chance Nutty wants a challenging brother?"

"I doubt it. And Nutty might need a foster home, anyway, if I get arrested."

Nikki shook her head and let the cat go. "Stop it right now. No one's getting arrested. Well, hopefully, someone is, but not you. So she knew about the rescue. That's not a bad thing. Maybe she'll spread the word, once she clears us of all wrongdoing." She went back to the counter, finished filling dog bowls and counted them.

"She only knew about the rescue because she thought you trained me to be a killer. How is that a good deal?" Stan asked.

"We need more publicity. There's only so much I can do on Facebook when I'm driving a million miles a week. Come on, help me feed the mutts. I have some cutie-pies." She smiled sweetly and blinked her own big brown puppy dog eyes.

"Coming. But I'm not adopting a dog. When's Justin coming back?"

"Tomorrow. Just in time for the adoption event Saturday."

Justin loved animals as much as she did. Nikki didn't give men the time of day if they didn't get her work. Justin did. He helped out with the herd every day and even went on transports.

"Oh, speaking of that. I have treats in my bag."

"Awesome. They'll all be clamoring for you to adopt them. Come on. Grab some bowls." Nikki pulled on a pair of cowboy boots, balanced as many bowls as she could carry and headed out the back door.

Stan picked up the remaining bowls and followed her friend outside into the fray. The dogs were lined up, howling in anticipation. All shapes and sizes: puppies, adults, big, small, shaggy and short-haired. They were adorable. Nikki tried to keep it to ten per trip, but she usually failed. There were so many dogs running out of time in the shelters in the South. She often spoke about how awful it was, especially the ones that still used gas chambers. Nikki had even started a program in schools to talk to younger kids about caring for animals. Gotta start somewhere, she always said. And if the little ones can teach their parents something, she had done her job.

"You can start there." Nikki directed her to the other end of the kennel. "Just put the bowls in the corner and fill up the water if they need it."

Stan went to work. She hoped it would quiet her brain, but it wasn't working. Nikki's assessment of the possible murder weapon bothered her. But it was something she should know, given her line of work. It didn't mean she was a killer.

She handed food to a boxer named Mitch, a bulldog mix named Queenie and a German shepherd named Crew. The next cage seemed to be empty, so Stan almost passed it by. Suddenly she caught a glimpse of something through the small door leading inside. She pulled the latch and entered the run. Went all the way to the back, where the dogs could go through the opening. Peered in. A small, shaggy, messy dog watched her anxiously.

"Well, hello there," Stan said. "Would you like an early dinner?"

The dog's stubby tail wagged hesitantly.

"Why don't you come outside?" Stan asked. "Otherwise, I have to go all the way around. Come on, come see me." She knelt and held out her hand. The little dog, suddenly brave, trotted out and licked her face. Jumped right in her lap and proceeded to scarf down the food Stan offered.

Stan smiled. The dog was adorable, despite its desperate need of a haircut. Probably a newcomer who hadn't yet encountered Nikki's groomer. And he—she?—didn't seem to want to move out of her lap. Settling down on the ground, she let the dog eat, enjoying the cuddle time. Nutty wasn't a huge cuddler. Only at night when he wanted to get warm, and then it was more about the blankets than about Stan. She handed over another treat, and the little dog inhaled that, too.

"Making friends?" She turned to find Nikki hanging over the fence, grinning at her.

"Yeah, we're just hanging out." Stan ruffled the dog's floppy ears.

"That's Scruffy. She's a schnoodle. She had twenty-four hours to live. And you should sell those treats somewhere other than my bake sales. I swear, every kind I've seen you with has been a hit."

Stan waved her off. "They're dogs. They'll eat anything."

"No way." Nikki pointed to a golden-retriever mix lounging in the sun. "That dog? I offered her five different treats during transport and she turned her nose up at every single one. Yours, forget it. She barely chewed them."

"Oh. Well." Stan shrugged, embarrassed. "They're healthy."

"I'm telling you. You should package them and sell them. Scruffy's up for adoption, by the way." Nikki blinked innocently at Stan.

"I know, I know. Sorry, Nik. Can't do it right now."

"Oh, why not? You just moved to a big house. You have one cat and a fenced-in yard. You could have two dogs. More." Her eyes twinkled, but she was serious. Nikki had been encouraging her to adopt for ages. Stan had resisted, blaming her travel and overall work schedule. Getting a sitter for Nutty alone had been hard enough, especially when she and Richard had the same travel schedule.

"Right, but I have some things to figure out. A recruiter called me. I have an interview next week."

Leaning against the fence, Nikki wrapped her long fingers in the chain link. "Same type of job?"

Stan nodded.

"I don't understand why you'd put yourself through that again. Especially if you don't have to."

"I do have to. It's not responsible to stay voluntarily unemployed."

"It is if you're trying to figure out what you really want to do with your life instead of what you think you want to do." Nikki's tone challenged, and Stan felt her hackles rise.

"I'm thirty-five years old, Nik. I'm a little past the what-do-I-want-to-be-when-I-grow-up stage, I would hope. I'm good at what I do."

"That doesn't mean you have to keep doing it if it doesn't feed your soul. Come on, Stan. You've finally planted roots in a place that could make you happy, instead of some dark condo with shitty neighbors whom you tolerate because it's close to your office. Give yourself a break. Take the time you need. There are other things that make you come alive besides press conferences. I know it because I've known you for more than twenty years. Don't sell yourself short to prove something to some fantasy audience."

"Jeez. You want me to adopt a dog that bad that you have to stomp all over my career to get me to do it?" As soon as she said it, Stan wished she could take it back.

Nikki's eyes darkened. She let go of the fence. "I don't need to beg people to adopt dogs. Most people realize the kind of friendship they're getting without me having to jam it down their throats. And, surprisingly, some of those people are even big-shot corporate types. They just might be a little more enlightened than you."

Stan continued to pet the schnoodle, thankful for the distraction keeping her from responding right away. She didn't know her friend had felt that way about her job. Or about who she had become because of it.

"I know I needed a change. I'm just going to check the job out. But I will do the responsible financial thing."

"Knock yourself out, then." Nikki's voice was cool. "I'll be up at the house." She walked away.

Great. Now Nikki was mad at her, too. Stan took another treat out of her bag. Scruffy's ears perked up and she licked her lips, rolling out of her relaxed pose so she was ready to receive. Stan handed her one. She took it very politely and devoured it. Then she waited expectantly for another, wagging her tail.

She did like the little dog. She pushed the thought aside and left Scruffy's kennel. There was enough going on without worrying about a dog, too. She finished dropping off bowls of food and gave out the rest of the dogs treats. They all devoured them and barked their disappointment when she displayed the empty bag.

As she walked back to the house, Stan turned around one last time. Scruffy stood at the fence now, watching her as she walked away. She had stopped wagging her tail.

* * *

Stan drove home slowly, trying to chase away the nagging feelings of doubt about her best friend. She'd known Nikki for more than twenty years. She hadn't done anything wrong. Stan would swear on her life.

But she'd known Carole in the past. Knew animals that had died in her care. She shook off the nasty thoughts. Trooper Pasquale needed to step up her game and find the real killer quickly. This business of suspecting everyone she saw on the street had to stop. And she was spending so much time trying to prove Stan guilty that her time to find the real killer had to be limited. She hadn't seen the police dragging her neighbor off for questioning, even though they had been publicly threatening each other two days before Carole's murder. Although that seemed crazy, too. Sweet, petite Amara Leonard, who meditated on the grass and practiced homeopathy.

Whom Carole had called a two-bit hack. Was that because she was jealous or threatened, or was Amara a hack? Amara had called Carole a hack right back, so who knew?

But Stan hadn't looked Carole up on the Internet before promising to bring Nutty for an appointment. She was slipping. It must be what happened in small towns with all that peer pressure to use each other's services.

She needed to do some research on her now. Maybe she'd find some bad reviews with names she could show Pasquale. She should probably research Amara, too, before bringing Nutty in to see her. It was the responsible thing to do, and she didn't want to make the same mistake she'd made with Carole. If Carole had known something about Amara that would have destroyed her if it had come out, all the more reason. Meanwhile, the simple answer might just be to ask Amara about the fight.

She really hoped Amara wasn't the killer. That would really devalue the whole block. Plus, where else would she find a homeopath right next door?

Chapter 13

Amara Leonard's little house buzzed with activity. Stan dropped her car off in her driveway and walked over. Two cars and a contractor's van filled the driveway. The house was under construction. A ladder stood against the side. At the top a man scraped paint. A red Honda was parked in the driveway behind a black Ford Focus.

This had seemed like a good idea earlier, but now Stan wasn't so sure. What was she supposed to say? *"Hi, I heard you having an argument with the dead vet the other day. Do you mind telling me what that was about?"* It sounded ridiculous. Maybe she should just go home.

Before she could, Amara appeared from around the side of the house, brandishing a pair of hedge clippers almost as big as she was. A pink Boston Red Sox baseball hat covered most of her forehead. Despite the heat, she wore long pants and a long-sleeved T-shirt, probably to prevent bug bites or allergy issues from working in the yard. Diane

Kirschbaum, the animal control officer, was right behind her. Amara saw Stan and waved.

No turning back now.

"Hey! Did you come to make Nutty's appointment?" Amara asked.

Diane hung back, arms crossed, observing Stan. Her curly brown hair had withered into frizz from the heat. She wore Bermuda shorts and a T-shirt that had cats on it. Sneakers and ankle socks topped off the outfit. Stan felt herself judging. *Stop critiquing. These women are my new neighbors!*

"I did," Stan said, convincing herself it wasn't really a lie. She could do that while she was here, too.

"Cool. Have you met Diane?" Amara pulled the other woman forward. "Diane Kirschbaum. Town animal control."

Diane walked over slowly and shook Stan's hand. Strong grip. *Diane and Amara are friends?* Stan smiled and held out her hand. "Nice to meet you. Stan Connor."

"You too," Diane said.

"Come on in, then," Amara said. "We'll find a time to get Nutty over."

"I was just leaving," Diane said.

"I'd love to come in," Stan said. "I won't stay long. You're busy."

"Eh." Amara waved her off. "I'd rather talk to potential clients than do yard work any day. Elmore!" She shouted toward the man on the ladder. "I'm taking a break. Do you want anything?"

Elmore smiled and waved. Amara sighed. "He

doesn't speak much English," she explained to Stan. "Ray Mackey found him for me."

"Amara, I'll call you tomorrow," Diane said.

"Oh, please don't leave on my account," Stan said. "Besides, I love to get to know more people from my new town."

Diane's expression resembled a deer in headlights at the suggestion. "I have to get back to work."

"Bye," Stan murmured, watching Diane walk over to the Focus, slide in and drive away.

"Don't mind her. She's shy," Amara said. "But she does wonderful things for animals."

Stan followed Amara into a kitchen that looked straight out of *Country Living* magazine. Wallpaper in an apple design plastered the room. The yellow linoleum floor reminded Stan of her grandmother's kitchen. By contrast, Amara's white table looked chic and out of place. She'd covered one of the walls with a blue velvet tapestry depicting the sun and the moon. A small stereo on the counter played soft jazz. A red candle burned in a metal holder on the wall, emitting a cinnamon scent. The dog she'd heard barking, the beautiful golden retriever, ambled over to see her. His large tail swung in a happy arc. Shoot, she'd given all her treats to Nikki's dogs.

"That's Beau. He's a muffin."

"He's adorable." Stan rubbed his head. He rewarded her with a lick; then he dropped at her feet and put his head in his paws. "And your house is too."

"It needs some work," Amara said, waving at the

walls. "I bought the fixer-upper. Had to look past the cosmetic stuff to see it was a good house and a good deal. And the town's great, truly. Aside from the . . . unpleasantness you've encountered."

It seemed too soon to start talking about why she was really here, so Stan stayed quiet.

"I wanted somewhere to expand my business, and so far, so good." Amara rapped on the wooden pantry door to seal her luck. "Hopefully, bigger and better things are in store. So let's talk about Nutty." She grabbed an appointment book off her counter and motioned to Stan to sit. "Water? Lemonade?"

"Water is great. Thanks." Stan sat.

Amara filled a glass with iced water for each of them and placed them on the table. "Okay. So Nutty has IBS symptoms. Bloody stool?"

"At first, he did. He improved quickly after the food change and I was able to take him off his meds."

"Hang on." Amara hurried out of the room, returning a moment later with a laptop and a bag crammed full of papers and books. "I do all my own scheduling and office work right now, since I don't have an office yet and can't really justify the overhead." She opened the laptop and hit some keys. "And just so you know, this history is all part of his first appointment. When you bring him, I'll look at him. But if I gather it now, he won't have to spend as much time. Is that okay?"

"Of course."

"Great. The first appointment fee is one hundred seventy-five dollars. The follow-ups are less, and most of them can be phone check-ins." She waited until Stan nodded in agreement, then continued. "So tell me what you cook for Nutty."

Stan recited some of her typical meals. "I keep it basic, since I didn't have a lot of time up until recently."

"It's all great stuff. That's wonderful. And it's helped him, so what more can you ask?"

"It has," Stan agreed. "By the way, would you object if I brought Beau some of my homemade treats? I usually have some on me, but I'm empty today."

"Of course I wouldn't mind. I'm sure he would love them. Wouldn't you, Beau?" Amara scratched the golden's ears. He thumped his tail. "Does Nutty go outside?"

"Oh no," Stan said. "He was a stray. I found him outside of my old condo. He had been injured somehow, maybe a car. So I kept him. He likes it inside so much better."

"And he doesn't take medication anymore at all?"

"Doesn't need to."

"What did your other vet say? Your traditional vet."

"Well, I didn't use him very much, but he would've preferred to give Nutty a steroid or something. Some vets are very open-minded about natural medicine, while others don't want to hear about it."

"Darn right, and it's such a shame. Animals would benefit from different vets collaborating. It's not about if I'm right or they're right. It's about working together for the best outcome for the animal. And if we worked as partners on a regular basis, animals wouldn't need half the pharmaceuticals or surgeries they need today." She leaned forward, her eyes blazing like one of those TV preachers during a particularly important sermon. "But that's the problem. Because a lot of traditional vets—not all, you're right, there are some enlightened ones—but most think the only way to heal is with a pill and a knife. I'm *very* lucky, you see. My fiancé, Dr. DiMauro—have you heard of him?—is a traditional vet and he's very open. Vincent struggles with his closed-minded colleagues constantly about this."

Well, Amara is certainly passionate about her profession. "So, did you have issues with that when you moved here? With Dr. Morganwick?" Stan held her breath.

Amara cocked her head, eyes immediately becoming hooded. "What do you mean?"

"Just curious. She saw us talking on the green that day, and she was at my door an hour later asking me to bring Nutty to see her."

That made Amara angry. Stan could see it, although the other woman tried to brush it off.

"That's how she operated. Listen, I'm not trying to speak badly of a dead woman. I feel terrible about what happened to Carole, but she wasn't very enlightened when it came to alternative therapies. People like her, it sounds awful, but they stall change. This town needs someone with a different mind-set when a new vet moves in. There's so much potential here. But it's a farm town, and sometimes that mind-set is hard to shake. It's a challenge, but a worthwhile one. So . . . let's get back to Nutty."

People like her stall change. Sounded like Carole Morganwick being gone, one way or another, worked out for her competition. And, wow, did Amara get worked up when the topic arose!

Amara went through another series of questions before she declared enough history. "Now, do you want me to come to your house and see him? I can't wait to meet him."

"That sounds great. How about next Friday?"

Amara scanned her screen and hit some keys. "I could come by at ten."

"Perfect."

Amara keyed in the appointment, then reached into her bag and handed Stan a packet. "My card, some information on classical homeopathy and my credentials. When I said I was just starting out, I meant here, with an official home office. I've worked in other people's practices before. And I trained under a doctor in London."

"Impressive." Stan tapped the card on the table. "Can I ask you a question?"

"Of course."

"The day I moved in, you and Carole were . . . arguing."

Amara's whole body tensed up, but she said nothing.

"I know you already told me you two didn't see eye to eye. But did you always disagree so vehemently?"

"Why are you asking?"

"I'm wondering if she was that disagreeable with everyone." *Put it on Carole. Maybe then Amara will talk.*

Amara pursed her lips. She ran her fingers over her keyboard, then rested them on the table. "I have no idea who got along with her and who didn't. She was angry at me for a couple of reasons, aside from what I told you earlier about her views on my way of treating animals." Her gaze was cool, and her tone just a little bit defensive. She didn't offer the other reasons.

Stan sighed. She could see her mother shaking her head, hear her voice: *"Why would you start such a ridiculous conversation?"* She could hear Billy Joel in her head. *"Big Shot."*

"Look. I'm not trying to pry. I found this woman dead, and the whole town knows it. I think people think I killed her, or something crazy like that."

Amara's eyes narrowed. She shoved her chair back and stood up. "So you're suggesting I killed her because we had an argument?"

Was I? "No! Of course not. I'm just trying to get some information. I have no idea what dynamics were going on between Carole and the rest of the population, but it doesn't seem she had a lot of friends. Our resident state trooper suspects me. If there were people Carole harassed the way she was harassing you that day, then maybe they're worth checking out."

"This is crazy." Amara stalked to the window; then she turned around and stalked back to the table. "Look, I'm sorry you're in this position, but

I resent your implication. That woman was nuts. She thought I was stealing her clients. But the reality is, she wasn't a very good vet. Not to mention, people are finally starting to see the benefit of what I do as an alternative. I won't let you trash my name, too."

"I'm not trying to trash your name," Stan protested.

"I don't care. You should leave now. I'm not sure I can help Nutty, after all."

Now she'd done it. That impulsive streak had just punished her cat, who really needed a good doctor. Plus, she'd turned a potential new friend into an enemy.

"Amara, please. I didn't mean to insinuate anything of the sort."

"I said, I think you should leave."

Stan had no idea how to clean up the mess she'd just made. She rose and picked up her purse. "I really am sorry," she said.

Amara didn't answer. Stan turned and left.

Chapter 14

Theme song: "*My Favorite Mistake.*" Stan lay in bed the next morning and thought maybe Richard was right and Frog Ledge had been a mistake. Maybe she did belong back in the city, looking for another corporate job and staying out of murder investigations. What kind of person bought a house in a strange town because it was cute, anyway? She buried her head back under the pillow against the bright sun and blue skies trying to tempt her out of bed. But it wasn't the solution, no matter how unemployed she was, or how much she angered her neighbors. Stan Connor did not hide under the covers.

Although today the possibility sounded tempting, she had treats to bake. And Nutty would want breakfast. Stan never slept this late. Not that she had technically been sleeping, just tossing and turning and fending off troubled dreams and frightening possibilities of what could happen next.

Today called for extreme coffee. She loaded her coffee grinder with her stash of extra bold and leaned against the counter with her cup, waiting for the liquid to drop into the carafe. Just the thought of having to be productive today made her want to cry. She had no desire to go outside and see anyone.

The pot had filled enough for her to pour some, which she did gratefully and took the first greedy sip. The first dose of caffeine shot through her veins. A few more sips and her head started to clear. She could feel her mind shift from *poor me* to strategy mode. The conversation with Amara hadn't gone as planned, but so what? She couldn't mourn a friend she hadn't really made yet. And survival was the goal right now, not friends.

Draining her first cup of coffee, Stan poured another and arranged her ingredients on the counter. The apple cranberry oat treats had been a big hit with Nikki's dogs, so she measured out extra ingredients for that kind. She didn't want to sell out of anything tomorrow. And treats might come in handy today, with the errand she had to run. A conversation with Diane Kirschbaum might be in order, before Amara got to her. That is, if she hadn't already. Besides, a trip to the dog kennel might not be a bad idea for a new resident.

Stan packed up a variety of fresh snacks and the food she'd made for Savannah, Char and Ray's dog, and got her bike out of the garage. It was hard to justify using her car for anything around town, unless it involved taking Nutty in his carrier. She dropped the food off first; then she biked past the town hall and the library, past Izzy's shop and almost barreled past the street before she saw the sign for the dog pound obscured by a leafy tree. She took a hard left and coasted down through a residential neighborhood. At the next sign she took a right. The houses faded away to woods. After another half mile, she finally saw a sign: FROG LEDGE MEMORIAL PARK. Underneath the sign, a smaller one read, DOG POUND THIRD LEFT. The signs were ugly green metal. Obviously, Gene had not crafted them.

Stan drove into the expansive park, past picnic areas, walking trails and even a small lake. She passed clumps of families on blankets, kids playing games, Rollerbladers and skateboarders practicing their technique, until she got to another sign. It pointed down a dirt road. Crappy place for a dog kennel. It didn't exactly encourage visitors, unless someone happened to be visiting the park and noticed it. Stan hoped that had no superstitious significance for the animals who ended up there.

She coasted into the parking lot and halted in front of the building. It was hideous. Small, square and gray, it resembled an old bomb shelter more than a hub of animal care and adoption. Chainlink runs stretched out along the sides and back, abutting the woods. Diane's white ACO van was parked haphazardly outside, as if she'd backed up to the door and unloaded an animal in a hurry.

Propping her bike against the side of the building, Stan hung her helmet off the handlebars and headed for the open front door. No dogs barked at her arrival. Quiet, except a voice holding a one-sided conversation. She peered around the corner and saw Diane's back, half hidden behind a wall

separating the office from the presently empty
kennels.

Stan didn't want to interrupt, so she hung back
in the "welcome area." It consisted of a dirty welcome mat, a few cracked plastic chairs and a sign
warning people not to put their fingers through
the fences. It smelled moldy and damp and faintly
of Lysol. No dogs in sight. The notices tacked to
the bulletin board warned about an animal abuser
who might be in the area and advertised a reward
for a lost cocker spaniel named Mitzi. Stan tapped
her foot impatiently. Maybe if she wandered inside,
Diane would see her and hang up. As she went to
step around the corner and reveal herself, Diane's
words filtered across the room.

"It's got to be easier with her gone. We need
to get access to that building." A pause. "Amara's
still going for it, but it might get held up depend-
ing on who owns it on paper and what happens
with the will."

She had to be talking about Carole's practice.
Not wanting to miss a word, Stan stepped into the
room, sticking close to the wall, intent on the conversation. And she kicked a collar with a bell,
which was on the floor, sending it jingling across
the dirty cement. Damn. She darted back to the
door, pretending she'd just walked in.

Silence from behind the wall. Diane's chair
creaked as she leaned back. She saw Stan, frowned
and said, "Gotta go." She hung up the phone,
pushed the chair back and stood up. Her outfit
today was a uniform, and she didn't look as
frumpy as she had in Amara's yard.

"Yes?" she said.

"Hi. Stan Connor. We met at—"

"I remember you."

All righty. Stan crossed to pick up the collar. "It was on the floor."

Diane stayed where she was. Stan put the collar on a shelf against the wall, next to an assortment of collars and leashes. "I was out for a bike ride and wanted to see where the kennel was."

"Why?"

Why? Apparently, not many people cared where the kennel was. "Because I should know where things are in my new town."

"So you're not looking for a dog?"

"Not right now, no. Which might be good, since you don't seem to have any."

Diane either didn't get her attempt at humor or didn't care. "They're out back. It's their exercise time."

"Oh, well, that makes sense." Stan glanced around, trying to figure out what to say next. *Perhaps "Who were you talking to?" Or, "Why do you want Carole's building?"*

Instead, she voiced aloud, "Does the public come here to adopt?"

"Sometimes. Did you want a tour or something? Because this is pretty much it." Diane waved a hand at the runs. Sparse but clean. Each had blankets and bowls and toys. "We have a cat room out back, but there aren't any cats right now. I can show you the dogs, if you want. Quickly." She looked at her watch. "I have an appointment."

Another friendly sort. Maybe Amara had already warned her about what a troublemaker Stan was. She'd better ask what she wanted now, because she might not get another chance. "I'd love to see the dogs, and I wanted to talk to you about Carole. Morganwick," she added, in case there was any confusion.

A whole slew of looks chased each other across Diane's face. The one she probably thought was nonchalance stuck. She would have been terrible at poker. "What about her?"

"Yeah, Stan, what about her?" her internal voice probed. "Did you work with her often?" Stan asked.

Diane shook her head no. "Not usually. She didn't take in strays or surrenders or anything. Even when I asked her to." Her tone turned sour on that. "Why?"

"I saw you outside her clinic on Monday."

"So?"

She decided not to tell Diane about Trooper Pasquale questioning her as a suspect. It hadn't elicited the sympathy card with Amara, and Diane seemed a much tougher nut. "I just wondered if anyone knew any more about what happened. It was shocking for me, you know, to find her like that. . . ." Stan trailed off; Diane said nothing.

"So, can I see the dogs?" Stan asked, since she didn't seem to be getting anywhere. "I brought homemade treats for them."

Diane looked at her strangely, but she nodded. "Sure." She led her outside. "We can't go in. They're under observation right now."

Stan followed her outside to the fenced area. Six adorable pit bulls, ranging from huge to puppy, waited at the fence, tongues hanging. They barked a welcome chorus when Stan and Diane appeared. The largest dog, mostly brown, stood up and howled.

"That's Henry," Diane said. "They're all friendly. You can give them treats from over the fence."

Stan stepped over and offered her hand for Henry to smell. He did a thorough sniffing, then licked her fingers. Stan held out a treat. He plucked it from her hand and devoured it. The other dogs watched intently. Henry stepped back and woofed. The other dogs seemed to take that as a signal that everything was okay, and the rest clamored for their turns.

Stan fed them all. She caught Diane wearing a tiny smile. When Diane realized she'd been seen, the smile vanished. A car drove into the parking lot. A door slammed.

"Diane! You ready?" a man's voice shouted.

"Back here," Diane called. "I have to go, and I can't leave you here," she told Stan.

A man with a shiny bald head, who was wearing a karate uniform, came around the corner. His smile faded when he realized someone else was present. He nodded at Stan. "Hello."

"Hi." Stan started to step forward and introduce herself, but Diane interrupted.

"I'm ready. Let's go. Thanks for bringing the treats," she said to Stan.

"No problem."

She followed them to the parking lot and got on her bike. They waited until she rode away before starting the car.

* * *

Stan biked away from the park and headed back toward the center of town. Another piece of the puzzle: Diane wanted to get into Carole's clinic. Maybe Carole had something in there Diane wanted back, or maybe she wanted the town to turn the building into an adoption center. It would certainly be more conducive to getting animals adopted than where she was now.

Or maybe there was something linking her to Monday's events she wanted to destroy.

But the police would've found that. Stan pedaled faster, her brain humming with thoughts. *Diane is odd, but is she a killer?* Maybe it was paranoia taking over. But you really never knew who you were standing next to.

As she neared the green, Stan decided to swing by the library. She'd promised Betty she would sign up for a library card, and this would be a good chance to nose around for more potential information. Or at least some gossip.

She parked her bike out front. She thought about locking it, then remembered where she was. People may get murdered in their own vet clinics, but Cyril hadn't written any stories that she had seen about thievery.

The buildings in Frog Ledge had that just-old-enough look about them without looking run-down. They had history. And a lot of them were, in fact, historical buildings or homes. She loved that. The library was housed in a two-story white structure that apparently had been the old town schoolhouse. It looked like it had received all new siding recently. Stan wondered if it had been red. The carved wooden sign out front was shaped like a book and said, *FROG LEDGE MEMORIAL LIBRARY*. Another Gene creation.

She pushed open the front door and went inside, stepping into a foyer-type area. Immediately to her right, a cozy living-room arrangement had been set up with chairs, a couch and a gas fireplace. The books were on built-in wall shelves, just like a real living room, and the shelves had signs taped to them: BETTY'S PICKS, JAMES'S PICKS, LORINDA'S PICKS. There was a play area with toys and kids' books. There was also a table with snacks and pitchers of iced tea, covered with plastic wrap, filled to the brim with lemons and ice, waiting for readers to pour a cup and sit with a book.

Stan loved libraries almost as much as cemeteries. They had been her favorite place when she was a kid. Her sister had no interest, except for the magazine section. Stan, however, would browse the stacks for hours, or sit with the latest issue of *Highlights for Children* and learn about all kinds of things. She hadn't set foot in a library in about five years. Maybe longer. Something else she'd given away in exchange for living the dream.

Well, that was going to change. She was here today for a purpose, but as part of her new routine, she would visit the library every week. Get acquainted with some old favorite authors and find some new ones. Read some magazines. When was the last time she'd read an issue of *The New Yorker* or *The Atlantic*? Or even *Lucky*? Reading *Money* and *Forbes* was fine, but it had become all she read, because God forbid someone mentioned a recent article and she couldn't jump into a well-informed conversation. She'd forgotten a lot of things that were important to her.

And now, it was important to get these things back.

She moved down the hall and found the main desk, a wooden, circular affair with piles of colorful flyers stacked on it and the usual book drop slots cut into the front. A woman with long, curly black hair and overdone makeup looked up and beamed a smile at Stan. She had a smudge of lipstick on her front tooth.

"Good afternoon! Welcome to the Frog Ledge Memorial Library. Can I help you find something?" she asked, dropping the papers she was sorting through and coming to the front of the desk.

"I need a library card, and I wondered if Betty was here?"

"Wonderful on the library card, and, yes, Miss Betty is here! Let me page her for you." The chipper librarian picked up her phone and pressed buttons. Her nails were longer than Nikki's, which was saying something.

"Betty! You have a guest," she sang into the receiver. "Well, you know, I forgot to ask." She cupped her hand over the mouthpiece. "What's your name?"

"Stan Connor."

The woman frowned. "'Stan,' you said?"

"I did."

She repeated that into the receiver, then nodded and hung up. "Betty's on her way. Meantime, let's get that library card going!" She fussed on her computer. "Is your name really 'Stan'?"

"It is. Short for Kristan."

"Oh. Well, that's a relief. I was just about to ask what your momma was thinking." She made herself laugh. "I'm Lorinda, by the way. What's your address?"

Stan gave it to her.

Lorinda paused. "That sounds so familiar." Then it dawned on her. "Oh, I know who you are. You're the girl who bought the green Victorian."

At least she didn't say the girl who maybe killed our vet. "Yes, that's me."

Lorinda typed a bit; then she looked up at her. She scanned a key tag and handed it over. "Here you go. Now I'll show you to our sitting area. Betty will be right down."

When she came out from behind the desk, Stan got a kick out of her outfit. She wore a short black skirt, gray leggings and a red sequined top. Teetering on impossibly high snakeskin heels, she led Stan to a small alcove behind the children's section. It looked out over a small flower garden area with benches.

"Enjoy!" Lorinda sang out. With a hair toss, she clicked back over to her post.

Stan didn't have to wait long for Betty. She came down the winding staircase and welcomed Stan with a hug.

"Did you get your card?"

Stan held it up. Betty clapped. "Marvelous! So glad you stopped by. Are you going to spend some time and look around?"

"I plan on it, but not today. I wanted to ask you a question." Stan glanced around to see if anyone was within hearing distance. Satisfied there wasn't, she spoke but dropped her voice, anyway. "Turns out a friend of mine knew Carole when she was Carole Cross. She had some, um, problems with her work, too. This was in New Jersey. I wanted to see if you had any insights."

Betty snorted. "'Insights'? I gave you my insights. She was a terrible vet. Those state troopers should have enough suspects to interview for the next two weeks. What you just told me doesn't surprise me, not at all. Doesn't matter what name she used. But you should look up some reviews for her. You'll see it wasn't just me. Do you want to use a computer and do it now?"

"Oh, I can do it at home," Stan said. "Thanks for the info."

"Anytime," Betty assured her. "Did you find someone to mow your lawn yet?"

"How did you know I needed a mower?" Stan asked; then she chuckled. She was forgetting where she lived. "Yes, I did. Gene sent his apprentice."

"Gene has an apprentice?" Betty asked. "Since when?"

"I have no idea," Stan said, "but he came and he mowed."

"Well, that's good for you. I'm glad." Betty patted her shoulder and stood. "I'm very glad you have your card. Visit us often. And check out books."

Chapter 15

Richard called as she was letting herself into the house. Shoot, she suddenly remembered, they were supposed to have dinner. She debated ignoring the call, because she really didn't want to go out in public, but at the last minute snatched it up.

"Hey, babe." He sounded like he was in a good mood. "What are we doing tonight? I'm coming to you."

"You are?" When he'd left her on moving day, it sounded like coming back to Frog Ledge was the last thing he wanted to do.

"I am. Anything interesting going on out there?"

Stan had to bite back a hysterical laugh. *Just a dead vet and a cop who thinks I killed her. And a whole bunch of unfriendly townspeople.* "Not really."

"Find any good places to eat? Or do you want me to bring some food from your Thai place? That way we can talk where it's quiet. I know you had something to tell me."

Her stomach felt like it had been in a constant state of nausea since Monday. The thought of food, even food she couldn't smell yet, made her want to be sick, especially combined with discussing the murder. She swallowed, forcing her voice to sound carefree. "That sounds great."

"And then we can go out for a couple of drinks. I'm sure there are a few good places to have a beer or two." Richard sounded like he had this all planned out. Stan knew she should be grateful he was engaged and trying, but she really just wanted to sit in the house and lock the doors until her life straightened out again. "It'll be fun."

"Sure. Fun," she echoed. Stan hung up, feeling like a trip to the firing squad was more imminent than dinner and drinks.

Richard was in a good mood. That meant he talked a lot. The sales conference had been quite successful. He wanted to tell her all about it, partly because she knew all the players and partly because he was excited about his new leads. They were sitting in the sunroom eating the Thai food he'd brought and drinking red wine. Stan half listened to his stories while forcing down as little food as she could get away with, grateful that she knew both him and the event well enough to know when to interject which reaction.

"And the food was crap as usual," Richard said, winding up. He slurped up the last noodle from his pad Thai and paused, weighing his next words. "Lots of people were asking about you. I just told them you were on to the next thing."

Stan shrugged. "True enough."

"Do you remember Randall Bennett?"

"Of course." Bennett was a big shot in gambling and casinos.

"He was very interested in what 'the next thing' meant for you. He's looking for a PR person."

"Really?" Stan laughed. "I'm not the Vegas type."

"He's got stakes in lots of games, no pun intended. I told him I would pass the info along." Richard pulled a card out of his wallet and tossed it on the coffee table. "If you're interested. I didn't make any promises, like you said. Just told him I'd pass it along."

Stan left the card where it was. "Thanks." She could see the annoyance flicker in his eyes, but he let it go.

"What's the story you wanted to tell me, Stan?" he asked, changing the subject.

She had been both wondering when he would give her his attention and dreading telling it. She placed her fork carefully on her plate. "The craziest thing happened the other day." She explained about meeting Carole and her invitation to bring Nutty in. Richard's eyes were glazing a little like they did when she went on too long about the cat or something else he didn't have much interest in. He topped off his wineglass; she brought him back with a bang. "When I got there, she was dead."

His eyes widened. "'Dead'? Like, not breathing?"

"I mean *not alive*. Dead. Murdered, actually."

"'Murdered'?" He stared at her. "Are you serious?"

She nodded slowly. "Someone killed the vet. I found her. The police—well, the one cop who works in this town—have been questioning me about it."

"Why? Do they think you did it, or something?"

"It's absurd, right? I think they just haven't spent a lot of time doing their homework on this lady yet. She had a lot of enemies."

"How did she die?"

"They didn't release the autopsy results."

"So maybe she just had a heart attack or something. Why would they think she was murdered?"

"Because she had a needle stuck in her neck."

"You're kidding."

Stan shook her head.

Richard studied her. "Stan, are you in trouble?"

"I didn't do anything! I didn't even know this woman. Why on earth would I kill her?"

He came to sit beside her on the lounger. "Do you need me to find you a lawyer?"

"I'm fine. I don't need a lawyer, and I can find one if I need one."

"Are you sure?"

"I didn't kill this woman, and I'm not going to act like I have something to hide. I've been answering all their questions. I'm handling it, Richard. But thanks." She didn't tell him how people were already whispering about her around town, or about her fight with Amara.

"Okay, then." He nodded, as if the problem had just solved itself. "So where are we going for drinks?"

"You really want to go out?"

"Yeah, why not? It's early still. Not even eight. Wasn't there a brewery or something out here?"

She thought of McSwigg's and Jake's invitation to her and Nikki; then she immediately pushed it out of her mind. She didn't want to take Richard there. "I think so," she said. "Next town over."

Richard pulled out his iPad. "I'll look it up."

Stan cleared the plates while he did. She should go change. Put on some makeup. Get excited about going out with her boyfriend. Plus, if she didn't show her face in public, it might look like she was hiding out of guilt. But she didn't want to socialize. Or run into Amara. Not to mention Jake's sister had practically arrested her in front of half the town yesterday.

She finished loading the dishwasher and turned around to tell Richard she was going to freshen up a bit. "Hey, look at this," he said. "There's a place about two miles from here. Your favorite. An Irish pub. McSwigg's. Let's check it out."

McSwigg's parking lot overflowed onto the street. People streamed in and out in various stages of laughter, and conversation loudly trickled through Richard's open window. The pub was about a half mile out from the center of town, a stone's throw from Carole's clinic and the town hall. The building stood alone and looked like it had once been some kind of historical landmark. Jake must have completely redone it. It was black, save for the stone front flanking heavy mahogany doors, with an Irish flag waving above them. Lights on each side of the doors gave off a welcoming, homey feel. One of Gene's creations, this time in the shape of an Irish top hat, pronouncing MCSWIGG'S, protruded from the side of one of the doors.

And the place was slammed with people. Friday night at the only game in town. Of course it would be busy. Stan wondered how many people would stare and whisper when she walked in. She felt like the woman with the scarlet *A*; only hers would be an *M* for "murderess."

Richard was already out of the car, despite the fact he normally wouldn't consider leaving his beloved Jag parked on any kind of street. Despite Stan's tale about the murder, he must think the little town was safe enough.

Stalling, Stan pulled down the visor and checked her makeup in the mirror. She looked good, if not a little green. But at an Irish pub, no one would notice. Richard leaned in and smiled at her. "Ready?"

She pasted on a fake smile. "Ready."

He took her hand as they walked up to the door. A heavyset man reminding Stan of a club bouncer opened it with a mock bow. Irish music poured out, reminding her of an Irish step-dancing show she'd attended a few years ago. She'd not yet made it to Ireland, but she had a suspicion this was how a pub there would feel.

McSwigg's knew how to pack them in. The room was full, but not uncomfortably so. And it was cozy. Wide-open, with tall and short tables scattered around, surrounded by padded stools in greens and golds with Celtic knots. The live band played in a small area near the back. Wooden floors gleamed, despite their obvious overuse. She could smell pub food and good beer. The bar itself was a shining mahogany masterpiece, accentuated by droplights positioned to shine on each person's space. Jake had another Irish flag displayed on the far wall behind the bar, and another carved wooden sign, with a Gaelic saying above it: *AN ÁIT A BHFUIL DO CHROÍ IS ANN A THABHARFAS DO CHOSA THÚ.* She wished she knew Gaelic to translate it.

The dim room was cozy in a way that announced, *I'm in my living room enjoying a glass of wine.* The whole scene looked like an ad for a bar at a fancy resort. If Jake had done all this, he'd poured a lot of time, money and heart into the place.

A couple who had been standing in front of them talking moved, and Stan saw Jake filling a pint behind the bar. He laughed at something. There were two other people working with him, a guy and a pretty young girl. She had long brown hair and white teeth that sparkled when she laughed. She was doing a lot of that with her customers. Izzy would probably say Jake stocked the bar with her ilk.

Jake placed the beer in front of its owner, turned and saw her as he scanned the room. He smiled when his eyes landed on her, and she felt her stomach flip a little. Probably her Thai food not agreeing with her. Then Richard leaned over and said, "Where do you want to sit?" She could feel Jake still watching her.

Richard didn't wait for her answer. "The bar,"

he decided, and put his arm around her waist to lead her there.

She felt like a spotlight shone on her as she made the walk to the back of the room. Her imagination or not, she felt people turn and stare at her as she passed. Then a sleek ball of gray suddenly shot out from under a stool and bounded toward her in a full-on sprint. Somehow Duncan managed not to knock anyone over or spill any drinks on the way. Thank goodness Stan didn't have a drink in her hand, because Duncan jumped right up, paws on her shoulders, like he did when they met at the green. Richard stepped back, alarmed, and Stan wasn't sure if it was because he was afraid of Duncan or surprised to see a dog in a pub.

Jake shook his head. "Duncan!" he yelled over the music and chatter. "I don't know what it is about you," he said to Stan when he reached them and pulled the dog off her. "He doesn't do that to anyone else." He turned to Richard and held out his hand. "Jake McGee. I own the place. Welcome. This is Duncan. He's not well behaved, in case you haven't noticed."

"Uh, hi. Richard Ruse." Richard shook his hand.

"Should I be flattered or concerned that he's got some obsession with me?" Stan rubbed the dog's head. "I'm prepared this time." She pulled a bag of treats out of her purse and handed him one. He gobbled it, still wagging his tail. He would love her with or without treats, she could tell. That was a dog for you. Sometimes she wondered if Nutty would stick around if she didn't cook for him.

"Come on over. We have a couple seats. What are you drinking?" Jake motioned for them to follow him. He nudged a guy sitting at the bar. The guy took a look at Stan, smiled and gave up his seat, which was next to an empty stool.

"That's not necessary," Stan began, but the guy laughed.

"When the boss here says to move, we move," he said. "And it couldn't be for a prettier lady." He glanced at Richard, found nothing else to say, saluted and melted into the crowd.

Stan shook her head. "That's no way to keep customers."

Jake grinned. "I have no trouble keeping customers. What are you two drinking?"

"I'll have a Sam Adams Summer Ale." She looked at Richard. "Vodka and tonic with a twist," he said primly. Stan wondered if he was sorry that he'd suggested going out.

Jake went behind the bar to get the drinks. Duncan plopped at Stan's feet, looked up and wagged his tail. "Not a Guinness girl, huh?" Jake commented.

"No. Too dark. So how do you get to bring Duncan in here?"

"I own the place." He grinned and slid the bottle at her, following it up with Richard's drink.

"Thank you. Where's the restroom?" Richard asked.

Jake pointed to a hallway next to the kitchen door. "Right that way."

Richard nodded. "I'll be back," he told Stan.

Jake watched him walk away. "Boyfriend?"

Stan felt her cheeks heat. What? Was she in high school again? "Yeah." She took a sip of her beer.

"Too bad."

Caught between a laugh and a swallow, Stan choked on her beer. Jake poured a glass of water and placed it in front of her.

Stan drank some and shook her head. "You're crazy."

"Just saying it like it is."

She changed the subject. "This is a nice place. The music is perfect."

"It is," Jake agreed, following her gaze around the room.

"Was this a house?"

"Yep. Still is, if you want to get literal about it. I live upstairs."

"Do you?" Stan glanced around, surprised.

"I don't have a sign pointing the way, if that's what you're looking for. Wouldn't want any of my customers wandering upstairs to my bed. You know what I mean? Well, in most cases."

She rolled her eyes. "That might work on your bartender," she said, nodding at the young woman.

Jake laughed. "I hope not. That's my sister. My *other* sister. Obviously, not the one you've met."

"Oh." *"Nice job, Stan,"* her inner voice chided. "How many sisters do you have?"

"Just two. Brenna, and, of course, you know Jessie. That's enough." He glanced behind him, shook his head as he watched his sister lean forward, elbows on the bar, engrossed in whatever one of the male patrons was saying. "She's just messing with him, but she's real good at it. Gets rockin' tips that way."

"Seems like an odd thing for a big brother to encourage," Stan said.

"What am I gonna do? She's gonna do it somewhere. May as well be where I can keep an eye on her. Or punch somebody out, without too much fear of repercussion."

"I don't know about that," Stan said. "Your other sister is pretty hard-core. She might close you down."

A strange look passed over Jake's face and his lips moved into a thin line. "Yeah. That's one way to describe her."

Richard returned to his seat, glancing between her and Jake as he did so. Someone yelled Jake's name from the other end of the bar. He raised a finger to tell them to wait. "Well, enjoy your evening. And please let me know if you need anything else."

"Thanks," Stan said.

Richard nodded stiffly. After Jake walked away, Richard said, "You didn't tell me you knew the owner."

"I met him out running. I don't *know* him."

"Well, you two seem pretty cozy." Richard took the straw out of his drink and made a show of drinking half of it in one gulp.

"'Cozy'?" Stan laughed. "Jealousy is not becoming on you, Richard. And, really, people have already found a few reasons to stare at me. Let's not give them another." She took a generous swallow of her drink. This had been a bad idea. She knew it, but she still agreed to come here with him. Would she ever learn to follow her instincts?

As if sensing her agitation, Duncan sat up and

howled. The patrons around them turned to see what was upsetting their usually calm mascot.

"It's okay, Duncan." Stan patted his head.

"Everything okay, young lady?"

Stan turned to the voice a few bar stools down and recognized Gene, the sign maker.

"Fine, thank you," Stan said. She smiled, but it felt more like a grimace. Richard leaned over to get Jake's sister's attention, pointing at his glass. She held up one finger, still listening to another customer clearly in the middle of a story.

But Gene had recognized her now. "It's the bike rider. How was your trip the other day? See anything interestin'?" He got up and limped over to her.

Just a car stalking me. "I rode through that beautiful cemetery. It's enormous."

"Our cemetery's something to be proud of. Folks from all over the county choose it, hands down. Unless they have some tie to their own town. Or their relatives are too lazy to drive." He chuckled at his own joke. Stan held the polite smile. She hated pretending stupid jokes were funny. Gene didn't seem to notice. "How'd you like them eggs?"

"They were absolutely delicious," Stan said. "And I need to pay you for them still." She reached for her bag, but he shook his head.

"I'll bring ya more this week. Leave a bill for two cartons. Ok?"

She nodded. "That's great. Thank you."

He indicated Richard. "He with you?"

"Yes, that's Richard." She turned to him, but now he was chatting up Jake's sister, who had turned her attention on him. Great form of revenge. Hitting up a twentysomething. "Well, he's busy right now." Jake's sister looked like she wanted to be anywhere else but listening to him. Probably droning on about his latest sale at work. And his commission. Trying to impress the college kid.

"Friendly fella," Gene commented.

"Yeah." Time to take control of this conversation. "So you had an appointment with Carole the other day? The day she died?"

A mixture of emotions Stan couldn't identify fled across his face. "Junior did. Yup."

"Were you friends with Carole?"

"Knew her growin' up, but I already told ya that."

"Was she a good vet?"

Gene narrowed his eyes. "Weren'tcha there with your own cat?"

"I was."

"Well, helluva time to be asking me now, ain't it?"

Stan wondered if she'd offended him, but she couldn't tell from his poker-faced expression if he was kidding or not. "It was my first time going."

"Ah."

She glanced over at Richard. There was another empty glass in front of him. Still talking to Brenna, who was looking around for an escape. Stan decided to take advantage of the situation.

"Does Carole have family around?"

"None I can think of. Just that brother of hers. I suppose they called him to figure out what to do. He don't come around much, but I bet he stepped up to do a nice funeral. They're doin' a wake Monday. Took a while, I guess, with the autopsy and all. Funeral's Tuesday, but they ain't inviting anyone." He leaned against the bar, completely invading the man's space next to Stan and ignoring his dirty look. His eyes were watery enough to make Stan wonder if he'd had a few too many drinks. She wondered how Jake handled his townspeople and friends leaving the bar snookered, especially when he knew that one of his sisters might be waiting outside to arrest the lot of them.

"It's a private service?"

Gene snorted. "It's a crock, you ask me. No one but relatives allowed. Funny thing is, like I just told ya, she don't have many. It'll be a short service—mark my words."

He looked like he was about to say more, but a man came over and slung an arm around him. The top of his head gleamed smooth. As he stepped into the light, Stan recognized him. He was the karate guy who had come to the kennel to see Diane. "Need another drink, my friend?" His tone was jovial, but Stan sensed an undercurrent of hostility.

Gene did, too, because he immediately stiffened. "Sure, why not. Nice ta see ya, Don." It didn't sound like it was all that nice. He didn't introduce Stan.

The man named Don looked Stan up and down. His gaze was neutral and he didn't say anything. Instead, he kept his arm around Gene and walked him away from the bar.

Stan turned back to Richard, who was working on a new drink. Jake's sister had moved on, and Richard looked foul again. "Did you see that?" she asked.

"What?"

"That man who came over. It was like he didn't want Gene talking to me."

"Who's Gene?"

"The guy who was just standing here. If you'd stopped flirting for a few seconds, I could've introduced you." Stan craned her neck to see if she could see them, but they'd vanished into the crowd.

Richard didn't catch her dig. He caught Brenna's eye again and raised his glass. Brenna's smile looked to Stan more like a grimace, but she grabbed a glass and poured the drink. Satisfied, he looked at Stan. "You having another one?" he asked.

Stan opened her mouth to snap at him that no, she wasn't, and he shouldn't, either. But she didn't get a chance. Instead, she covered it with both hands as Brenna slid the drink down the bar with just the tiniest flick of her wrist, and the quickest gleam of satisfaction in her eye. It tipped and spilled, flowing over the shiny mahogany right into Richard's lap.

Chapter 16

If Stan wasn't hearing it for herself, she wouldn't have believed it. First thing in the morning, crowing roosters really did sing *cock-a-doodle-do!* She thought that had been a cartoon exaggeration from her youth, but no. It happened regularly in Frog Ledge, and at six on a Saturday, too.

She rolled over and covered her head with the pillow. She'd forgotten to shut the blinds, so the sun beamed in, making it more impossible to ignore the morning. Richard would snarl and complain if he was there. But he wasn't. He'd left in a huff last night after dropping her off, still wearing his alcohol-soaked pants and complaining how he better not get pulled over on the way home smelling like a brewery.

Stan didn't bother to point out that he'd had plenty to drink, and it wasn't just the booze he'd worn contributing to the problem. She also didn't point out his attempts to flirt with Jake's very young sister had been poorly received. After the spilling incident Stan had been intent on getting out of the bar before either of them made anyone else mad. But she wished she'd had a chance to find out about the man named Don, who clearly had wanted Gene to stop talking to her.

Footsteps on her porch had her out of bed and at the window, in time to see a young boy pedal away, a newspaper bag slung over his shoulder. New edition of the *Frog Ledge Holler*. Cyril had gotten delivery help. Stan's stomach immediately flipped, the familiar sense of dread settling in. What had Frog Ledge's renowned investigative journalist come up with this time?

Nutty meowed loudly, as if to say, *You don't want to know. Stay in bed.*

Stan sighed, threw the covers off and dragged herself up. She forced her normal routine to take over. She hit the bathroom first; then she headed down to the kitchen and started her coffee brewing. Once that was done, she took a deep breath and headed to the front door.

The newspaper had landed just to the left of her welcome mat. She stepped out to get it and bent over. She barely had time to brace herself when she heard panting and pounding paws. Duncan leaped up her stairs and landed on her.

"Whoa! Jeez, Duncan!" Stan braced herself by grabbing her door frame, grabbing his collar with the other hand. "What the heck are you doing here?" Was Jake around? He had to be. Suddenly self-conscious, she finger-combed her hair. She wished she'd washed her face, but she didn't see him anywhere. Not even across the street at the green.

"Come on inside." She grabbed the paper and ushered the dog through the door. "I'll call your dad." Although she didn't have his phone number, and, of course, Duncan's collar had no tag on it. "Your daddy needs to keep a better eye on you."

However, Duncan had already careened down the hall toward the kitchen. Seconds later, Nutty scrambled out like a cartoon cat, sliding on the long fur around his paws. He fled up the stairs. Stan held back a giggle. She followed Duncan. He had both paws up on her counter and had the treat jar sliding dangerously toward the edge. "Duncan! No. Wait." Obediently he plopped down on his haunches and waited, tongue hanging, for her to serve him.

Stan tossed him a few treats and looked around for her phone. She found it on top of the toaster. She looked up the number for McSwigg's and dialed. A female voice answered.

"Hi, I'm looking for Jake," she said.

"He's still upstairs. Who's calling?"

"This is Stan Connor. His dog just showed up at my door."

The girl gasped. "Oh, my God. Hang on." Stan heard the phone clatter down, followed by yelling. After about five minutes Jake picked up.

"Yeah?"

"Uh, it's Stan. Duncan's at my house."

A pause. "Well, what the hell is he doing there? And why didn't my sister just give you my number? Hey, Brenna," he yelled away from the phone. "Next time give her my number. Forget it, I can just give it to you." He started reciting, but Stan interrupted.

"Hang on. I don't have a piece of paper." Stan grabbed a pen out of her junk drawer. She imagined Jake shoving his rumpled hair back and jamming one of those caps he always wore on his head.

"Ready." She scribbled the number he recited. He paused.

"Do you . . . ?" she started to say.

"I guess I'll . . . ," he said at the same time.

They both stopped.

Stan cleared her throat. "Do you want me to bring him to you?"

"No. You shouldn't have to do that. I'll swing by. Unless that's not convenient?"

"That's fine. I'm here for a while."

"Okay. Gimme a few. What's wrong with that dog?"

"Maybe he really likes my treats."

"You know," Jake said, "I wouldn't doubt it."

That made her blush. Stan raced upstairs to change out of her pajamas into a pair of cutoff sweats and a tank top. She washed her face and ran a comb through her hair. She left the bathroom; then she ducked back in and swiped powder over her face. She went back downstairs and threw the dirty dishes from last night into the dishwasher. Like he would even notice.

Get a grip. Go about my business. Trouble was, she didn't have much business right now. Her eyes darted around the room and landed on the paper she'd tossed on the table. Which had started the whole morning. Picking it up, she forced her eyes to the headlines:

LOCAL VET MURDERED WITH OWN MEDICATION
POLICE NARROW THE SEARCH FOR KILLER

The autopsy performed on the body of Carole Morganwick, Frog Ledge's veterinarian, determined a potassium injection was the cause of death, according to resident state trooper Jessica Pasquale.

Morganwick was found stabbed with a needle at her clinic early Monday.

Pasquale said an autopsy performed by the state medical examiner determined the needle contained potassium, which can cause a heart attack in about thirty seconds if it's administered rapidly.

The doorbell rang, startling Stan out of the article. With shaking hands she tossed the paper aside and went to answer it; Duncan trotted obediently beside her.

Jake stood on the porch, cap on, bleary-eyed, just as Stan had pictured him. She swung the door open. Duncan wagged his tail.

"Hey," Jake said. "And you," to Duncan, "what do you have to say for yourself?"

Duncan bolted back toward the kitchen.

"I guess not much," Stan said. "Come on in."

"Sorry about this." He stepped in and looked around. "Place looks nice."

"Oh, thanks, but it's not even close to being done. Want coffee?"

"I'd love some. You sure I'm not intruding?"

"Not at all."

"Your boyfriend here?"

"No. He had to go home last night." *And change clothes.*

"He like the bar?"

Since he was behind her, Stan had to look back to see if he was busting her chops, but his face remained carefully blank. She thought back to Richard's reaction to the drink in his lap and decided in this case a white lie would be preferred.

"He had a great time."

"Probably until my sister dumped his drink on him."

"There was that."

"From what she said, he deserved it."

"He was annoyed with me."

"So that means you flirt with a twenty-two-year-old? In front of your girlfriend?"

This didn't sound like something a player would say. Izzy would tell her it was all an act to get her on his side. She shrugged, not knowing how to respond.

"If Brenna hadn't done it, I probably would have. But my little sister isn't shy. Apparently, Duncan likes what you've done to the place, too."

The dog had plopped down on the small rug in front of the sink, watching them. When Stan looked at him, Duncan's tail wagged.

Stan poured Jake a cup of coffee and placed it on her table. "He's so cute. And I feel like I'm still really behind in getting settled. With . . . everything going on, unpacking hasn't taken priority, although it would probably get my mind off everything. So how did Duncan get out?"

Jake sat down and took a sip. "Good coffee. I

don't know. I'm thinking my door from my
apartment didn't shut all the way and he got
into the bar. Then, when people started coming
and going this morning, he snuck out."

Stan shook her head. "Dangerous."

"I know, I know." He wagged a finger at the
dog. "Getting me in trouble."

"I have to feed Nutty. Can I give some to
Duncan? It's a turkey, cheese and carrot mix.
With calcium powder."

Jake raised an eyebrow. "For the cat?"

"Yes, for the cat."

"That . . . sounds crazy."

"Why? I make all his food. Not just treats."

"Get outta here."

Stan crossed her arms defensively. "He has
stomach problems."

"Hey, do what you gotta do. Sure, Duncan can
have whatever he wants."

"I'm presuming he didn't eat breakfast yet
today."

"Cut me a break, would ya? I went to bed at
three. And he has food at the ready all the time."

Stan wrinkled her nose. "What kind?"

"I don't know. It's in a bag."

That made Stan think of the kibble showered
over Carole on the day of her death, which de-
flated the fun of the banter. She busied herself
with getting the food onto plates. Decided she'd
bring Duncan his own stash of good-for-you meals
so he didn't start running away to get them. She
heated them up enough to take the chill out;

then she handed Duncan his. He attacked it, with his tail wagging the whole time.

"Be right back. Have to find Nutty. He wasn't happy about the visitor." She went upstairs and found him on the windowsill. He glared at her, his expression clear: *I know there's a dog in the house. Please remove it.*

"He's just visiting, Nutter. Eat your breakfast."

She went back downstairs. Jake was reading the paper. He glanced up at her as she came in.

"This whole Carole thing is crazy, but it looks like they're narrowing it down."

"Yeah. Your sister will show up with handcuffs any minute now." *Either here or at Nikki's.* She moved to the coffeepot and poured another cup. Her hands still shook. "More coffee?" She was surprised to find her voice sounded normal.

"Sure." He passed her the mug. "Listen. I heard about what happened at Izzy's. I'm sorry. My sister is . . . loyal to this town and the people. For a cop she has some trouble believing the worst about people she's known forever. She'd much rather blame the people she doesn't know, because that's where she's had the experience. I think it gives her an illusion of safety. Believe me, she has her reasons."

"I wish I weren't the one in her sights." Stan topped off the mug, handed it back and did the same with her own before returning to the table. "It's just because I was there and I found her. I also heard the killer leaving, but no one cares about that."

"You heard the killer leaving? What do you mean?"

"I heard someone going out the back door that morning. That's why I went down the hall. I thought she had been out back or something and hadn't heard me come in. There was no receptionist, so I walked down to tell her. But it hadn't been her, so whoever killed her was just leaving."

And could have killed me, too. If whoever it was had seen her, or recognized her car, then he or she could come after her, too. That person might think she could implicate him. So not only were the police watching her, the killer might be as well.

From the look on Jake's face, he was thinking the same thing. He was quiet for a minute; then he said, "Brenna's friend worked as her receptionist. Carole let her go a couple of weeks back."

"Really. Why?"

Jake shrugged. "Not sure. Brenna said there wasn't enough work. I guess her friend was bummed because she wants to work with animals and couldn't find another job around here."

"So Carole fired her receptionist." Maybe the receptionist was angry about it, too. "What was her name?"

"Amy Franchetti. She wants to go to vet school, and the job seemed like a good way to get some experience. But she didn't work there very long." Jake shrugged. "Now she's waitressing for me."

"You get all the college girls, huh?"

He grinned. "My customers like them."

"Do you know some guy named Don?"

"Don. You mean Don Miller? The councilman?"

"Bald? Kind of unfriendly-looking? Some kind of karate person?"

"That's him. He runs a school for martial arts. Why?"

"Gene was talking to me last night and Don came and pretty much strong-armed him away. I'm wondering why."

"What was Gene talking to you about?"

"Carole. I asked him how well he knew her. He seems to be one of the only people I've met around here who liked her." She cocked her head and looked at Jake. "Did you like her?"

Jake drained his cup. "Didn't know her. Can I get more? This coffee rocks."

"It's Izzy's." She waited to see if he had any reaction to that. He didn't. She motioned to the pot. "Help yourself. Did you take Duncan to her?"

"Nope."

"Who did you take him to?"

Jake sighed. "Another chance for you to tell me what a bad parent I am for him. I was in between vets for Duncan. The rescue where I got him—"

"Oh, he's a rescue. That's great."

"Wow, you approve of something I did with the dog. Can I write that down? Anyway, they had done all his vet stuff. I only adopted him about a year and a half ago, so I haven't gotten my own vet yet."

"Where do you take him if he gets sick?"

"He usually doesn't. He has an iron stomach and decent genes. Plus, all the leftover booze he cleans out of the glasses for me every night has to help. I'm kidding," he said at Stan's horrified gasp. "No, there's a twenty-four-hour place a couple towns away. It's my backup for now. Are you going to throw something at me, or just report me?"

"Probably throw something at you, but not when you're expecting it. I'm curious to see how many people went to Carole from around town."

"Honestly? I didn't hear great things about her. And from what Brenna says, Amy was less than thrilled with the actual experience of working there."

"Why?"

"Not sure. I don't usually ask for details on stuff like that."

"So she's got no family except for a brother and a son no one's seen in years. What did she do around here? Who did she hang out with?"

"No idea, sunshine. Why are you so interested?"

"I want to know who hated this lady enough to kill her."

"Stan, really. My sister knows you didn't do it."

"She doesn't know any such thing, and she's made that clear enough."

Jake was silent for a minute. Stan couldn't read his face.

"Were Carole and Mona Galveston buds? That was quite a speech the mayor gave the other night."

"Not even close. A lot of history there."

"History? Tell me. I can make you breakfast."

"Bribing me for information?" Jake grinned. "I'll take you up on it."

"Omelet?"

"Sure."

Stan went to the fridge and began pulling eggs and vegetables out. "The history?"

"I don't know everything. You just hear things around town, and who knows when they stopped being true, right? But Carole's father was a vet, too. He did large animals, and he was the vet for the Galvestons' racehorses. Somewhere along the way they had a falling-out."

"What kind of falling-out?"

"He wasn't the best vet, from what I hear. Kind of lackadaisical about things one would expect him to care about in that line of work. Bloodlines, that type of thing. Those folks took their horses pretty seriously, and something happened to one of their rising stars under his care. The horse died. I don't know the whole story. But the Galvestons—this was the mayor's father at this point—pretty much saw to it that his career was over."

"Was Carole involved?"

"No. Carole and Mona were kids then. Friends, actually. But it turned into one of those Hatfield and McCoy things that happen in small towns. Right down to the kids."

"But they eventually got friendly again?" She finished chopping vegetables and poured the mixture into her cast-iron pan.

"No. They hated each other's guts until the day Carole died."

"So what was up with the whole speech thing the other night at the memorial?"

"Just the way it is," Jake said. "That's how people operate, sweetheart. Don't tell me you don't know that."

"I never paid attention to this stuff before." *I also never found a dead body before.* "But where I worked, yeah, a lot of the same stuff. Minus actual dead bodies."

"Where did you work?"

She told him.

"Not anymore?"

"Nope."

"Why'd you leave?"

"My position got eliminated." *Why am I offering that up?*

"I'm sorry. You miss it?"

She shrugged. "Sometimes." She folded the omelet perfectly in half and slid it onto a plate, handing it to him. "But it's fine. I'll find something else."

"I'm hiring a cook. And waitresses."

"Gee, where can I apply?" She smiled to soften her words. "Hopefully, your sister won't arrest me before I find another job. Those background checks are pretty awful, even if you never did anything wrong."

"My sister will figure it out. She's not as bad as she seems. And she's smart. Like I said before, her only problem is she gives a bigger benefit of the doubt to people she's comfortable with. Me, I'm not as convinced that just because you've known people forever means you *actually know* them."

After Jake left, Stan packed her treats carefully in the cooler and collected the paw-shaped bowls she used for displaying at Nikki's adoption events. It would be nice to get out of town for the afternoon. She changed into a Pets' Last Chance T-shirt and jeans and made an iced coffee for the road, called a good-bye to Nutty and went out the front door, stopping to check it behind her to make sure it was securely locked.

Then she saw Trooper Pasquale's car parked across the street at the green. The officer leaned against it, engaged in a lively conversation with Jake, who didn't look happy even from this distance away. Duncan did, as usual, sitting at Jake's feet, tail swiping the ground like a short-circuited windshield wiper.

Jessie must've seen Jake's truck at her house and waited until he left to give him a thrashing for associating with her prime suspect. She would probably succeed in swaying him over to her side . . . eventually. She was his sister. Then Jake wouldn't talk to her, either. Just stare at her, like half the town did when they saw her.

Jaw set, Stan ignored them as she crossed to her car. She'd just loaded up her stuff when a car pulled into the driveway. Richard. Followed by a second car. *Good visit or bad visit?* Stan's money was on bad. Knowing Richard, he had brought some kind of corporate recruiter with him. Richard got out of the car and went over to the man parked behind him. He said something to him; then he led him over to where Stan waited, with her hand on her car door, ready to escape.

"Hey," he said, coming up and giving her a peck on the lips, any traces of annoyance from last night gone. "I brought someone to meet you. This is Keith Cronin. He's an attorney. Your mother and I were concerned about what's going on, so he's here to talk with you."

Cronin wore thin, wire-rimmed glasses and had thick, wavy black hair shot through with gray. His features were almost feminine, and they matched his too-skinny body. His three-piece suit looked expensive, but it seemed wilted from the heat. He stepped over and held out a hand. Stan shook it unenthusiastically. It was damp and his handshake was limp. Her friends from corporate law would have a field day with this guy. And her mother was involved. That was perfect. "What do you mean, 'what's going on'?" Stan asked.

"Well, you know." Richard glanced around as if fearful a reporter or television camera lurked, ready to capture his every word. "The unfortunate death of that woman."

Cronin watched from a few feet away, sympathy wrinkling his smooth, babyish face. "It's lovely to meet you, Kristan," he said. "Should we talk inside?"

Stan gritted her teeth. "It's Stan. I'm on my way out. And I don't believe I need your services."

Richard and the lawyer both stared at her. Richard spoke first. "What do you mean?" he said with a nervous laugh. "Aren't they trying to pin a murder on you? Be reasonable, Stan."

Stan took a deep breath, trying to keep her temper in check. This was just like Richard. He blew it off last night because it didn't suit him to worry about it, but now something had caused him concern. The *Hartford Courant* had probably picked up the story. She could see Jake and his sister across the green, looking in her direction without trying to appear they were. She wanted to tell them to mind their own business. She wanted to ask Richard and her mother's lawyer to leave. And she wanted to go sell pet treats.

"Gee, Richard, I thought you weren't worried about it. But I didn't kill anyone, and I'm certain they'll figure out soon enough who did," she said. "I don't think I'm in danger of being arrested, but if I am, I'll certainly give you a call, Mr. Cronin. If you'd like to leave me your card, please do so. Otherwise, I'm late for an appointment."

They both stared at her as if she'd completely lost her mind. Maybe she had. But at the moment she didn't care. She was tired of people trying to run her life, even if they had good intentions. She was old enough and smart enough to solve her own problems, and it was about time everyone accepted that.

Cronin looked at Richard, unsure of his next move. "I really think she and I should talk," he said to him.

"Hello?" Stan waved at him. "I'm right here, so if you need to say something to me, please don't direct it at anyone else. I don't think we need to talk right now. But again, I'll be happy to call you if I do. If you don't have a card, I'm sure Richard can give me your number."

Richard sent her a foul look, but he kept his cool. More for the lawyer's benefit than for hers. "That's fine," he said. "I believe Keith has a card. Right, Keith?"

Cronin looked uncomfortable, but he reached into his back pocket and took out a leather wallet.

He extracted a business card and handed it to her. "I'll be available when you need me," he said. *When.* Not *if*. "Your mother has put me on retainer."

Great. Her own mother figured it would only be a matter of time before she got arrested. She took the card and stuck it in her back pocket. "Thanks. Now can you both move your cars?"

Richard's look would've wilted wildflowers, but only because his back was to the lawyer. "Of course, sweetheart. I'll call you." He pasted a polite smile on his lips, air-kissed her again, then turned and walked back to his car.

Cronin glanced at her one last time. "Nice to meet you," he said.

"Likewise," Stan said, her gaze steely.

He scurried back to his own car and backed out of the driveway. Richard didn't look at her as he peeled out, way too fast for this small street. Stan made a mental note to mention that to him later, *if* there was a later. He probably had to go report to her mother about her bad behavior, and that could take a while.

Chapter 17

Emma's Waggin' Tails was a high-end pet supply store, offering handmade clothes, high-quality food and toys from recycled products. Nikki loved having events there. High prices, rich clientele. If they didn't adopt, they usually threw money at the problem. She always brought an extra-large donation jar.

Stan arrived at the same time as Nikki and her crew. Justin had returned from California in one piece, looking like he'd just jumped off his surf-board. His long hair was still damp, curling into ringlets. He wrangled two Boston terriers and a boxer out of Nikki's van while she directed some of her younger volunteers to set up cages and place flyers and other information.

"Can I help?" Stan deposited her goods on an extra table.

"Oooh, the treats." Nikki clapped her hands. "We need a sign for those. Emma!" she called to the woman behind the cash register. "Can we get some poster board?"

Emma hurried to oblige after waving hello to Stan.

"We can set the treats up on that table," Nikki said. "You have different kinds, right?" At Stan's nod she flashed a thumbs-up. "Just set them out and make sure we identify each. Cara, we need the cages stacked with blankets between them. Otherwise, the cats will be harassing each other all day." She turned to Justin. "You good?"

He flashed a smile at her. His teeth were so white that they gave off a glare. Stan always wondered what the draw of New England was for such an obvious California boy. "We're great," he said. His three charges were huddled together in a pile in the small pen he'd set up.

"Those three are too cute. I have to get the cats. Cara, if you're done with cages, come help me." Nikki bounded through the front door again.

Stan watched her go, then shook her head. "No idea where she gets her energy."

Justin laughed. "She kills me most of the time. So how's your new house, sweetie? I felt bad I wasn't around to help you move in."

"It's great. I'm sure California was a better time."

"Nikki probably whipped the place into shape for you, didn't she? I know she wanted to be there on official moving day, but she got tied up. It's why she was so bent on getting back early Sunday."

Sunday? Nikki hadn't been back to the area until late Monday. "Didn't she—" Stan began to answer, but the front door crashed open again. Cara stumbled through with two huge cat carriers.

"Careful!" Nikki's voice floated behind her, lost

in a stampede of dog feet. A Rottweiler and a few other mixed-breed mutts dragged her in the door. The cacophony of their barking set off the Bostons and the boxer. Nikki sent Emma an apologetic look.

Emma didn't look fazed in the least as she worked carefully on the poster. Stan stepped over to take a peek. She drew different-shaped treats interspersed with stick figure dogs and cats around the words *GOURMET ANIMAL TREATS, BAKED FRESH!*

Nikki handed off a couple of the dogs to Justin. Once the tangle of leashes had thinned out, Stan noticed the little dog she'd spent time with at Nikki's the other day hanging back behind the crowd, her nub of a tail pointing down.

"Oh, there's my friend! Hi, Scruffy!" Stan dropped to her knees a few feet away.

Scruffy's tail immediately wagged when she recognized Stan. She took a few tentative steps over, but the Rottweiler blocked her path. She stomped her little feet and *woo-woo-wooed* at Stan until she came over and led her around the other dog.

"You must smell the treats. Come on, over here." Stan led her to the table and chose one of the apple cranberry oat–flavored treats. "Try this one." While Scruffy wolfed it down, Stan went to work arranging the different kinds in their bowls and setting up a sign for each. "How much are we charging?"

"Want to do a buck apiece, two for one-fifty?" Nikki asked.

"Sure." She added the price to the poster Emma

had proudly taped to the front of her table. "So Scruffy's up for adoption already?"

"Well, she didn't get groomed yet, so not technically. But I wanted to see how she did. She's kind of shy."

Stan watched the little dog stand up against the table, sniffing for another snack. "She doesn't seem that shy to me."

"Around other dogs she is, but she'll get over it. How're you doing with the cats, Cara?"

"Good. They're so cute!" Cara squealed.

Nikki checked on the other girl's handling of the cages and helped her arrange an adorable litter of kittens.

"I didn't know you had so many cats. Have you been taking more in?" Stan reached through the cage door and petted one of the babies.

"I've pulled a few. The rest just seem to show up. A pregnant mom wandered into the dog area a while back, so I set her up in a room. These are her babies." The black-and-white kittens tumbled over each other, playful and full of joy, blissfully unaware of the danger they had been in before their mom chose Nikki as her guardian angel.

"Ladies—oh, sorry, and gentleman, of course," Emma corrected, and shot an apologetic look at Justin, "are you about ready? I have to open the store."

"We're good. Let 'er rip," Nikki said. "You want to watch Scruffy, or do you want me to put her in a pen?"

"She can hang with me." Stan rumpled the dog's ears.

"Don't let her eat all the treats. That's how we make the most donations at these things."

Nikki was only half teasing. Stan leaned down and whispered to the dog, "Don't worry. I have plenty more."

The first customers came in the door—a family with two young boys, who both began to shriek excitedly when they saw the animals.

"Don't touch that dog!" the mother exclaimed as her younger son made a beeline for the Rottweiler.

"Don't worry. He's probably the friendliest dog here," Justin said, shooting a warning glance at Nikki. She tended to have little patience for uninformed people who discriminated by breed.

The Rottie named Blaze licked the little boy's hand. The mother shot both the dog and Justin a dirty look and dragged her children to the other side of the store.

"I hope it's not going to be one of those days," Nikki said.

After the first family, the potential adopters improved. Two hours later two kittens had been adopted, and someone had filled out an application for one of the Boston terriers. Stan's treats had netted twenty-five dollars so far, although most of the money had come from one woman whose Great Dane had inhaled nearly one whole bowl before she realized he'd done so.

Scruffy hung out under Stan's table the whole time while she and Justin chatted and helped the younger volunteers with their charges. She'd wrapped Scruffy's leash under one of the chair legs, but the dog didn't seem to be in any hurry to leave her side. Every now and then, Stan slipped her a treat.

"What kind do you recommend?" An older woman stood in front of the table perusing the treats, holding in her arms a tiny Yorkie who had a red bow in her hair.

"The cheese ones are a big seller, but your dog might like this one." Stan selected a pumpkin spice treat and handed it to the woman.

She hesitated. "I'm just not sure Nellie will like it."

"Don't worry. It's a free taste test."

The woman perked up. "Really? Free?"

Stan broke off a half and handed it to her. "Really."

Nellie sniffed it delicately; then she took it between her teeth. "Let Momma break it for you," the woman cooed. She crumbled the cookie up and let the little dog eat it out of her hand. Nellie crunched contentedly, then sniffed for more.

"Looks like she's sold! That's lovely. I hate feeding her processed treats. Especially with all those terrible ingredients from China. I'll take two more. The apple cranberry and"—she browsed the other plates, tapping her finger against her lips—"the broccoli and cheese. Nellie likes vegetables. Is the first one still free?"

"Of course." Stan accepted the money and wrapped the two cookies. "I hope Nellie enjoys."

Nellie and her person walked away; the woman cooed baby talk at the dog the whole time.

Emma approached the table with a man trailing behind her. He wore a purple suit, complemented by a shiny gray tie. His brown hair was feathered just a bit on top. Stan swore she could see a makeup line around his chin.

"Excuse me, Stan? I'd like to introduce you to Sheldon. Sheldon Allyn. I presume you know of him?" Emma raised her eyebrows as if to say, *You'd better.*

Stan didn't, but she was good at faking it. "Of course." She rose gracefully and held out her hand. "I'm Stan Connor. Lovely to meet you."

"Yes, yes, you as well," Sheldon said, shaking her hand. His was cool and smooth.

"We're fortunate, because Sheldon is one of our neighbors," Emma said. "His Pomeranian, Bessie, is a regular. Where is Bessie today?"

"Oh, she's a bit under the weather," Sheldon said. "But these treats might just perk her up! I've seen a steady stream of animals enthralled with them," he told Stan. "Emma told me you bake them yourself."

"That's right. I have some recipes, and the others I just experiment with until they come out right."

"Fascinating." Sheldon picked up one of the cookies, held it to his nose and inhaled, with eyes closed. Stan glanced at Emma. She shrugged.

"What ingredients do you use?" Sheldon continued to sniff, but he opened his eyes and looked at Stan.

"Well, it depends on the flavor, but I use fruit, rolled oats, spelt flour, cheese, pumpkin, all kinds of things, really."

"No preservatives of any sort, I presume."

"Of course not!"

"Local ingredients?"

"As much as possible. In fact"—she pointed to her apple cranberry oat selection—"these have a smidgen of local honey in them to sweeten the flavor a bit."

"Delightful! Do you mind if I sample?"

"Sample the pet treat? I don't mind, but why would you. . . ." Stan trailed off as Sheldon Allyn nibbled on the cookie, eyes closed again. Behind him, Emma made a choking sound as she tried to hold back a giggle.

"Stupendous!" Sheldon declared, his eyes flying open. "Ms. Connor, might you be able to step away from your post for a moment and discuss some business with me?"

"'Business'? Uh, sure, I guess," Stan said. She sent a look to Justin that pleaded, *Help me.* He had been watching the scene with amusement, too.

"I got you, sweetie. I'll make sure no one steals any treats, and I'll keep an eye on Scruffy," Justin assured her. "Go on and talk."

"Emma, may we use your conference room?" Sheldon asked.

"'Conference room'?" Emma repeated. "I don't have a *conference room.* But you're welcome to use my kitchen." She led them to the back of the store and pushed a door open, revealing a half office, half break room. "Voila."

"Thank you, thank you." Sheldon held the door for Stan and followed her inside and held out a chair. She sat. Instead of sitting himself, Sheldon perched on the edge of the table. Totally in her space. Stan inched back in her chair as much as she could.

"I'm sorry to be so abrupt with my offer, but your food is a delight and it's just what I'm looking for. You know Every Sweet Thing's reputation, I'm sure."

Stan gaped at him. Now she recognized the name. Every Sweet Thing bakeries were upscale—gourmet pastries at its finest—sprinkled throughout classy New England towns. There was only one in Rhode Island, in downtown Newport. They tended to land in places like Boston's Newbury Street. What the heck did the owner of Every Sweet Thing want with her dog treats? "Yes, I know Every Sweet Thing."

Sheldon nodded as if he wouldn't expect anything less. "I'm expanding my reach. And to do so, I'm expanding my line. I'm doing some cupcake shops as a separate line in order to open more stores, and I'd like to do a pet pastry line. I've been searching high and low for a creator who will do this justice. I've already thought of the name. Every Sweet Thing for Pets." He drew the words out as if enjoying the taste on his tongue; then he beamed at Stan. "And I've had terrible luck so far. Just terrible. Everyone who is referred, they are pompous fools and don't understand what I want. I want classy. Tasteful, as well as tasty. I want gourmet!" His voice rose on the last words as he swept his hand into the air. His passion for the project was evident.

Stan waited. Sheldon waited.

"Well?" he said finally. "Do you have anything to say?"

"I'm . . . not sure what you're asking me."

Sheldon smacked his forehead with the palm

of his hand. "My apologies. When I get excited, I talk in circles. I need a pastry chef. Your pet treats tell me you have potential. I don't want a pompous fool baking for the 'fancy' animals who will eat these creations. I want *real*. And *beautiful*. My poster child for pets. So, will you be my pet chef?"

Stan's mouth dropped open. *A pet chef? Is this guy for real?* "You—you mean you want someone to make dog treats?"

Sheldon sighed heavily. "No, no, no. Cannolis. Birthday cakes. Mousse. Pupcakes. Pet pastry. Do you understand?"

She didn't, actually, but this man seemed a bit unstable. "I, um, I think so. But how do you know I can do that? I appreciate your enthusiasm, and it sounds lovely, but I've never—"

"Ah!" Sheldon leaned forward and, to Stan's shock, planted a kiss right on her lips. "Perfection! I knew I made the right choice. All the greats doubt themselves in the beginning. We will learn together! It will be the first venture of its kind." He leaped up and clapped his hands. "I'll get a contract together. Please e-mail my assistant with your information. But first, your phone number." He waggled a finger at her. "I don't want you getting away from me."

Stan recited her phone number, not even sure what she had agreed to do. Sheldon programmed it into his phone, pulled her to her feet and bussed her cheek. Then he hurried out the door, still raving to himself about his fabulous idea and the amazing team they were going to make.

Chapter 18

Stan stayed in her chair after Sheldon's exit, wondering what, exactly, she'd just gotten herself into. The guy had to be out of his mind. She should go ask Emma. But before she could leave the room, Emma appeared at the door. Her face was flushed with excitement.

"So? How'd it go?"

"It was interesting. Tell me the truth. Is that guy for real?"

Emma gaped at her. "You're kidding, right?"

"Actually, no. I have no idea who he is."

"Holy crap." Emma dropped into the nearest chair. "You don't know Every Sweet Thing?"

"I do know Every Sweet Thing. I know they have good pastry. I just didn't know who the owner was. . . ." Stan realized she was talking herself into a corner.

"Well-known is an understatement. If you're familiar at all with the food industry, you would know Sheldon Allyn. He's, like, a visionary." Emma's eyes took on a weird shine as she described him. It made Stan think of cult members talking about their crazy leaders.

"So, bottom line, he's for real?"

"He's *so* for real! What did he ask you?"

"He wants a pet chef. For some reason he thinks he wants me. Apparently, because I can bake bone-shaped treats, he thinks I can bake doggie cannolis."

"Oh, my goodness!" Emma's squeal was loud enough that Justin came running from the front of the store.

"Are you guys okay?"

"Wonderful! Stan's gonna be famous—"

"Hang on," Stan interrupted. "Don't get carried away, Emma."

"'Carried away'? He wants her to be his pet chef!"

"Really?" Justin looked impressed. "Will you get a TV show?"

"A TV show?"

"Yeah. Sheldon's been in discussions about something on the *Food Network*. Last I heard, anyway," he said.

"You know him, too?"

"Of course." Justin looked at her like she'd asked him if he brushed his teeth every day. "Who doesn't know Sheldon Allyn?"

Emma giggled.

"I didn't have time to watch The Food Network! Cut me some slack," Stan said.

"Maybe he can do a spin-off on *Animal Planet* or something." Justin was getting excited now. "Wow, that's really cool, Stan!"

"He just talked to me about it. We'll see if it even happens, guys. He seemed flaky."

"His croissants are flaky. He's one of the most brilliant men I know. He can turn anything into an amazing recipe," Emma said defensively.

"He seemed lovely. Just not the type of business deals I'm used to."

"You better tell Nikki," Justin said.

"Good idea. Where is she, anyway?"

"I think she's out back. She had to talk to someone about a dog." Emma pointed at the far end of the store. "You can go that way. It takes you right into the parking lot."

Stan went out the back door, shading her eyes from the sun, and looked around for her friend. Not seeing her, she turned to go back in the store, when the lettering on a white van caught her eye: FROG LEDGE ANIMAL CONTROL. She paused, about to chalk it up to coincidence. Then Nikki walked around the side of the van, her head bent close to Diane Kirschbaum's, deep in conversation.

Diane Kirschbaum was at Nikki's adoption event, an hour away from Frog Ledge. If Nikki knew her, why had she never mentioned it? First Perri Galveston, then Carole Morganwick/Cross, now Diane. She'd thought her friend's first experience with Frog Ledge had been when she'd seen the house.

Seemed she had been wrong. It didn't give her a good feeling, especially after Diane's cold reception and Nikki's admission that she'd known Carole.

"Hey, Nikki!" Stan called.

Nikki looked up, startled; then she said something to Diane. "I'll be right there!" she yelled back.

They went around the back of the van again,

out of sight. Stan leaned on the rail and waited. A minute later, Nikki reappeared. Diane climbed back into the van and drove out of the parking lot, her eyes never meeting Stan's.

"Hey, you need me?" Nikki jogged over. "We're getting a lot of applications for the dogs, huh?"

"We are. And I have a funny story to tell you."

"Cool. Let's go in." Nikki started for the door, completely ignoring the elephant in the room.

"Hey, Nik?"

"Yeah?" She half turned, still holding the door.

"Why was Diane Kirschbaum here?"

"She needed to place a pit bull and someone passed my name on." She shrugged. "Just helping out."

"That's pretty far for her to come to talk about a dog, no?"

"I guess, but this sounded like a personal thing, not a town thing."

"So where's the pit bull?"

"What?"

"The pit bull. Did she bring him to you?"

"Her. And I have to assess her first. What's with the third degree, Stan?"

"No reason." Stan followed her in. "You seem to know a bunch of people from my new town, including the dead person."

"One person's hardly a bunch. And I told you, I don't know her. I was just asked to help out. Any new apps?" she asked Justin.

"Don't forget Perri," Stan reminded her.

"Okay, so what's the big deal? I didn't know I had to report back about every person I spoke to." Her harsh tone stung.

Justin sensed it, too. He glanced from Nikki to Stan, then held up some papers. "Apps on the other Boston and all three of those guys." He nodded toward the pen with the smaller breed dogs. "Most of Stan's treats are gone. Did she tell you her fabulous news?"

"No, I didn't get a chance." Stan brushed by her friend. She could give the cold shoulder, too. "I'm going to take Scruffy outside."

She unwrapped the dog's leash from the chair leg and led the little dog out. Her nub of a tail wagged the whole way. They walked along the parking lot to the grass behind the store. Nikki had certainly seemed annoyed at her questions. If there was a simple answer, she wouldn't be so defensive. But it seemed like a natural piece of conversation, to mention knowing someone in the town your best friend moved to—especially since Stan didn't know anyone.

Maybe she was being oversensitive. Or Nikki was having a bad day. She did get upset at the way pit bulls were treated.

She sighed, watching Scruffy sniff out the perfect spot to do her business. *Maybe I shouldn't have stormed out like a child.* Scruffy hopped out of her squat and pawed at Stan's leg. She was adorable.

"Do you like cats?" Stan asked, squatting in front of her.

Scruffy licked her nose.

"Why am I asking you that? I can't adopt another animal right now. No matter how cute you are." Stan stood up and sighed. Scruffy sighed, too. Stan swore she did. Now she was letting the dog down as well.

She hoped the rest of the treats really were gone. It was time to go home.

When they got back inside, Nikki came flying over to her and gave her a huge hug. Her attitude from fifteen minutes earlier was seemingly forgotten. "I heard Sheldon was here! That's so amazing! Wow, Stan. See, I told you cool things were gonna happen for you!"

"Thanks. I don't think I agreed to anything yet."

"Well, you'd be crazy not to. Sheldon can get you places. Didn't I tell you your treats are awesome?"

"He wants more than treats. He wants a pet pastry chef. I have no idea if I can be that."

"Of course you can be that, if you want to be! That sounds like fun for a change. You could use some fun in your life. Hey, I'm sorry to snap at you earlier. I've just been overrun by pit bulls, but I can't ever turn them away. My problem, not yours. Forgive me?"

"Sure."

"Cool." Nikki didn't seem to notice Stan's lack of enthusiasm. "Hey, can you do me a favor? I have to drop these dogs off for training and then follow up on this new dog. I don't suppose you'd want to watch Scruffy for a while?"

"Um. Sure, I guess. How long?"

"Not sure. Overnight, at least. Depends on if I can get away tomorrow. But I'd like to see how she does with cats. So maybe longer."

"You have cats."

"I know, but she's not inside that much at my house. *Please?* She'd love the personal attention."

Sitting between them, Scruffy wagged her tail.

She wasn't sure how Nutty would feel about it, but what the heck? "Sure. Sounds fun."

"Excellent. Here's her toy." Nikki dove into her duffel bag and pulled out a ratty stuffed sheep. "She doesn't go anywhere without it."

Scruffy immediately jumped up when she sighted the toy, her tongue hanging out, panting slightly.

"She likes to play chase," Nikki said.

Stan took the toy. It was chewed up, stained and dirty. She looked at the dog. "Sounds like we're gonna have a fun evening, me and you."

Chapter 19

Stan drove home with her sunroof open and windows partway down so Scruffy could enjoy the fresh air from the backseat. She wagged her stubby tail the whole time, sticking her head out as far as she could so the wind whipped her ears around. They took the long way, since Stan really had nowhere to be. *"Life Is a Highway"* played in her head, so she didn't bother with the radio. She figured she wouldn't see Richard again tonight, and she had no other plans. That is, other than not to get arrested.

Or she could do some of that research she'd been meaning to do. A relaxing evening on the sunporch, with perhaps a fresh tomato, basil and mozzarella salad and homemade blackberry iced tea while she Googled information on potential murderers. She laughed out loud at the absurdity of it. How in the world had she ended up in this situation?

But when she drove through Frog Ledge again,

especially past the clinic, her thoughts sobered.
Someone was dead. Nothing funny about that.

The green was abuzz with activity. A bunch of
teenagers hauled chairs around, arranging them
in a half-moon shape facing the library parking
lot. Two vans were backed up to the same spot,
their back doors thrown open as people carted
out equipment. Kids ran shrieking around the
circles of adults, throwing balls and chasing dogs.
Someone set up a popcorn cart. She remembered
the sign she'd seen at the other end of the green
for a concert and dance tonight. It was some historical thing that involved costumes. It sounded
like fun. And she hadn't had popcorn in such a
long time. Carnival-type popcorn was almost as
good as movie theater popcorn. She salivated for
a minute, thinking about it. Then she remembered her reality. If half the town didn't think she
was a killer, she might consider going. But since
that wasn't the case, she resigned herself to a
quiet night at home.

She experienced instant relief when she pulled
into her driveway and found no one waiting for
her. She had a clear path inside. *I don't have to talk
to anyone. . . . Ha! What a joke my life has become.
Well, still is.* She slammed her emergency brake up
and shut the car off abruptly. It was exactly like
her existence in her old place, only she'd really
hoped it would be different here. She wanted to
meet people, make new friends, get out and do
things. But the murder had squashed all that.

Then she felt bad for whining, even if it was in
her own head. The murder had been harder on
Carole, certainly. She opened the back door and

grabbed Scruffy's leash and toy, along with the empty containers from her pet treats. "Let's go. We have a rockin' good time ahead of us."

Her relief at no visitors soon changed to apprehension when she noticed the envelope sticking out of her front door. Hesitant, she approached, wondering if she should even touch it. At this point she wouldn't be surprised if it jumped up and bit her. But she had to get in the door, and the stupid envelope was, in effect, blocking her way. Stan sighed and ripped it free from the frame. Plain white envelope, nothing written on it. Unsealed. She lifted the flap and pulled out the single piece of paper. She unfolded it.

A bill from Leonard Homeopathic Veterinary Care for 250 bucks. Stan resisted the urge to rip it up. Amara might be watching right now. Instead, she calmly tucked it in her purse, unlocked the door and led Scruffy inside.

Nutty waited in the hall, anticipating either Stan's return or the visitor she brought. His tail went up at the first sighting of Scruffy, but he didn't bolt like he had when Duncan was in the house. Scruffy's tail vibrated with excitement as she strained the leash, trying to get to Nutty. *Crap. Is she going to try to eat him or wrestle him?* Stan's bets were on Nutty, either way.

Keeping her on the leash, Stan led Scruffy over to the cat. Scruffy was surprisingly reserved, approaching cautiously, tail as straight up as such a tiny nub could be. Nutty didn't back down. He let the dog sniff him all over; then she licked his face. He blinked his eyes and rubbed against her; then he sat at her feet.

"Wow, I guess you do like some dogs. That's good news. She's visiting for tonight," Stan told Nutty, unclipping Scruffy's leash. "Why don't you two go play?"

Instead, they both followed her to the kitchen. Dinnertime.

"I should have known. I'll get it ready now."

Depositing her stuff on the table, she took some food out and heated it on the stove while she checked her voice mail. She'd had her phone turned down all day, anticipating fallout from her mother over the lawyer visit. And she wasn't disappointed.

"Kristan, what in the world is going on? Richard told me someone was murdered and you were . . . in the vicinity. Now the state news has picked up the story, he said. I sent the best lawyer in the state and you turn him away? Please call me."

She knew it. The *Hartford Courant* had picked it up. Stan deleted the message and threw the phone back in her purse. She wouldn't return that call. It explained Richard's sudden concern. He and her mother were both so predictable.

After she fed the animals, Stan put on a new pair of shorts and a T-shirt. She sliced the fresh mozzarella and tomatoes, which she'd picked up at the co-op, on top of fresh basil leaves. She drizzled balsamic vinegar and a touch of olive oil and sprinkled pepper; then she grabbed her laptop and her iced blackberry tea and headed for the sunroom.

The salad was delicious. She allowed herself a few bites before opening her laptop and pulling up Google. But instead of searching for Carole or

Diane or anyone else in town, she typed Sheldon Allyn's name into the search bar. A number of hits came back within seconds: the official Every Sweet Thing website, some articles on the pastry chef, including a spread in the *New York Times,* a YouTube video of the man himself demonstrating how to make meringue—a practice that apparently required a fierce amount of praise directed at the ingredients—and some clips of his guest appearances on some of the great *Food Network* shows.

His enthusiasm was contagious. He loved his pastry. Anyone could tell by watching his meticulous measurements, his praise of what each ingredient brought to the table, his pride at the finished product. For the first time Stan allowed herself to feel something other than disbelief or skepticism. She thought about what it might be like to control her own destiny, to wake up in the morning and do something that made her happy. Not the kind of happy bred only by money and beating the pants off the competition, but the kind of happy a person made for herself by doing something she loved.

Could she really be Sheldon Allyn's pet pastry chef?

Why not?

Outside, through her open windows, noise and chatter started to filter in off the green. People arriving for the party. The band was tuning up, testing equipment. She could see fireflies flitting through the woods on the side of her property—even they were taking part in tonight's festivities.

Stan turned back to her computer and pulled

up the search bar. She typed in **Carole Morganwick, Connecticut** and sat back.

The results started filling the page. The *Frog Ledge Holler* articles topped the list. Cyril Pierce had an online edition as well. He must spend an awful lot of time at his beloved paper. Stan had to admire him. The world needed a good media presence. Of course they needed good PR people, too.

Reviews of Carole's practice were right below it. This was where her gut told her the clues could be. And her gut was right. Only five reviews, but four of them were poor. One with one star, three with two. The fifth review had five stars. Stan wondered if Carole had created it, or put someone up to it.

She skimmed the poor ones. Comments ranged from **Terrible bedside manner** to **My dog got sick after his vaccine, and she overcharged me too.** There was a commentary about a cat that sounded suspiciously like Betty's story.

The doorbell rang, interrupting Stan's reading before she could get to Carole Cross' reviews. Scruffy frantically *woo-wooed* and shot to all fours. *Now what?* Stan took one more bite of mozzarella and hurried to the front of the house, with Scruffy leading.

She peered through the narrow side window before approaching the door. It was Jake. What was he doing here? She swung the door open wide, one finger in Scruffy's collar so she wouldn't run away. Duncan stood there, wagging his tail. He barked excitedly when he saw Scruffy; his tail flapped hard enough to dent the wooden railing. Stan was pleased to see he was on a leash.

"Easy," Jake said, yanking him back. "Hey, Stan. New dog?"

"Just babysitting. Well, dog sitting. Come on in."

Stan let Scruffy go. She and Duncan frantically sniffed at each other, tails wagging. Jake looked at Stan. "I guess they're okay with each other," he said, unclipping Duncan's leash.

"I guess they are," Stan agreed as the two dogs chased each other through the house. A crash, sounding suspiciously like a kitchen chair tumbling, followed. Jake winced.

"Sorry. Dunc's a rough one. I wanted to see if you were coming to the dance tonight."

"No, I don't think so."

"Why not? It's actually pretty fun."

"Don't you need to be at the bar?"

"Brenna's there, and Travis. Travis is second in command. He's more the bar-social type than the community-social type. They'll be fine."

"I can't go to the dance."

"Why not?"

"Because everyone thinks I killed Carole. Haven't we gone over this? People stare at me, Jake. The lady at the general store didn't even want to ring me up. I'm surprised she didn't let me walk out the door with the stuff for free."

"Abbie?" Jake made a dismissive motion with his hand. "Abbie's just a gossip. Most people in town aren't like that."

"Doesn't matter. I'm sure people listen to Abbie. Her place is the hub, right?"

"'The hub'?" Jake laughed. "Where'd you get that?"

"Never mind. It's not just Abbie." Stan threw

her hands up in frustration and walked back to the sunroom, stopping to right the upended chair on her way. "Point is, I'm not going."

"That's not very sociable of you."

"Huh! Did your sister think I was being 'sociable' when she saw you over here this morning?"

Jake said nothing.

"See, didn't think so." Stan sat back down and waved at the other chair. "Feel free to sit."

Jake did. She closed her laptop.

"My own family and supposed boyfriend already called a lawyer." Stan viciously hacked her tomato into bite-sized pieces. "Can you believe that? A lawyer!"

She hadn't realized that had bothered her so much until now. She knew her mother had a misguided way of offering help, but hiring a lawyer before she even got arrested? That didn't show a whole lot of faith.

"Is that who the suit was in your driveway this morning?" Jake smiled. "He didn't get very far."

"Yep, you guys had front-row seats. I bet your sister was annoyed when she thought I had someone who wouldn't let me talk."

"Stan, I know you're angry at my sister, but she really is trying her best to get to the bottom of this."

Stan had nothing to say to that. She swiped her last piece of mozzarella around her plate to pick up the remains of her balsamic vinegar; then she pushed the dish away. Jake watched, his expression slightly amused.

"I know why you should come to the dance," he said.

She glared at him.

"To get a decent meal, at least. All you're eating are some leaves and cheese for dinner?"

"A decent meal?" Stan snorted. "What, are they grilling hot dogs?"

She didn't mean to sound so snarky, but the stress was definitely getting to her. Jake didn't take offense, though. He didn't look like much of anything got him riled. He just laughed and stood to go.

"I'm heading over there now. I'd love it if you came with us. Bring the pooch. It's fun. Don't worry about not having a costume," he said, anticipating her next line of protest. "A lot of people don't dress up. Including me."

Stan knew she should decline, but she really did want to go. He'd obviously made an effort. Whether it was because he genuinely felt sorry for her or was trying to apologize in his own way for his sister's behavior, she wasn't sure. Being a jerk to someone who actually still wanted to talk to her wouldn't help her cause. As if on cue, *"I Hope You Dance"* floated into her head.

She sighed. "Okay."

He looked surprised. "Really?"

"Sure, why not?"

Jake grinned. "Your enthusiasm is truly overwhelming."

Chapter 20

Frog Ledgers were serious about their parties. Their history, too, if the costumes were any indication. People packed the green, eating, showing off their period hats and dresses, staking out spots for the show. The band had set up on the grass, with a space sectioned off for dancing. Jake led Stan into the fray, and Scruffy strained her leash to keep pace with Duncan, who greeted everyone he met. People were equally enthralled with Scruffy and kept exclaiming over what a precious dog she was, and so beautiful.

Scruffy wagged her tail proudly after each compliment and kept glancing back at Stan to make sure she'd heard. Stan focused on the three people Jake was introducing her to: Fiona, his neighbor, a middle-aged woman whose interest in costumes had nothing to do with history, if her zebra pants and teased-out hair gave any indication; a fellow named Louis, who judged poultry in the town fair; and then Terri, who worked at the small soda factory in the next town.

"Hey, that's Amy." Jake pointed to a young woman standing near the small stage, talking animatedly with one of the band members. "She's the girl who used to work for Carole."

Stan perked up. "Can I talk to her?"

"I don't see why not. But don't be so intense, okay? Maybe I can just introduce you tonight."

"'Intense'? If you were a hair away from being arrested for murder, you'd be *intense,* too," Stan shot back. Then she realized Trooper Pasquale stood a few feet away and could clearly hear their conversation.

Only, tonight Jessie didn't look like Trooper Pasquale. Dressed in a simple orange tank dress, and holding on to a little girl's hand, Pasquale looked like any other small-town soccer mom, only prettier than most. But her face still had cop written all over it, at least in Stan's eyes. She observed them, with her expression unchanged. Stan didn't think she'd even say hello to her brother, but the little girl began to squeal. She looked like a mini version of her mother.

"Unca Jake! Unca Jake! Mommy, it's Unca Jake and Dunkie!" The child started running toward them, stopping when she realized her mother still firmly held her hand. "Come *on,* Mommy!" She stomped her foot impatiently.

Pasquale looked like someone was leading her to a particularly vicious crime scene, but she allowed her daughter to lead her over.

"Hi, peanut." Jake scooped up his niece and gave her a kiss on the forehead. He nodded at his sister. "Jess."

"Jake," she returned, her gaze raking over Stan. "Ms. Connor."

"Hi," Stan muttered.

"Lily, this is my friend Stan. Can you say hello?" Jake asked.

Lily giggled. "That's a boy's name."

"It can be a girl's name, too," Jake said.

Lily thought about that; then she turned to Stan and waved. "Hello."

"Hi, Lily," Stan said.

"Can I have my kid?" Pasquale asked Jake.

"Give her a break, Jess. She wants to see the dogs." Lily squirmed away from Jake, trying to reach Scruffy while shrieking with excitement as Duncan kept jumping to lick her face. "Besides, you're off duty. Take a break."

"Thanks for the advice. Hold on to her then while I go get something to eat?"

"Sure."

Without even a thank-you, she turned and walked to the food tables, her dress dragging along the grass.

Stan looked at Jake. He smiled. "I'm sorry."

"Don't be." She smiled at Lily. "Do you want to meet Scruffy?"

"Yes!" Lily wriggled free of Jake and dropped to her knees in front of the little dog. She started cooing and petting her; Scruffy sat perfectly still, soaking up the attention.

"She's a nice dog," Jake said.

"Yeah."

"You keeping her?"

"I can't."

"Why not? Cat hates dogs?"

"No, they actually seem to like each other."

"Then why not?"

He certainly asked a lot of questions. And they hardly knew each other. "I'll probably be going back to work soon. It wouldn't be fair to her."

"Found something already? That's great."

She didn't have time to explain. Izzy strode up behind them, her brown eyes fiery. Great, she'd assume Stan was fraternizing with the enemy. But Izzy ignored Jake and walked right up to Stan. "We need to talk," she said in a low voice.

"Right now?" Stan glanced at Scruffy, still being coddled by Lily.

"Yes, right now." Izzy crossed her arms and tapped her foot, waiting. She had ignored the costume option, too, and was dressed in a flowing peach-colored skirt and a white tank top.

"I'll hold the dog," Jake offered.

Stan glanced at him, then back at Izzy and sighed. She handed him the leash. "Thanks."

She followed Izzy to a quiet spot halfway down the green. "What's so urgent?"

"What's urgent is that friend of yours, getting herself in trouble. And you, probably. You'll get yourself in trouble, you know, if you lie for her." She wagged a finger at Stan.

"Whoa, whoa, whoa, Izzy. I have no idea what you're talking about. Or who. I didn't lie about anything. Lie to who?"

"That rescue friend of yours! You told the trooper she wasn't here the day the vet died."

"She wasn't."

"Not according to my sources."

"Your 'sources'? What are you talking about?"

Izzy reached into her purse and pulled out her iPad. She touched a few buttons. "This her van?" She turned the device around.

A grainy picture taken during some form of darkness clearly depicted Nikki's blue van, unmistakable with the smiling dog on the side of it. Stan couldn't tell if it was dawn or dusk, but the tinge of light creeping around the edges made her think morning. She could just make out the back of Izzy's shop behind the van.

"This is from Monday."

"Really. Where's the date?" Stan heard the unsteadiness in her own voice and hoped Izzy couldn't.

Izzy pointed to the tiny dateline. "My watcher took it. E-mailed it to me Monday, but somehow I missed it. Not staying on top of my e-mails this week."

"Your 'watcher'?"

"I told you, I had some problems when I came here. There are a couple of kids who keep an eye on things for me."

"Kids? No security cameras or anything? You sure that's dependable?"

Izzy raised an eyebrow. "They like money. So, yeah, they're dependable."

Stan thought of the group of kids she always saw skateboarding around town in various parking lots. They probably were the logical choice, because during early mornings or later in the evenings, they had full access to parking lots when stores were closed.

"The question is, what was she doing outside my shop at five A.M.?"

Stan had no answer for that. She didn't know if what Izzy told her was true, but she didn't have any reason to doubt her. Nikki, on the other hand, had already proven she could withhold information, even from her alleged best friend.

Izzy still waited for her answer. "Listen." Her voice softened. "If you didn't know, that's one thing, but I think it's weird. Pasquale asked you if she was here, and now it looks like she was. Don't you agree?"

"There has to be a mistake, Izzy. Nikki wasn't back from her South Carolina run on Monday morning. She didn't get back until later in the day."

"How do you know that?"

"Because she told me." Stan realized as she spoke them how weak the words sounded in light of everything else. In the back of her mind, Justin's words suddenly shouted at her. *She was hell bent on getting back early Sunday.*

"Yeah," Izzy said. "Maybe you need to ask her again. With a polygraph."

After Izzy left to help with the refreshment table—making sure people had decent things to drink, she said—Stan stayed by the tree, thinking. If Nikki had been in Frog Ledge the day of Carole's murder, that would mean she lied. On more than one occasion. Stan couldn't imagine why she might have been here. Something to do with rescue animals would be the rational explanation. And if it wasn't . . . Stan didn't want to think about that. Izzy's shop was uncomfortably close to Carole's clinic. Of all days to be parked there—it looked bad.

Jake walked up with the dogs. Lily was nowhere in sight. He probably had orders to return her to her mother before he started carousing with the alleged murderess.

"Everything okay?" Jake passed Scruffy's leash to Stan.

"Everything's fine."

"That doesn't sound convincing."

She didn't respond.

"Come on, then. Want a drink?"

"I don't know. I think I need to go home."

"Why? Stan, what's going on?"

Part of her really wanted to confide in him. She didn't know if it was because her list of confidants was dangerously short, or because she trusted him. Either way, she didn't have much to lose. She was just opening her mouth, when a girl dressed in a skimpy tank top and tiny skirt sauntered up and slid her arm around his waist.

"I've missed you!" Ignoring Stan, the girl planted a kiss on his cheek. To his credit, Jake looked embarrassed.

"Hey, Kate."

"Are you gonna dance with me?" She pressed even closer to him. Stan figured soon she'd pee on him to make sure everyone was clear that Jake was her property.

"Maybe later, okay? I'm in the middle of something here."

Kate pouted, shooting a look at Stan that commanded, *You're in my territory.*

Maybe what Izzy had said all along about him was true. This girl looked a lot younger.

"It's okay. I'll talk to you later," she said, smiling at Kate. "I'm Stan. I was just leaving."

Confused, Kate glanced at Jake, then back at Stan. "Oh. Well. Nice to meet you. I'm Kate."

"Lovely to meet you, too. Jake, I'll see you later." She turned and slipped into the crowd with Scruffy. She didn't look back to see his reaction. "Let's go home, Scruff. This was a bad idea," she told the little dog. Scruffy wagged and trotted along beside her. Before she could get halfway down the green, she heard her name.

"Stan! Stan, wait!"

Turning, she saw Char waving frantically. As usual, she was difficult to miss. Today she wore a flowing green dress one shade away from neon. As Char moved closer, Stan could see her fingernails and toenails were painted the same shade.

"Honey, you are so wonderful." Finally reaching her, Char nearly swallowed her in a hug. "You saved my Savannah's stomach! And skin! My goodness, it's only been a couple of days and that dog looks a hundred times better!"

Her food. She'd almost forgotten. Well, that was good news, at least. "I'm so glad," she said.

"Me too! We have to discuss how we'll handle this going forward. Can I order in advance? I'd like a week's worth at a time. What do you charge?"

"'Charge'?" Stan repeated.

"Well, yeah, doll, of course you'll charge us. And you better not lowball the price." Char waggled a green-tipped finger in her face. "This is a valuable service. Do you have other orders to fill? Are you advertising?"

"*Advertising?*" *What is she talking about?* Stan shook her head. "No, I just gave you some portions of what I make for Nutty. I don't, like, sell the food. As a business."

Char stared at her. "Well, why in heavens not?"

"I . . . never thought about it?"

"Well, then, it's your lucky day. You just sit down with Izzy Sweet and she'll tell you how to start your own business. She built that shop from the ground up, you know. She'll get you going. In the meantime, then, call me tomorrow after you think about a price."

Stan could only nod her assent before Char squeezed her arm and plunged back into the fray. She saw her slide her arm through a soldier's, jostling his fake rifle, and realized it was Ray. He waved the gun at her when Char pointed her out. Stan waved back.

"That's some good news, anyway," she said to Scruffy. They continued through the crowd, walking against the flow of people, which only got thicker as the band started to play behind them. Not wanting the little dog to get trampled, she bent down and scooped her up until they were away from the crowds. They crossed the street, finally reaching her lovely little house, with the welcoming porch, where she'd hung flowers just yesterday, and the light beckoning them to come in and be safe. But she stopped before she reached the door. Her feeling of impending safety took off down the street like a runaway dog chasing a squirrel.

On her front porch, propped against her door, was a bag of kibble. The same kind that Carole sold in her clinic, unmistakable by the large picture of a mother dog and puppy smiling from the front; and by nature of deduction, the same kind that had been strewn over Carole's dead body.

The bag had a large slash through it. Food spilled out of the wound, puddling on the floor.

Chapter 21

Getting a decent night's sleep had become a distant memory. Stan slept on and off, her dreams plagued by costumed characters, larger-than-life needles and a woman drowning in a sea of dog food. The Rockwell song *"Somebody's Watching Me"* served as the soundtrack, until she finally hauled herself out of bed at six and took Scruffy out into the backyard.

After she fed her charges, Stan went to the TV room and turned on a yoga DVD. Got halfway through the routine before her lack of focus made her lose her balance during a prayer twist. She dropped onto the mat, forcing back tears. Nutty, who'd always had good ESP for when she was upset, wandered in and sat on her stomach, kneading at her with his sharp claws. At least now she could pretend his needle-sharp plucks were her reason for crying.

A noise on the porch made them both jump. She'd never removed the bag of dog food. The whole thing had creeped her out, and she hadn't wanted to spend an extra minute out there, exposed in the dark.

She hoped a raccoon or possum hadn't discovered it.

"Come on, Nutter, we better go see."

He followed her obediently downstairs, where Scruffy stood in front of the door *wooing* at it. Nutty jumped on the windowsill to observe, while she pulled the door open cautiously, an inch at a time, half expecting someone to be waiting outside with a needle to plunge into her carotid artery.

Instead, she found Duncan, sound asleep next to the now-half-empty bag of dog food. He'd cleaned up every piece of kibble from the porch for her, and then some. It looked like he'd worked a paw into the hole in the bag and helped himself until he was stuffed.

Stan groaned. On a good day this stuff was not an ideal choice, loaded with preservatives and who knew what else. But this bag hadn't been left by someone with good intentions. She hoped nothing was wrong with it. How did the dog get out again, anyway? Meanwhile, Scruffy wiggled her way through the crack in the door, thrilled to see Duncan once more. He rolled over when he saw her, and Scruffy dropped next to him and they engaged in a lickfest.

"Dunc, get in here. You too, Scruffy."

Duncan immediately jumped up, tail thudding the porch, and hurled himself at her, planting sloppy kisses wherever he could reach. Scruffy followed suit. She must think this was a new game.

Stan returned the hug and ushered them inside with one last glance around. In the sunny-morning hours of daytime, the sinister events of the night seemed almost surreal. Except for the ominous bag of kibble, that is.

As she closed the door, she noticed another *Frog Ledge Holler* near the front of the porch. Cyril was on a roll lately. She scooped it up and went inside, glancing down at the news above the fold. He hadn't disappointed:

POLICE CONTINUE MANHUNT FOR VET KILLER

By Cyril Pierce

Nearly a week after local veterinarian and beloved neighbor Carole Morganwick was found murdered in her exam room, state police from Troop L are pursuing at least one person of interest, said Frog Ledge resident state trooper Jessica Pasquale.

"We are pursuing all appropriate leads and hope to apprehend the murderer and close this case in the very near future," Pasquale said.

She would not confirm the person of interest's identity. She said, however, that their search has been focused on the immediate Frog Ledge area.

"We don't think this was a random act," Biggs said. "We believe Dr. Morganwick was targeted."

Stan crumpled up the newspaper without finishing the article and stuffed it in her trash can. Was this Cyril's way of letting her—and the rest of the town—know she'd be behind bars soon? The dangerous outsider who came to town and all hell broke loose. It was like a Stephen King novel. She stewed for a few minutes, then remembered Duncan, sitting at her feet, wagging his tail.

"Yikes, I have to call your dad. Where did I write down that number?"

She searched around the kitchen and came up empty-handed. Looks like she would have to call the bar again.

The same female voice answered on the fourth ring, again sounding out of breath. "McSwigg's."

"Hi, this is Stan Connor. Duncan's back. He was on my porch this morning."

"Oh no! How does that dog do it? I'm so sorry. This is Brenna. Jake's not here right now, but I'll call him."

"I can drop him there. It's no problem. Just give me a half hour or so."

"Are you sure? It's our fault."

"No problem," Stan assured her. "I just worry about him being out on the street like that."

"I know. We do, too. He's slick."

Stan hung up and surveyed the dog, who'd eaten himself into complete lethargy and was sleeping on her kitchen floor. Nutty had vanished. He was not a fan of Duncan. "Make yourself comfortable while I shower," she told the sleeping dog, and went upstairs.

Half an hour later she, Duncan and Scruffy were in her car, heading to McSwigg's. She wondered where Jake was. With Kate? She mentally kicked herself for the thought. But she did note that she hadn't even yet thought about Richard, when she should probably call him and assess the damage from the lawyer incident. Maybe tonight she'd go see him. Show up at his place, go out to dinner. Maybe he was only trying to help her.

The McSwigg's parking lot had only a few cars in the far end, presumably staff. She pulled up near the front door and parked. The dogs clambered out behind her. She pushed the heavy front door open. Duncan immediately bounded in, raced to where Brenna set a table and planted kisses on her face.

"What a bad boy!" Brenna scolded, but she nuzzled his head. "I'm so sorry about that. I can't believe he got out again."

"I just worry he's going to get hurt," Stan said. "I have no problem with him visiting."

"Well, thanks. My brother would thank you, too, although I'm not sure where he is." Brenna shook her head. "He does that sometimes. Disappears."

I'm sure it's more than sometimes. Stan smiled noncommittally. "Have a good day," she said, and turned to leave. Brenna stopped her, though.

"Hey, I'm sorry about the spilling thing. With that guy." She twisted her dish towel around one hand.

"Don't be. He asked for it."

"Oh." She relaxed her grip on the towel. "Okay, then. Is he your boyfriend?"

"For now."

Brenna smiled. "Fair enough. So you cook food for dogs?"

"I have a cat. I cook for him. People have asked me for food for their dogs, though."

"Do you think sometime you could teach me how? I'd like to get a dog when I get my own place, and I know the food out there is pretty much crap."

"Of course," Stan said. "Anytime you like."

"Well, thanks." Brenna smiled. "I'll tell my brother you saved the day. Again."

The kibble still sat on the porch. Stan had hoped it would somehow be gone, vanished from reality. But since it wasn't, she figured she should let Trooper Pasquale know about the gift. She would give her a hard time about not calling someone when it happened, but oh, well. Pasquale had been at the dance, so she couldn't have done much, anyway.

The person answering Pasquale's phone put her through to voice mail. Twenty minutes later her doorbell rang. Stan was expecting it. She opened the door and pasted on a smile.

"Good morning," Stan said, keeping her voice cool. "You got my message."

"I did." Pasquale knelt and examined the bag of food without touching it. "Have you touched this?"

"No. But Duncan ate some. Ripped a bigger hole in it, actually."

"Duncan? Why?"

"He wandered onto the porch and it was there."

Pasquale pursed her lips. Disapproving. She stood. "So you just came home last night and here it was?"

"Yes."

"So why did you wait until now to report it?"

"I—I don't know. I wasn't sure anyone would take me seriously. I also knew you were off duty." It sounded lame, even to her.

"You're aware the barracks are full of troopers with jurisdiction?"

Stan gritted her teeth. How could this foul woman be related to Jake and Brenna? "Yes."

Pasquale gave a curt nod. "We'll look into it." She snapped a pair of gloves on her hands, picked up the bag and walked back to her car.

Scruffy had joined her on the porch. They watched her drive away. Scruffy looked at Stan as if to say, *What now?* Stan looked at Scruffy and shrugged. "I guess we'll call Nikki and see when she's coming for you."

Scruffy's ears went down.

Nikki's phone was off, so it wasn't an issue, at least for the time being. Then Stan remembered the farmers' market that afternoon.

"We need to do some more baking," she told the dog. "I almost forgot all about it."

She didn't have any stock left from yesterday's adoption event, which was good for Pets' Last Chance, but it meant she had to bake fast if she wanted to try her hand at the farmers' market. And Izzy was expecting her now, so she had to get started.

Three batches, two hours and a couple of doggie potty trips later, Stan packed up her treats, clipped Scruffy's leash on and went across the street. The green had been transformed into a carnival of produce, dairy products and other locally made trinkets, clustered together under an enormous white tent, others on separate tables strategically placed throughout the grass. At least a dozen tables were in some stage of dressing, and there were already people milling around trying to get a sneak peek at the goods.

Stan waited on the edge of the green with her containers of treats, unsure, much like those times as a child when she was unsure if there was an open invitation to join her classmates' kickball or hopscotch games, or if everyone would turn and stare at her. Or worse, see through her facade to realize how terrible she was at games and yell at her to leave. Scruffy, however, couldn't wait to join the fray. The little dog strained at her leash, *woo-wooing* every time she spotted another dog already at the party. *May as well get on with it.* Stan channeled Kelly Clarkson—"*What Doesn't Kill You (Stronger)*"—and walked slowly into the crowd.

Shouts and conversation punctuated the story of the day. The tone seemed hopeful. Anticipatory. Competitive. Merchants casually sought out their nemeses, sized them up, then decided if they could up the ante. Or lower the prices. Stan

wasn't sure where her table—well, Izzy's table—
was. She should've found out if she needed a li-
cense or something. Or a certificate to prove she
was legit.

These people, with the exception of Izzy, were
real farmers. They could hold their heads high
above their produce table and say they belonged
there. They slaved over the soil with their pitch-
forks and tractors. Their cows produced this milk
eight hours ago. They churned this butter at four
in the morning. Their chickens had been laying
eggs all day. What could she boast? That she
turned her oven on to 350, mixed a few ingredients in a bowl and set a timer? She was a fraud.
This was not a press conference, and she didn't
belong here.

But she couldn't be a quitter, or a chicken. So
Stan held her head up and headed into the fray,
Scruffy prancing along beside her. Along with her
sellable items, she had a small bag of treats tucked
in her shorts pocket for Duncan and some of her
other pooch friends and cash for the items on her
list: goat cheese, fresh tomatoes and local honey.

She noticed Jake right away, helping an older
woman put up a tent to protect her wares from the
sun. He laughed at something she said. He had a
nice smile. And he used it a lot. Duncan sat obediently next to him, supervising the process. When
Jake turned around, Stan averted her eyes before
he noticed her, not wanting to be caught staring.

She needed to get a grip. She veered off toward
the first table in her path, which happened to be
the Happy Cow Dairy Farm. She wondered how
Hal Hoffman was doing after his bar brawl; then

she smiled. Maybe she was getting the hang of the small-town thing, after all.

The woman behind the table finished counting change for a young boy and handed him a bottle of milk from a cooler. He took it and ran off, clutching his money in his free hand, shouting for his mother. Stan stepped up and smiled. It was the same woman she saw around the farm. Hal's wife. Char had said her name was Emmalee.

"Hi, I'm Stan. Your new neighbor," she said.

"Oh, hello! Lovely to meet you. Emmalee Hoffman." Emmalee stood and shook Stan's hand with a farmer's grip. Strong and sturdy. She was taller than Stan. Everyone around here was tall, it seemed. Grays shot through the brown hair pulled back in a braid. "How are you liking the neighborhood?" Then her face fell. "I'm sorry, maybe that was a stupid question, after what's happened."

"Oh, my goodness, no. I love it," Stan said. "It's very cozy."

Emmalee Hoffman looked dubious. "Even with the cow manure? You don't look the type to like the smell of cow manure."

Stan laughed. "I wouldn't say I like it, but it doesn't bother me. Honestly, I don't smell it much. Anyway, I like cows."

"Well, you came to the right place, then." Laughing, she sat down again. "Would you like a sample of our cheddar cheese?" She reached into a second cooler without waiting for an answer and handed Stan a chunk.

"Sure." Stan nibbled it. Not goat cheese, but still

delicious. "Yum. This would be perfect shredded into my cat treats."

"Oh, you make cat treats? How adorable." Emmalee pulled a block of cheese out and set it in front of Stan. "That's ten dollars."

Emmalee Hoffman knew how to make a sale. Smiling, she reached into her wallet and pulled out a bill. "I do make cat treats. I refuse to buy my cat that junk from China they sell in the grocery store."

"Amen." Emmalee tucked the money into a silver lockbox. "Thanks for stopping by. I'm sure I'll see you around." She turned her attention to the man waiting patiently behind Stan and began her cheese sample routine all over again.

Stan left her to it and wandered around, looking for Izzy's table. She spent a few minutes looking at jewelry and shelled out another twenty-five dollars for a bracelet she couldn't live without. And then she realized she hadn't gotten anything on her list yet. Not even information. Nor had she set up her own goods. She should find Sadie Brown and her goat cheese, and get moving to wherever Izzy was.

"Stan!"

She turned at the sound of her name, and there was Izzy, waving at her. "I saved you half the table."

Stan hurried over, grateful for one friend, at least. "Thanks."

"No thanks necessary. Elvira vouches for your food, and that's good enough for me. Here, I brought you a tablecloth."

Stan stared dubiously at the rest of Izzy's display. Instead of the fresh fruits and vegetables, organic honey, bee pollen and local dairy products that the weathered farmers peddled, Izzy's table belonged in a magazine. Gourmet coffee and tea were arranged in a beckoning display, a catalogue of her fancy chocolates propped in the middle. Samples of iced coffee beckoned from the cooler, with bottles of chocolate and strawberry liqueur hidden next to them.

Definitely a different vibe from the rest of the vendors. Izzy wouldn't have any trouble getting customers, especially if the non-locals were out stocking up on local food, which Stan imagined they would be. Stan arranged her tablecloth and began setting out her containers. Scruffy settled under the table, her tail wagging occasionally.

"This isn't going to look as nice as the rest of your table," Stan said, uncertain.

"Are you kidding? I didn't do anything special with the display."

"If that's not special, I'd hate to see what is," she said, but she arranged her goods. Apple and oat, blueberry and carob, carob chip.

Izzy had turned her attention to a woman browsing her coffee. "That one's the best." She pointed to the organic bold blend. The woman took her word for it and bought the bag. "Thanks," Izzy said, handing her change. "Now, do you have a dog?"

"I do," the woman said.

"Then you should buy him or her one of my

friend's fabulous, homemade treats right there. This is her first farmers' market. She's new to town."

"Really." The woman moved down the table. "Homemade, you say?"

"Yes. All organic ingredients."

"How much?"

"Two dollars each."

"Why not? I always get Rexi a treat when I'm out." The woman handed over the money and chose the blueberry kind.

Izzy watched the transaction with approval. "See? People love organic and homemade."

"Thanks for the referral."

"We gotta look out for each other. Oh, goody. Here he comes." She wrinkled her nose; her gaze was focused to Stan's left.

She turned to see Jake and Duncan heading across the green toward them. Duncan pranced along, happy as always, tongue hanging out. Then he saw Stan and bolted toward her, almost taking out one of the produce tables in his clumsy haste to get to the promised treats. Jake cursed and took off after him, waving an apology at the glaring woman behind the table. Scruffy saw him too and bolted toward him. Stan came out from behind the table, hoping to head him off before he knocked Izzy's stuff over and gave her another reason to hate Jake.

Duncan lunged at her, tongue hanging out, and slobbered her with kisses like he hadn't seen her in months. Scruffy bounced up and down beside them, trying to wiggle her way into the love fest.

"Okay, okay, easy!" She laughed. "I brought them. You have to get off me."

"Duncan, down!" Jake commanded, coming up behind him. "Bad dog."

Duncan hung his head and looked appropriately ashamed, while keeping one eye on Stan's moves as she took out the treats.

"You really should have that dog on a leash, Mr. McGee!" The offended woman stood up and pointed at them, causing heads in the immediate vicinity to swivel their way. "My dogs don't behave like that, and they're pit bulls!"

Stan's eyes widened and she had to smother a giggle at the woman's schoolmarm tone. Jake turned, hands raised in defense, a disarming smile full of white teeth catching the woman off guard.

"You're absolutely right, Mrs. Graham. My mistake," he said. "See, I was busy helping Rosie Barnes over there"—he pointed to an old lady making her way slowly across the grass with a walker—"and Duncan just saw one of his favorite people. I have his leash right here." He held it up to prove his point.

Mrs. Graham seemed slightly appeased. "Well, like I said," she grumbled, "he would've bruised my tomatoes."

Stan bit her lip to keep from laughing out loud. "Mrs. Graham, I'm sorry, too," she said. "I'm looking for some nice tomatoes. Want me to take those off your hands?"

The woman's lips relaxed into something not quite a smile, but she motioned her over. "Well, sure. Bad-mannered dogs shouldn't keep me from a sale."

"Okay, one second." She turned and winked at Jake; then she slipped Duncan a treat. The dog trotted behind her to Mrs. Graham's table, where she paid for the tomatoes. His tail was swinging in such a wide arc that he put the squash in danger, too, until Jake managed to clip the leash on and pull him back.

"Who are you?" Mrs. Graham asked. "I haven't seen you around before."

"My name's Stan. I just moved in last weekend." She pointed behind her at her house, but Mrs. Graham was gawking at her. "What's wrong?"

Mrs. Graham clamped her lips together and pushed the tomatoes across the table. "Nothing. Nothing at all. Here you are." She handed her change. Too much. Stan shook her head and held out two dollars.

"You don't owe me that much," Stan said.

"No, I think that's right. You just don't worry about it now. Thank you." Mrs. Graham busied herself with something under her table.

Mrs. Graham must realize she was a person of interest in Carole's murder. Stan glanced at Jake. He had noticed the reaction, too, but shook his head as if to say, *Forget it*. Stan walked over to him.

"Don't worry about it," he said before she could say anything. "She's a piece of work, anyway."

"Doesn't matter. This is stupid. What? Does she think I'm going to kill her for her tomato money?"

"Go man your table. Izzy's selling snacks for you." Jake pointed.

Izzy had moved over to her half and was bagging treats for at least three people. Stan walked over. Her feet felt like they were dragging through cement.

"Girl, your stuff's outselling mine," Izzy said when she returned. "You're all out of the blueberry."

"That one seems to be a winner. Thanks for handling those people."

Izzy waved her off. "What's Dee's problem?"

"Mrs. Graham? She's paying me off not to kill her."

Izzy gave her a weird look, but she had to turn her attention to the woman and her two shrieking kids who approached the table. One of the kids made a grab for the candy. Stan left Izzy to it.

Chapter 22

No answer on Nikki's phone again. Stan hung up, frustrated. She needed to ask her about being in Frog Ledge on Monday, so part of her was glad she didn't answer. But she had to talk to her sometime. Right now, she needed to get out of Dodge. For the night, at least. She wanted to go to McSwigg's and have a drink. She knew that would be bad, so she would play it safe and surprise Richard. Take him to dinner. Or bring Scruffy and get takeout. No, Richard was too uptight. Not really an animal person. He'd be worried about dog hair on his couch.

"I'll make sure it's a quick dinner," she told Scruffy when she took her outside before she left.

After a shower and the resurrection of her favorite summer dress, which was too fancy for dances on the green, Stan fed the animals and kissed them both good-bye.

Richard lived in the suburbs out past Hartford, in the town where most of the Warner Insurance executives lived. He lived in a gated community, which had never made Stan feel warm and fuzzy. He wasn't quite at the executive level yet, but that didn't stop him from trying.

Stan pulled into the driveway. The condo was dark.

Shoot, that's what I get for not calling first. She pulled out her cell and dialed his number. Voice mail. Maybe he was at her mother's, planning another visit from a lawyer. A wasted trip, but it had been a nice night for a ride, anyway. And she wasn't far from her favorite Afghan restaurant. Takeout from there would help make it an unwasted trip. She still had the restaurant on speed dial. She called and from memory ordered her favorite dish; then she drove over.

The food would take fifteen minutes; Stan arrived in ten. She headed inside to wait. The woman at the hostess stand recognized her. She held up a finger and vanished out back in a swirl of flowing fabrics, reminding Stan of Char, but a skinny version. Stan sat on the low-slung red couch in the waiting area and glanced around, looking for something to occupy her time.

And a flash of big hair caught her eye. She stood, peered around the corner into the dining room for a better view. "Well, I'll be damned," she muttered.

Flouncing past the swirly hostess, who was on her way back from the kitchen with a bag and a smile, Stan went into the dining room and approached the table. Richard faced her and saw her coming, eyes widening as she approached. And that go-go dancer, bottle-blond hair—his companion could only be one person. Michelle

Mansfield. A Pamela Anderson look-alike, with Botoxed lips and too much cleavage. It would've been funny if the whole thing wasn't so clichéd.

Stan walked up and stood right behind his companion. She folded her arms and gave him a brilliant smile. "I guess this is why you're not home," she said. "How are you, Michelle?"

Michelle spun around; her tiny brain, under all that hair, was likely working overtime to process the situation. She settled on a fake smile and jumped up to offer Stan an even more fake hug. Her dress dipped in a V, almost to her waist.

"Stan! So nice to see you," she said. "Richard and I were just prepping for an early-morning sales presentation tomorrow. How are you doing?"

Michelle also worked at Warner. A lifer. Done twenty years so far in various positions. She didn't have a reputation for actually getting things done in any of them. Nowadays she worked closely with Richard and his sales team putting client presentations together.

Usually not on a Sunday night, unless things had really changed since she'd been gone. Not to mention the lack of paperwork on the table, or the open bottle of champagne, which didn't exactly scream, *We're working!*

"I'm fabulous," she said, bussing the air next to Michelle's cheek.

Richard still hadn't said a word, which clinched Stan's suspicion their dinner had nothing to do with a sales presentation. She felt angry tears threatening to bubble up from her throat all the way to her eyeballs, but she held the tears back.

Michelle, at least, looked like she was enjoying

herself. "So what are you doing now?" she asked. Richard continued to sit, still apparently with no voice. "Did you find work yet?"

Stan smiled. This was the part she had to admit she enjoyed. "I haven't been looking for work," she said. "Don't really need to."

Michelle laughed. "Yes, severance can feel pretty good for a while, can't it? But it does run out."

Stan wondered how she knew that. Michelle had never been laid off and couldn't possibly understand the humiliation. "My severance is just being rolled into my investments, anyway," Stan said. "I have plenty of income without it."

Michelle glanced at Richard, confused. "I thought you said you weren't working."

"I'm not. I'm just a damn good investor. Have been for years." She smiled and turned to Richard. "Have a *great* dinner," she said, emphasizing "*grrrreat.*" Then she continued, "Sorry to interrupt. Nice to see you, Michelle. Have a wonderful night."

Richard finally stood. "Stan, wait."

Stan glanced over her shoulder and shook her head. "I have to go, Richard. My food is waiting. But I'm glad I took a ride here, anyway. It was a real eye-opener."

She waved cheerily at them and went to the front, paid for her food and headed out to her car. The mad took over, once she was driving, manifesting through her foot on the gas pedal. Michelle, of all people. She wasn't even that attractive. Her hair was an attention-grabber, sure, but anyone with eyes could tell it was fake. And once you got past the hair, well, that was another story.

Stan pounded the steering wheel in frustration. She hated being snarky. Sometimes it couldn't be helped. But it really wasn't Michelle she was angry with. It was Richard. And herself, for not admitting what was right in front of her.

Richard didn't love her. Not really. They had been good when they worked together, because they had the same focus, same drive, same big ambitions. The lack of common interests and philosophical differences weren't as obvious when you spent most of your time at work, traveling for work or talking about work. Now that they didn't have that in common anymore, the cracks in the foundation were expanding like spiderwebs of shattered glass.

Stan knew it might be different if—when— she took this other job. Different company, but the same industry. They could easily fall back into the old pattern. But she was sick of the old pattern. His attention, concern and support for her was less than what she should expect for herself. Even showing up with that lawyer was a sad attempt at controlling, more than helping. Plus, it had been her mother's referral, not even his. It still made her sad. Now she had to add "cheating boyfriend" to the list of really sucky occurrences of the week.

She lifted her foot off the gas. Halfway home already. She had better slow down or a ticket would round off the day. Her cell rang. Richard. She debated shutting it off, but figured prolonging the aggravation wouldn't be productive, either. She hit the speaker button. "What?"

"It's not what you think," he said.

"What do I think?"

Silence. "Well, you know. Dinner with Michelle and all. But we were working on a client presentation."

"Yes, Richard, I'm aware of how important your job is, and how closely you and Michelle have to work together. I understand. It brought some things to the surface that should have been apparent a long time ago."

"What's that supposed to mean?" Now he sounded annoyed. Like she'd done something wrong.

"Just tell me. Did you actually cheat on me yet? Or were you in the pre-cheat stage still?"

Silence. Which Stan took as answer enough. She snorted in disgust. "Forget it. I'm done."

"Done? What do you mean done? You know I wouldn't cheat on you—"

"I don't know any such thing. And frankly, I don't want to have to even ask the question."

But instead of being chastised, Richard just seemed angry. "You know, Stan, you've been a real piece of work lately. You are being incredibly irresponsible—"

"Irresponsible?" She didn't mean to screech, but couldn't help it. "How do you figure?"

"Losing your job. Picking up and moving to some remote location. And now? A suspect in a murder? What's happened to you, Stan?"

Like any of that—aside from the moving piece— was her fault. Anger almost made her drive off the road, but she wouldn't give him the satisfaction. She tried the old count-to-ten trick before she responded, but it didn't help. The mad was back.

"I'm done talking to you." She turned the phone off and threw it in her bag. Flicked on her high beams and slowed down as she hit the long, winding country road that led out to her house. She drove faster than she should. There were no cars on the road, as far as her headlights could see. It was black, black, black. The moon had vanished somewhere in the clouds. Streetlights were hard to come by around here. Signs illuminated briefly as her car swept past them; then they plunged back into darkness. Somewhere in the distance she could hear sirens. They sounded like they were heading toward her, but she couldn't tell. The emptiness was disorienting. Headlights lit the sign telling her she'd be in Frog Ledge in a mile. Still no cars on the road, but the sirens were getting closer.

Stan slowed as flashing lights filled her rearview mirror. Not police cars. Fire trucks. Two of them. The Frog Ledge Volunteer Fire Department was in the opposite direction, so these trucks must be from a neighboring town. Heading into Frog Ledge.

Stan pulled to the side of the road as the fire trucks barreled past her, the noise deafening. She hated sirens. Hoped nothing had happened on her street, with Nutty and Scruffy in the house. After the trucks had thundered past her, she pulled out behind them.

The sinking feeling intensified as she realized they were heading in the direction of the green.

Right near her house. But the trucks didn't slow. She heard other sirens, too. An accident, possibly.

The fire trucks careened around the stop sign next to the library, heading into downtown. She thought of Jake's bar and hoped nothing had happened out there requiring this many emergency vehicles.

She should park in her driveway, enter her blissfully quiet house and forget whatever else was happening. It had nothing to do with her; and the more she stayed out of drama, the better off she'd be. She'd almost convinced herself and slowed down as she got to her house; then she changed her mind and drove past. Just a peek. Who knew when the *Holler* would have the story? It was too late for Cyril to print papers now, unless he was going to post an update online. And it wasn't necessary, anyway. All she had to do was walk outside tomorrow and someone would be talking about whatever it was.

She reached the library and turned right. The sirens had stopped; but as soon as she turned, she could see the lights flashing. Right on Main Street. Above them, thick black smoke curled into the sky.

Right above what used to be Carole's vet clinic.

Chapter 23

Police vehicles lined the road, blocking traffic in both directions. A couple of troopers and some blockades kept people at a safe distance. Stan reached for her phone, but then she let it drop. She wasn't sure who it was. Either the fire was so bad the locals weren't confident they could get it under control with their resources, or they were afraid of it spreading, or both.

She had a sinking suspicion that an accidental fire in the same place a murder had occurred less than a week ago would be too much of a coincidence. Whoever had killed Carole had come back and set her building on fire. That didn't make sense . . . unless there was evidence to tie the murderer to the clinic somehow. Perhaps there was evidence that could be uncovered when they started sorting through Carole's will, or tracking the ownership of the building.

She thought of Diane Kirschbaum's phone conversation about accessing the building, about Amara and that guy slinking around behind the clinic. Sirens sounded again. Now an ambulance roared up. Stan shivered. She hoped no one had been inside.

People poured out of their houses and gathered nearby, even though they couldn't get close. Stan pulled her car into the library parking lot and ran down the street as fast as her sandals would allow. She reached the gathering crowd; people stopping their cars, trying to get home from somewhere; others who lived close by coming outside in pajamas to find out what the ruckus was about.

"My Lord," a woman uttered. She was wearing a housecoat like Stan's grandmother used to wear. "How could this have happened?"

No one answered her. She saw EMTs, a glimpse of a stretcher being loaded into the ambulance, and then the doors slammed and the vehicle screamed away. Everyone's worst fears were confirmed. Someone had been in there.

The crowd went silent. Stan saw a man make the sign of the cross and she felt sick, fearing that a fatal injury might have occurred. If another person had died in that building, she didn't want to hear about it. She should go home. Odds were that Trooper Pasquale would show up at her door shortly, anyway, to find out where she'd been. Well, at least she'd been fighting with Richard in public. Something good had come out of that situation.

Cyril Pierce and someone wielding a camera arrived and tried to talk to the staties, but no luck. The hush on the street spoke volumes. The acrid smell of smoke floated down and covered the idyllic town. Troopers came and went from the cordoned-off area. Stan didn't see Pasquale anywhere. People spoke in hushed tones. Whispers and speculations. She heard something about an explosion. No one spoke to Stan. It seemed like hours that they had been out there; but when Stan checked her watch, it wasn't even nine o'clock. Less than two hours ago she'd faced off with Richard and Michelle in a completely different world.

When she was sure her lungs were turning black from inhaling smoke, she decided to leave. She'd hear the whole story tomorrow, surely. But as she moved through the crowd to get back to her car, a snippet of conversation caught her ear.

"I don't know if anyone talked to Jake yet," a man said.

Stan didn't recognize the man or the young woman he spoke to who brushed tears away. "We have to tell him and Brenna," she said, and Stan stepped in front of them. To hell with being rude.

"Tell Jake what?" she asked, and they both looked at her. The man's eyes were serious and sad.

"His sister was hurt. Trooper Jessie. She was there when the explosion happened."

Stan pulled into her garage and stepped out into the darkness. Her throat was sore; she smelled like smoke; she wished she could go to bed and sleep, but she knew it wouldn't happen. Brandishing her key, she hurried to the door, alert for anything out of the ordinary. Scruffy scratched at the door from the inside, trying to get to her. Stan stuck the key in the lock, then froze. A scream bubbled up in her throat as she sensed someone over her shoulder.

The scream turned into a hysterical giggle when she turned, karate kick at the ready, and found herself facing off with her very own hand-made wood-carved wagon, complete with a gigantic collection of flowers and plants inside it. She'd forgotten all about it in the week's excitement. It was gorgeous, and way too short to be a person.

She needed some sleep. She'd check it out tomorrow. She let herself in and greeted the dog and the cat, waiting at the door together. She got everything locked down, and then she realized Scruffy still needed to go outside. The one downfall of dogs. At least she would bark if anything was out there.

"Come on, then," she said, picking up her leash. "Let's make this short and sweet, okay?"

Scruffy wagged her tail—such an obliging dog. Stan got her all geared up and they went out front. Scruffy did her selective sniffing routine, found a spot and did her business. She had just finished when a pickup truck slowed in front of Stan's house. Scruffy barked like crazy. The truck stopped and, to her dismay, the driver's door opened and a shadowy figure came around the front of the car. Stan froze, knowing she should bolt into the house. The person waved at her.

"I dropped off yer wagon!" Gene called.

Relieved, she loosened her grip on Scruffy's

leash. "Yes, I saw! Thank you!" Stan called back, staying where she was. Scruffy continued to bark.

"You like it?"

"It's beautiful," Stan said. "Thank you so much, Gene. Can I drop off your payment tomorrow?"

"Yeah, tomorrah." He shrugged. "Not worried about it." He opened his mouth as if he wanted to say something else, but he changed his mind. Closed it again. "Lots of sirens tonight. You hear them?"

"I did. There was a fire," Stan said. "Downtown." She did not say where. She didn't feel like talking at all, never mind talking about that.

"A fire, huh." Gene shook his head. "So much bad stuff going on lately."

"I know. Terrible. Well, thanks for coming by. You have a good night. Come on, Scruffy." With a wave she dragged the protesting dog inside and locked the door behind her. She peeked out the window. Watched Gene limp back around to the driver's side of his truck and drive away.

Huddled in her bed with a cup of tea, and Scruffy and Nutty nestled beside her, Stan tried to process the newest development in this never-ending saga. Her appetite for her long-cold Afghan food had vanished with the smoke she'd seen tonight. She felt like she'd taken a massive blow to her windpipe when she'd heard the news of Jessie Pasquale's injuries. Her throat tightened up; she couldn't speak. A wave of hot nausea washed away the initial chill. Because it was Jake's sister? Or because she kept seeing Pasquale's daughter, playing with the dogs and tugging on her uncle's hand? It certainly wasn't because she was overly fond of Pasquale, although she would never wish harm on anyone.

But the part of her she didn't like spoke up, in a childish voice, saying, *"See, big shot, you got what you deserved, because you've been wasting your time making Stan's life miserable, and the real killer is still out there, Trooper."* That bratty inner-child voice came through loud and clear tonight in the privacy of her own home—and in her own mind—despite Stan's best efforts to squash that naughty kid and send her to her room. It was the truth. Jessie Pasquale had screwed up, and it could've cost her life.

On the heels of that thought came the guilt and the half-baked prayers: *Please, please, don't let her die. She has a kid, and Jake would be devastated. Who would the resident state trooper be?* and on and on. The warring emotions had her up and pacing like a restless ghost; Scruffy was on her heels, the little dog anxious at the change in atmosphere. Nutty just watched her, a concerned look on his face, his tail straight up on high alert.

She wanted to call Jake, but she wasn't sure if that was appropriate. The family had to be handling it. She needed a drink. Her head felt like it might explode. Processing the sighting of Richard and Michelle, the fire and finally this news tonight, she wasn't sure which end was up. Never mind Nikki. The other piece bothering her right now. She still hadn't heard a word from her friend. Nikki's phone had been off. It wasn't like her to be off the grid completely, even if she was on a transport, which she hadn't said anything about yesterday. All the crazy things Stan had learned this week made her nervous. Worse, they sent her brain down a path she didn't like one bit.

Draining her tea, she set the mug down with a snap. She couldn't sit here and worry all night, and she wasn't going to get any sleep. Grabbing her purse and keys, she hurried out of the house again, making sure her porch, driveway and garage were all ablaze with lights.

It was near, if not past, closing time at McSwigg's. Stan pushed open the heavy front door, scanning the room. A few diehards nursed their last drinks. Duncan galloped over to greet her. She didn't see Jake or Brenna. She and Duncan went up to the bar. A guy with a huge head of curly hair washed glasses.

"We're getting ready to close," he said.

"Actually, I'm looking for Jake."

The bartender shook his head. "'Fraid he's not here. Family emergency."

"I know. Do you know if he's coming back?"

"Not sure."

"Mind if I wait? I'm supposed to watch Duncan," she lied.

The guy shrugged. "Sure."

Stan settled on a stool; Duncan's head was in her lap. The bar emptied out. The curly-haired guy moved on to sweeping the floor. Stan sat there for the better part of a half hour as everyone else emptied out.

And then Jake walked in.

He came in the front door, so he hadn't gone up to his apartment first. Which meant he'd just returned from the hospital. Stan's heart started pounding. She was afraid to ask how Jessie was. Afraid of his reaction. She'd been snotty about his sister before. He'd understood, but the game had changed tonight.

As he got closer, Stan could see how tired he looked. And how troubled. But he smiled at her. Minus his usual teeth display. "Hey." He slid onto the stool next to her.

"Hey."

"What are you doing here?"

She hesitated; then she leaned forward and let the words tumble out. "I know you probably think I'm full of crap, but I'm not. I feel horrible about what happened. How's your sister?" *Great speech.*

He raised an eyebrow. "I don't think you're full of crap. I appreciate your asking. She's okay. Thankfully, she took someone with her when she responded to the call. He called out the troops as soon as the explosion happened."

"What happened? Why did she go in there?"

Jake started to answer; then he stopped and held up a finger. "Hang on." He went over and spoke to the curly-haired guy. The guy nodded, took off his apron and walked out the door. Jake followed him and locked up, then returned to the stool.

"It was an anonymous call," he said. "Saying

someone was in the building and it was on fire. But it wasn't on fire, so she went in the back. Someone had jury-rigged some half-assed explosive, which, thank God, didn't work right. Something blew up in the exam room right behind her. Of course she had to check if anyone was in there."

"So someone set her up?"

Jake's silence answered her question. "No one's supposed to know that. The cop she was with is a friend. He told me. They had agreed not to go in, just go to the scene and wait for the firefighters, because they were in town. But since the place didn't look like it was on fire, Jess did what she does best. She ignored the rules."

"How long will she be in the hospital?"

"A day or two, I think."

"What about Lily?"

"Her dad came and got her. He lives in the next town."

"I'm sorry, Jake."

He lifted one shoulder. "She'll be okay."

"It was the person who killed Carole, wasn't it?"

"I don't know."

"It had to be. Who else would try to blow up the place?" Stan got off the stool and paced around the empty bar. "This is crazy. They have to catch this person soon. Right?"

He watched her, his eyes hooded in the dim light. "I hope so."

She jammed her hands in her pocket and looked around, not wanting to keep eye contact with him for too long. Her gaze fell on the Gaelic sign again. She nodded at it. "What's it mean?"

He followed her gaze. "'Your feet will bring you to where your heart is.'"

Stan kept her gaze trained on the words until they blurred. "How nice," she said. "Well, I should probably get going."

He didn't speak for a few seconds. Then he nodded. "Sure. Thanks for coming by. Be careful going home."

Chapter 24

Monday: one week since Carole died; since Stan's life went off the rails. Theme song: *"Crazy Train."* Ozzy Osbourne seemed a fitting choice. She wondered what it meant that a lot of her theme songs dated back to her angst-ridden heavy metal days. And today was Carole's wake, on top of what would surely be a day of crazy town gossip and stories galore about the fire at the clinic and Jessie Pasquale's injuries. Cyril might have managed to get an edition of the paper together. It was that thought that drove her out the front door, first thing in the morning, before she'd even had a sip of coffee from the mug in her hand.

On the porch she had a visitor.

Stan was getting used to seeing Duncan waiting out there—Jake still hadn't mastered the art of keeping an eye on him—so she didn't blink an eye when she saw the dog curled in a ball. But she wasn't used to this lack of response when he saw her. Usually, he was on her like a jumping bean, bouncing up and down until she gave him a kiss.

Normally, he would be standing up on his hind legs, his paws on her shoulders, licking her to death. This morning, nothing.

"Duncan?" she called.

He didn't respond. "Duncan!" Dropping to her knees beside his still frame, she was relieved to see him lift his head half an inch, just enough to give her a baleful look. Then he dropped back to the floor again. At least he was moving. For an awful moment she'd expected the worst.

"Dunc, what's wrong? Are you sick?" Fear at seeing him like this manifested into anger. Where was Jake? And why was she suddenly responsible for two dogs, when she had only signed up for one cat, and a self-sufficient one at that?

"Hang on, I'm gonna call your dad." She stood to go inside and find her phone, but Duncan fixed sad eyes on her and gave a pitiful whine. Then he vomited where he lay.

He could've eaten trash on the way to her house. Lord knew he would eat anything. So, did he just have a bad bellyache, or was this something worse? She didn't want to take the chance. Abandoning her pride, still dressed in her pajamas, she sprinted for the stairs. She hit the lawn, running, and raced next door to Amara's, banging on the door and ringing the bell simultaneously.

No response.

Stan cursed again, about to launch into a tirade about people who held stupid grudges at the wrong time. Then she realized it was barely seven in the morning; she tried again. This time she could hear the dog barking.

The door cracked a minute later. Amara stared at Stan.

"I'm sorry," Stan said. "I know it's early and you're angry at me. But there's a sick dog on my porch. Please, can you come help him?"

Amara hesitated just long enough to piss off Stan. "You can add it to my bill," Stan snapped, and Amara narrowed her eyes and finally spoke.

"One minute." She shut the door in Stan's face.

Stan crossed her arms and waited, tapping her foot, peering over to her yard in a futile effort to see onto the porch. Amara returned wearing a baseball cap and carrying a small kit. Stan led her to the porch, to Duncan. Still in the same spot. That's when she noticed the other spots of vomit on the porch.

Amara dropped to her knees and took the dog's head in her hands. She checked his eyes, inside his mouth, gently rolled him to the side and probed his belly. "You just found him like this?"

"Yeah. He comes to my porch sometimes for food."

"So you fed him."

"No, not this morning. I came out and he was just lying here."

"Was he foaming?"

"No. Why? You don't think he has rabies?"

"Not if he's had his shots. He has no bite marks, anyway." Amara opened her kit and perused the small vials inside for what seemed like hours.

Stan fidgeted, unable to watch Duncan like that anymore. "I'm going to call Jake." She went inside, letting the door slam behind her. Nutty and Scruffy waited in the hall, both looking very concerned. "It's okay, guys." She hoped.

She picked up her phone and put it back down. Dreaded this call. Would dread it under normal circumstances, but he'd already had a rough night. Yet it had to be done. She hit the call button before she could change her mind.

He answered on the second ring. She pictured him sleeping with the phone next to him, waiting for news about his sister.

"Hey." Her voice came out hoarse and gravelly. She cleared her throat and started over. "It's Stan."

"Hey, Stan. I was just about to call you. I can't find Duncan. Is he over there again?"

"That's why I'm calling. Can you come over right away?"

Silence. "Is everything okay?"

"Duncan's sick."

"I'll be right there."

Something small-town America and corporate America had in common: the rumor mill. As soon as word got out about what had happened to the beloved mascot of McSwigg's, the story spread as fast and as far as a raging wildfire. It even overshadowed the accounts of the real fire from the previous night. Some went with food poisoning and blamed Stan, since he had been on her porch. Others said someone in the neighborhood—also possibly Stan—secretly had something against dogs and was leaving rat poison in desirable places. And on, and on, and on.

Once the poison rumors had been exhausted,

the townsfolk moved on to Duncan's miraculous recovery. Some credited Amara with saving his life and raved about her awesomeness. Others, mainly the older crowd, whispered that she was some voodoo doctor or witch. Still, others said the real rescue happened once they got Duncan to the emergency vet, but Stan knew differently. He had gone from alarmingly sick to quiet and alert in the time it took to drive to the emergency clinic. Stan insisted on accompanying him. Amara had sent the remedy along for her to administer throughout the drive, and Stan rode with Duncan's head in her lap.

The morning was a barrage of sounds and images crashing together: Jake repeating that it wasn't her fault, that she'd been right the whole time and he should be more careful about letting the dog escape so easily. The vet techs rushing Duncan out back, expecting a dire situation after Stan's frantic call about a possible poisoning. Jake comforting her when she cried, instead of the other way around. The verdict that Duncan had likely eaten something toxic, although the vet couldn't tell what without running extensive tests. The cautious relief when Stan and Jake were allowed out back and Duncan wagged his tail and gave Stan his paw.

Stan had given Amara the credit and showed the doc the remedy Duncan had taken every fifteen minutes on the way over. The vet's response had been neutral. She recommended Duncan stay overnight to make sure he didn't relapse, and to monitor that his organs were functioning properly.

And then they were in Jake's truck, heading back to Frog Ledge.

"You okay?" Jake asked.

"I should be asking you that."

"I'm glad he's okay."

"Me too. I feel awful."

"Why? You didn't do anything. You saved his life."

"Amara saved his life. I don't care that the vet dismissed it. She did."

"I believe it. And you made that happen."

Barely. Only reason Amara did anything I asked is because she loves animals more than she hates me. But Stan didn't say that to Jake. She thought of the bag of kibble on her porch Saturday night. Duncan had eaten a ton of it by the time she realized it yesterday. In many cases poison wasn't instantaneous, unless there was a very large amount. She wondered if this was really random, or if someone's hatred ran so deep they were willing to hurt defenseless animals.

"Stan?"

"Hmm?"

"I said, stop blaming yourself."

"Hard not to. I move to town and everything falls apart."

"That's a little dramatic, unless you killed Carole and set fire to her building. And poisoned my dog."

"Of course not!"

"See what I'm saying?"

"You don't understand."

"You're right. I don't. If you didn't do it, you didn't do it."

"Life's not always that black-and-white."

"In this case, it seems pretty black-and-white to me."

"Not when my best friend could've been involved." It was the first time she'd spoken the words aloud. She'd danced around the whole Nikki thing in her mind, sure, but mostly to justify why it couldn't be true. But the evidence seemed overwhelming. Especially with Nikki's van sitting in Frog Ledge the day of the murder, when she'd explicitly told Stan she was hundreds of miles away.

Jake didn't take his eyes off the road, simply raised an eyebrow. "Explain."

She hesitated, not sure she should confide in him with this level of information. But she needed to talk it through with someone, and that obviously couldn't be Nikki. So she did, beginning with Nikki's past experiences with Carole Cross/Morganwick and her furtive conversation with Diane Kirschbaum and Perri Galveston. She ended with Izzy's revelation about Nikki's van being in the area the day of the murder. She didn't notice Jake had kept driving, past the turnoff for Frog Ledge, until he pulled up in front of a coffee shop that she'd never seen before. He didn't turn the car off until she was done talking.

"Feel like a cup of coffee?" he asked.

"Sure."

They went inside and found a seat. He waited until they'd ordered before he spoke again. "Do the police know about all this?"

"I don't know. I haven't told them anything. Maybe Izzy told them about the van. I hate even entertaining the thought, but . . . people do crazy things every day. And something Carole said the morning she came to my house always stuck in my mind. She said how animal people are a little crazy. It was a generalization, but I know what she means. Nikki loves animals. She's passionate about rescuing them. Sometimes she does things other people could call crazy." Stan dropped her face into her hands and rubbed her eyes. It was then she realized she was still wearing the running shorts and tank top she'd worn to bed the night before. She had been so worried about Duncan that she'd run out the door without even thinking about it. She wasn't even wearing a bra.

Two weeks ago she wouldn't have gone out of the house without full makeup, armored in her business suit, carrying her laptop instead of a shield to battle the business world. Now she'd run out half dressed, probably had mascara smudges and hadn't even brushed her teeth this morning.

"But Nikki wouldn't leave a mutilated bag of dog food on my porch. She wouldn't hurt me. Or an animal." But what about the people standing behind her? "What do you know about Diane Kirschbaum?" she asked Jake. To hell with the lack of a bra. She couldn't fall apart now. If they didn't figure out who killed Carole soon, things would only get worse. With Jessie out of commission for a while, there was no telling who would be on the case. Trooper Lou hadn't inspired that much confidence.

"The ACO? Don't know her well. Jessie oversees

her. She always struck me as odd." Jake shrugged. "But people seem to like her. Well, the animal people seem to like her. Not sure she gets out much, otherwise."

"She's not very friendly. When I went to the dog pound the other day on my bike ride, she was almost hostile."

"I don't think she interacts with the public much."

"She's friends with Amara. Which seems odd, because Amara's sociable, when she doesn't hate you. She's pretty angry with me. I'm just glad she was able to put that aside for Duncan."

"Why is she angry at you?"

"I asked her why she and Carole were fighting the day I moved in."

Jake laughed. "She thought you were suggesting she killed her?"

"Well, I was wondering. Amara knows veterinary medicine, right? I know she's holistic, but she must have that background. Anyway, she didn't like the conversation. She threw me out and stuck a bill in my door."

"You better not run for office anytime soon."

"I don't think they elect convicted criminals, anyway. Do you think they tracked down Carole's son?"

"I have no idea. If they did, he might be at the wake tonight."

The wake. She'd nearly forgotten. Something else to look forward to. Plus, she had a job interview tomorrow. Exhaustion nearly overpowered her at the thought of it all.

She rapped the table in frustration. "There are plenty of people who didn't much like Carole, but

no one seemed passionate enough to kill her."
Something dawned on her and she looked up at
him. "Your sister's friend? The one who worked
for Carole. I need to talk to her. I never got to
meet her the other night."

"I told you I'd introduce you. I can still do that,
but Jessie already talked to her. She had nothing."

"Sometimes it's different when it's a cop questioning you." Stan drained her cup and rose. She
needed a shower. "Can you call her on the way
home?"

Jake tossed his empty cup into the trash and
walked outside. "I'll try her. And I'll be sure to
recommend you for a junior detective badge
when Jess recovers."

Chapter 25

"There's really no reason to go to the wake." Stan pulled a short-sleeved black dress out of her "really good clothes" closet, wrinkled her nose and tossed it aside. "I'm tired of people staring at me and whispering. I should just wear a sign with big letters that states, *'I'm not a murderer.'*" She accentuated those last words by rattling a hanger in time to each one. She pulled out a navy-blue-and-white dress and held it up in front of her mirror. Now she looked like a Cape Cod sailor.

Scruffy, her only audience, gazed at her adoringly, that little stump of a tail vibrating with excitement. Scruffy got excited about everything. Or she thought everything meant a walk or a car ride. Nutty couldn't be bothered with her continued drama and was off sunning himself somewhere.

Stan sighed and sat down on the side of the bed, glancing at her watch. The wake began at seven. It was six-thirty. She hadn't gotten to talk to Brenna's friend about Carole. Her cell had been off when Jake called. Still no word from

Nikki. And none of her "good" clothes were working. She wanted to forget she'd ever met Carole Morganwick. However, if she didn't go, it would look worse. Everything made her appear guilty. It was as bad as being a newbie in corporate America. Possibly more cutthroat.

"So I guess I'm going," she said to Scruffy, "and I'm wearing a skirt."

Scruffy *woo-wooed* and stomped her front paws.

"I know, I know. I'm not happy about it, either." Stan took a black pencil skirt off its hanger and paired it with an emerald green blouse. Open-toed black sandals, hair pulled back in a sleek ponytail, a little bronzer and eyeliner, and she was done.

Nutty strode into the room and fanned his tail. He reminded Stan of the head turkey who escorted her charges into the yard yesterday looking for birdseed, tail fanned out. Scruffy immediately dropped to her front paws in front of him in a bow. Nutty didn't move. Scruffy went back to her sitting position and held up her paw. Nutty headbutted it. Scruffy dove onto him and started licking him to death.

Stan laughed. These two were hilarious together. Nutty seemed to like her. Sort of. Stan winced as he grabbed Scruffy's beard with his claws and shook her face, then dashed from the room. Scruffy chased after him. Stan hoped Nutty wouldn't miss the dog too much when Nikki finally came back to get her.

Slinging her purse over her shoulder, she grabbed a black sweater in case the funeral home was cold and headed out to the wake, feeling more like she was going to her own funeral.

* * *

For someone who hadn't been all that well liked, Carole Morganwick's wake was packed from the moment the doors opened. Figaro and Sons Funeral Home, just past the center of town, hosted the event. The small—dare she say "cozy"—funeral home looked more like someone having a party at their house, with townspeople spilling out the doors, talking in the parking lot and gathering on the wraparound porch before they entered. The only hint that something else had brought them here was the attire, largely black. Stan hoped her green shirt wasn't too distracting. Maybe she should wear her sweater now.

But it was so darn hot. She decided against it, locked her car and headed inside, eyes peeled for a blue sedan in the parking lot. One of the Figaro sons, presumably, opened the door for her. He looked fairly young, maybe midtwenties, with slicked-back hair, which reminded her of an Italian mobster. Sweet eyes, though. He smiled as she passed into the blast of cool air.

Stan let her eyes adjust to the dim light. Quieter in here, but still a crowd of people. Stan looked around to find Char or Izzy—anyone still talking to her. She was a little nervous about the receiving line and meeting Carole's brother: *"Hi, I'm Stan Connor, and I'm a suspect in your sister's murder,"* she envisioned herself saying.

Someone jostled her elbow. When she turned, Izzy grinned at her. "Come on, let's sign in. Gonna be a long night."

They got in the guest book line, which didn't

seem to be moving fast. Izzy checked her watch and sighed. "I've been at the shop since six this morning. Crazy busy. The dogs spent most of the day there and they didn't even get a walk. They're not happy with me right now. Speaking of my babies, they wanted to know if you had any more goodies for them."

Stan frowned. "You don't have to say that, Izzy. I know the last thing people want right now is me feeding their animals. After what happened to Duncan."

"Now you just quit that right now. That's hog-wash. Anyone who listens to it has no right to breathe."

The woman in line behind Izzy gave her a startled look.

"It's true," Izzy said to her. "This lady is getting an unfair rap and it makes me mad."

"Izzy," Stan said, red-faced. "No one cares."

"Well, they should care. Right?" Izzy said to the woman. She looked like a soccer mom, the kind who stays away from confrontations and certainly doesn't speak to strange women in town. Her gaze moved back and forth between them like she was watching a tennis match.

"Right," the woman answered uncertainly.

"See?" Izzy said to Stan. "Some people realize you didn't kill Carole and you didn't poison any dogs."

Soccer Mom got out of line and moved to the back.

"You did that to get a rise out of her," Stan said.

"No way," Izzy said, but Stan swore she saw a hint of a smile on her lips.

They finally stepped up to the book. Stan scanned the names on the open page. She recognized a few: Lorinda, from the library; Emmalee Hoffman, from the Happy Cow Dairy Farm. Amara. Stan signed her name and stepped back to let Izzy do the same. The door opened behind them. Warm air wafted in with a stream of people. Jake McGee was at the front of the pack.

"Go ahead," she told Izzy. "I want to see how Duncan is."

This time Izzy didn't even remind Stan of how much she hated Jake. "Okay, find me in line."

Stan moved down the side of the line. Her palms were sweating and she could feel that familiar ball of fear in her throat. Jake swore he didn't blame her for Duncan being sick, but she couldn't help feeling responsible.

But he smiled when he saw her. "Hey."

"How's Duncan?"

"The vet called a little while ago. He's doing fine. Stop worrying, Stan."

"I can't help it." She smiled a little. "But I'm so glad he's okay." She motioned behind her. "I better get back in line."

Izzy hadn't made it to the casket yet, but she held court with a group of people, none of whom looked familiar. Stan joined them, but she hung back. She looked around to see who else was here and what was going on. Ray and Char sat with Mona Galveston. Ray saw her and waved. Char turned to see where he was looking and her eyes brightened. She stood up and beckoned Stan.

"Yoo-hoo, honey, come over and say hello!"

Her attempts at a stage whisper failed miserably, and her wooden bracelets were as loud.

Stan slipped out of the long line and crossed the room. Char leaned over the chairs and grabbed her in a hug that was more like a choke hold. "How're you doin', honey?"

A flashbulb exploded right in front of them. Stan's eyesight faded to silver spots.

"What the devil?" Char turned around and rolled her eyes. "Cyril Pierce, what in blazes do you think you're doing? Put that away and have some respect! We're at a wake!"

Cyril tipped his fedora at her. "Sorry, Ms. Char. I've got a job to do too," he said. "I'm covering Carole's funeral. It's only right, as a citizen of Frog Ledge, to give her an appropriate send-off." He nodded at Stan, Ray and Mona. "Folks." His gaze skipped back to Stan and lingered.

Stan could hear the question forming before his lips even moved. Luckily, so could Char.

"Well, go take pictures somewhere else." Char shooed him off with her suitcase-sized purse. "My word, some people just don't think."

"That's the media for you," Stan said. "It's why companies need spin doctors."

Mona Galveston hadn't said a word. She watched the whole exchange, but her expression was not unkind. Ray, as usual, took the polite role.

"Mona, Stan Connor. A new addition to town. Stan, our mayor."

"Yes, lovely to meet you." Stan offered her hand.

"Likewise." Mona's grip was strong, efficient, businesslike. "How are you enjoying Frog Ledge?"

The question had to be a test. There was no

way the mayor didn't know she seemed to be a prime suspect.

"It's delightful. The green is my favorite place to spend time."

"It is lovely, isn't it? You haven't had the bene-fit of spending holidays there yet. It's charming."

"I'm sure. I should probably get back in line. Nice to see you all."

"Stop by later, honey!" Char called after her. "We're hosting a small get-together. You know, a send-off for poor Carole."

By the time she joined Izzy at the casket, Stan felt like she'd been in the funeral home forever. It was almost nine. Her sweater had been unnec-essary. The room was stifling hot with such a large crowd. The air conditioners worked overtime and were still losing the battle.

Izzy moved up to the kneeler. Stan realized she was about to see Carole's body. Again. A cold sweat trickled down the small of her back. She must have gone pale; when Izzy rose and looked back at her, she looked concerned. "You okay?"

"Fine," Stan said. She braced herself and sank onto the vacated kneeler, thinking she'd just shut her eyes and try not to look. She made the sign of the cross and concentrated on not throwing up. But she couldn't help it. She had to see. Forcing her eyes to Carole's face, she was surprised to find the dead woman looking fairly peaceful. Defi-nitely a difference from when she had been on the floor covered in kibble.

Stan wondered if there was any left in that mass of hair somewhere, and she stifled a giggle. Hastily crossing herself again, she stood. Now would be the even weirder part—meeting Carole's family. The group was small. No sign of any son, at least not anyone who looked young enough. A man with the same white hair, only much shorter, stood next to the casket, looking solemn. A woman who was much younger stood next to him. She looked bored.

Izzy stepped up first. "So sorry for your loss," she said, holding out her hand. "Are you Carole's family?"

The man nodded and shook her outstretched hand. "I'm her brother. Elliot Morganwick."

"I'm a fellow business owner in town. Izzy Sweet. Again, so sorry."

The man pointed to his left. "My wife, Andrea."

Izzy moved down the line, leaving Stan no choice but to offer her condolences to Elliot Morganwick.

"So sorry," she murmured, hoping she wouldn't have to introduce herself.

Elliot nodded, leaning closer to hear her. "Thank you. And you are?"

"I'm new to town," she said hastily. "I was a client. Sort of."

He nodded, puzzled, but Stan had already moved on to his wife. Andrea Morganwick had short, dark hair and a pointy nose. She looked bored beyond belief. She also looked like she needed a sandwich. Stan could see her hip bones jutting out of the dress she wore. Her handshake was limp and she didn't make eye contact, just sighed a "thank you" as well-wishers passed by. Stan ducked out of line and found a black trench coat blocking her path. Cyril Pierce.

"Can I have a word?" he asked.

She sighed. "About what?"

Cyril glanced around to see who was listening. "You may want to talk in private. Although I'm not sure how private this will be in a few minutes."

Stan snapped to attention. "What are you talking about?"

Cyril motioned her to a quiet corner of the room. "I've had some accusations brought to me. I'd like your side."

"No comment. I already told you I didn't kill Carole."

"This isn't about Carole." Cyril pulled his notebook out of his trench coat pocket and made a dramatic show of uncapping his pen. "It's about Phineas Dobbins."

"Who?"

"Phineas is a dog. He belongs to Myrna Dobbins." He pointed across the crowd to a woman with Wednesday Addams hair and a sour expression. "Right now he's ill. With possible food poisoning."

"I'm very sorry to hear that, but I don't believe I've ever met Phineas. Or Myrna. What does this have to do with me?"

Cyril watched her with a reproachful expression. "Myrna Dobbins bought some of your dog treats at the farmers' market yesterday. It was the only deviation in Phineas's diet."

Chapter 26

Stan fled the funeral home without giving Cyril the benefit of a second "no comment." She ignored Izzy and Char, who both called after her. She was sure that somewhere along her path to freedom, she also passed Jake. He was about to rethink the idea that she wasn't to blame for Duncan's illness.

She made it to her car before the tears started, but she couldn't give herself the luxury of having a good cry. People were coming and going at a steady clip, and she didn't want to give the gossipers more fodder.

Poison an animal? Even people who didn't really know her should be able to tell how much she loved animals. She wanted to find who started that nasty rumor and beat them with her cake pan. She hoped Phineas would be okay, whatever had happened to him.

This was when she needed Nikki. There wasn't anyone else to whom she could cry. She dialed Nikki's cell again as she pulled out of the parking lot and headed home. Straight to voice mail. She pulled into her driveway, feeling more alone than she'd ever felt in her life.

The first thing she noticed about her house was the absence of her porch light. She distinctly remembered turning it on before she left. Already jittery, she went on instant alert. Fishing around inside her bag, she grabbed her old can of Mace, which Richard had given her for the nights she walked alone to her car in the parking garage. She had no idea if it was still functional, but it would have to do. And thank goodness she'd downloaded the flashlight app for her iPhone. She powered it up, grabbed her purse and keys and went up the front steps.

No slashed bags of kibble. A positive sign. Shining the light up, she didn't see anything out of whack with the light. Must be a faulty bulb. She stuck her key in the lock and started to twist, but the door gave under her hand.

She knew she had locked the door. She debated calling the police, but she dismissed the thought. They were probably busy building an animal cruelty case against her. "Nutty? Scruffy?"

Scruffy didn't run to the door to greet her. This didn't feel right. She hesitated; her brain was already screaming at her to leave, run, lock herself in the car and call the cops.

Then she heard a yowling sound. It was Nutty's upset voice—the voice he used when she tried to get him in the carrier for a vet visit. But still, he didn't come.

Nutty was in trouble. Stan whipped out her Mace, raced inside and down the hall, flicking lights on as she went. She grabbed her biggest butcher knife out of the holder on her kitchen counter and whipped around, trying to figure out where Nutty's cries were coming from. Then the doorbell rang, almost sending her through the ceiling. Was the danger in the house or outside?

Stan crept back down the hall and eased up to the side window to peek. Dark, but she could still make out Jake's silhouette. She went to yank the door open; then her hand stilled. Odd timing for him just to show up. No, now she was getting paranoid. They had been at the wake together. He'd probably heard the new story. He couldn't be a murderer, for God's sake. He was the trooper's brother. And there might still be someone in here, so she needed to move.

She whipped open the door, realizing a second too late she still held the knife and the Mace.

Jake raised an eyebrow. "You should just say you don't want visitors."

"Oh, for . . ." Stan shoved the screen open and let him in. "Someone broke in. The light was out and the door was unlocked. I heard Nutty crying, but I can't find him or Scruffy anywhere."

That snapped him into serious mode. "Did you call the police?"

"Is that your response to everything? No, I didn't call the police."

"It's my response to threats and break-ins, yes. Go call."

"I have to find the animals."

"I'll go look."

"I'll go with you." She followed him. "I was about to check upstairs. I want to know my animals are safe." Her throat prickled with tears. Scruffy would've come out by now. The dog wasn't in the house, and Nutty had stopped crying. She hoped he wasn't hurt.

Jake went left at the top of the stairs. She followed. They went into the spare bedroom. As he bent to look under the bed, something crashed in the closet. She shrieked and spun around, knife at the ready. Jake jumped up and pulled the door open.

Nutty bolted out and took off like he'd discovered the bogeyman was in there with him. "Oh, Nutty!" she called, and dashed after him. But he disappeared down the stairs.

Jake stepped out into the hall. "He okay?"

"Looks fine. But no Scruffy." The tears came now, a culmination of what seemed like the longest week of her life. The adorable little schnoodle who had followed her around adoringly. She had told Nikki she couldn't adopt the dog, and she had spent the last two days wondering when Nikki would come claim her. Now Stan would give anything to see her.

Jake relieved her of the butcher knife and put his arm around her shoulder. "Don't cry. We'll find her. We need to call someone, though. You're positive someone broke in? You didn't leave the door open by accident and she got out?"

"I've been religious about locking things up ever since . . ." She trailed off with a hiccup. "I don't know. My porch light was out when I got home and the door was unlocked. How did they get in?"

"Did you check the back door?"

Stan shook her head.

"Let's do that. Does anything look out of place?"

"I don't know." She glanced around, unsure. "I haven't really looked at anything."

"Okay. Don't worry about it right now. Stay here." He checked out the rest of the rooms upstairs. "No one here, but you'll have to see if anything's gone. I'm going to check the back door."

She followed him downstairs. "The basement," she said.

"Wait for me," he instructed.

Wired, she paced around, looking for Nutty. She found him in the TV room, hiding under the coffee table. She scooped him up and nuzzled into his long fur, wiping her face. He licked her nose. "What happened here tonight?" she asked him.

Nutty meowed.

"I'm sorry. I didn't mean to put you guys in danger. This is all my fault." She felt the tears coming on again and tried to swallow them.

"Hey, Stan." Jake appeared in the doorway. "You're gonna want to come out here."

Stan stood in her sunroom, still holding Nutty, observing her broken windows. She was over being upset. Now she was resigned. Once he figured out how they'd gotten in, Jake had investigated the front porch and found the lightbulb unscrewed. Whoever had left the kibble was back, and they wanted her to leave Carole's murder alone.

"So they broke in, took the dog and walked out my front door? Or did they break in to warn me, and the dog got out by chance?" She kicked at the scattered glass on her floor. "I'm sorry I ever came here."

They were waiting for the cops. Stan had finally given in and called. Jake looked troubled. He hadn't said much, but he seemed deep in thought.

Stan realized she had never even found out why he'd come over. "What are you doing here, anyway?"

"I heard about Cyril's stupid accusations and wanted to make sure you weren't paying any attention to those idiots. I swear, I love this town, but sometimes the people in it drive me insane."

Her stomach clenched, remembering Cyril's questions about poisoned dogs. He noticed.

"No one with any sense thinks you got any dogs sick."

"I don't know about that. They already did, because of what happened to Duncan." Her eyes filled with tears again. She turned away and busied herself getting a glass of water. Nutty stuck close to her. She'd almost tripped over him twice now. She picked him up and hugged him.

"Do you think he's trying to tell me what happened? I wonder if I should call one of those pet psychics or something." She was only half kidding, but Jake looked serious.

"Did you want to call someone?"

"I already called the police, remember?" The ice maker in her refrigerator had jammed. She opened the freezer door and shook the bin forcefully to clear it.

"No. I mean, your boyfriend."

"Ha! *Boyfriend*." She slammed the freezer door.

A piece of ice flew out of the chute and hit the floor. She hurled it into the sink. "That's funny."

"Why?"

"I don't want to get into it. Enough things are wrong right now."

"Okay." Jake emptied the dustpan and set the broom in the corner.

"Why does Izzy hate you so much?"

He opened his mouth to respond, but the doorbell rang. Of course.

She sighed. "Be right back."

Trooper Lou waited at her front door.

Lou. It figures. Here was the cop who had been on scene with Jessie at Carole's murder. He cocked his head when he saw Stan. "You're always in the middle of everything, aren't you?"

"Tell me about it." Stan led him to the kitchen.

Jake nodded at him. "Lou."

"Hey, McGee. How's Jessie tonight?"

"Doing better. Going stir-crazy in the hospital."

"I bet. So what happened, Ms. Connor?"

Stan went through the whole story. Lou went through the rest of the house, checked out the basement, the front door and the porch light, made notes, dusted for fingerprints.

"So nothing's missing?" he asked when he returned to the kitchen.

"Not that I can see. Nothing even looks out of place."

"I'll file the report."

"So what happens next?"

Lou slapped his notebook shut. "We look into it."

"What about Scruffy?"

"The dog? She may have gotten out in the confusion. Did you go out and look?"

"I was waiting for you," Stan said, exasperated. "Making sure no one was still in here."

"Oh. Well, I would suggest starting there."

He said it so seriously, like she would have been too stupid to think of that. She resisted the urge to make a snarky comment.

"What if the intruder took Scruffy? We need to find her. She isn't even my dog!"

Lou looked dubious. "I can't put out a report on a missing dog."

Stan looked at Jake, willing him to step in before she assaulted a cop.

"Lou. A little help here," he said.

Lou sighed. "We'll send a press release to the paper. You should put up posters. Check with Diane, too. Maybe she really did get out. If she did, chances are good she'll get picked up. Diane hates seeing dogs running around loose."

Chapter 27

Stan found Amy Franchetti running a five-minute mile on the Frog Ledge High School track. Brenna had tipped Jake off that she would be there. Stan had prepared herself for some serious running in case Amy couldn't stop to chat. She hoped she wouldn't be too winded to have the conversation, though she doubted she could sustain any kind of activity long-term.

After Lou left last night, she and Jake had searched for two hours for Scruffy, both on foot and in the car. They left a message at the pound. When they finally called it a night, she had to spend another half hour defending her decision to remain at her house and not spend the night on his couch or at Char's B and B. When Jake finally gave up and left, she spent the rest of the night hovering between being asleep and awake. Stan jumped at every sound, her Mace and cell phone clutched in her hand. The one bright spot had been waking up to hammering and pounding, which initially freaked her out. Once she realized it was Ray fixing her windows in the sunroom, after Jake had called him, she had been so touched and grateful that she cried all over him.

Now she had that darn job interview at Infinity in a few hours, and she needed to put up posters for Scruffy. Thank God she'd taken a couple of pictures on her phone. She was exhausted and un-raveled. But if Amy, the former vet tech, could help shed some light on the possible killer, the two roads might converge. At this point she was grate-ful for Nikki's silence. The last thing she wanted to do was tell her she'd lost one of her charges.

Amy ran at a pretty good clip around the track. Stan wished she'd take a break, but since that didn't seem likely, she jumped in and jogged along until she was close enough to call her name. Then Stan realized Amy wore headphones and couldn't hear her. She picked up her pace enough to match strides with Amy, then tapped her on the arm.

Amy yanked the earbuds out and slowed, ap-prehension all over her face. "Yeah?"

"Amy? So sorry to bother you." Stan explained who she was and what she needed. "I really want to be able to tell her brother everyone's trying to help. Could I have five minutes?"

The girl looked like she'd rather be asked to swim with alligators in a swamp. She glanced around, looking for some means of escape. "I don't think I can offer you very much, but I guess so. I'll meet you in the bleachers. I have to do one more lap." She picked up speed again.

Stan veered off the track and went to sit.

Amy finished her lap in no time and joined Stan in the bleachers after grabbing her bag off the side of the field. She took out a hat and slipped it on, shielding her eyes from the sun.

"So what do you wanna know about Carole? I already talked to the cops. I didn't work there that long. She was pretty dysfunctional. And disorganized."

"How long did you work there?"

"I started in February. So, not even half a year. She wasn't that busy, so I didn't work a lot of hours."

"Were any of her clients mad at her? Besides Betty Meany?"

Amy cracked a tiny smile, the first friendly sign Stan had seen. "Betty was mad, definitely. I don't remember anyone else being that outspoken. It's funny, because Carole was weird enough that I could see her killing someone instead of the other way around."

"Why do you say that?"

Amy jerked one shoulder in a shrug. "She had a temper. And she was just weird. Like, everything was a conspiracy. I remember when that other vet came to talk to her about selling the practice. Sounded like she would've been smart to take her up on it, but she got all nuts and threw her out. Thought the townspeople had banded together and were trying to get rid of her."

"What other vet?"

"That homeopath lady. I think her boyfriend wanted it more. He's a traditional vet. He teaches science at the college. I took his class last semester. Cool guy."

"Amara Leonard wanted to buy Carole's practice? When was this? Did you tell the police?"

Amy thought about that. "I don't think so. I didn't think it was important."

"Carole didn't go for it."

Amy snorted. "She told them to get out before she sicced a rabid pit bull on them." She shook her head in disgust. "She would say stupid things like that all the time. She really wasn't that into animals, if that makes sense. I wanna be a vet 'cause I love animals, you know? But she didn't get all excited about them or anything. I think she liked farm animals, though."

"Did she have a lot of clients?"

"Not too many. Mrs. McCafferty, my gramma's friend. And Mr. Holdcroft. He came all the time."

"With his dog?"

Amy looked at her like she was an idiot. "Of course with his dog. He didn't come for treatment."

"So she let you go."

Amy wrinkled her dainty nose. "She didn't, like, fire me or anything. She just said she wasn't getting enough business to support a staff. I was the only staff, though. So I'm not sure how she handled it when she needed two sets of hands." She shrugged. "Maybe she *was* gonna close up shop and sell. Who knows? But listen, I gotta finish my training for today. You all set with questions?"

"Sure," Stan said, disappointed. Amy didn't have any new insights.

"Thanks." Amy bounced to her feet; then she brightened. "Hey, since you're friendly with her brother, will you bring something to the funeral for him later?"

Since Amy had only deduced that, and Stan hadn't actually said it, she ignored the white lie. "What is it?"

"A bunch of stuff from the office. He knew I worked there. Carole must have been telling him stuff about the business. I wonder if he had a share in it or something. He tracked me down and called me at home. Wanted me to clean out her stuff from the office for him. Lucky I did it before the place burned to the ground. It's in my car."

"That is lucky. I'd be happy to," Stan said, trying to tamp down her eagerness. *Information from Carole's office! Score!*

"Nice. You're a rock star," Amy said, flashing her first real smile. "Come on, I'll get it."

Stan followed Amy to her car, a red Honda Civic. She opened the back door and searched around for a minute; then she triumphantly pulled a beat-up black leather briefcase out of a pile on the floor. The briefcase was scratched and so crammed with stuff that it gaped open. Amy shoved it at her, as if afraid Stan would change her mind.

"Thanks!" With that, she turned and jogged back to the track, falling into her stride as if she'd never taken a break.

Stan stood with the briefcase, amazed at her good fortune. And Amy's naiveté. Maybe she'd glean some information from something in there. What the heck, it was already open.

* * *

This job interview couldn't come at a worse time. Stan thought about rescheduling. But that was a no-no—even though these kinds of companies made you wait months and months before making hiring decisions, in most cases. So she put on her favorite suit, one she'd had nothing but good luck while wearing, left another message with Diane Kirschbaum about Scruffy and drove to Hartford, itching to open the bag of Carole's paperwork the whole time.

She checked her watch as she neared the city. Right on time. She was scheduled for two-thirty. But all she felt was sick.

The continued stress of her world, she assured herself as she walked into the building, a couple of folders from Carole's briefcase in her bag in case she had reading time. The place was bigger than her previous employer's. Normally, she would have researched every similarity and difference—ranked them as pros or cons—and have been über-prepared for this conversation. Today, not so much.

Bernadette, the happy scheduler, greeted her and showed her to a chair in the waiting area. She opened Carole's folder and flipped through. She started with the financials. Engrossed in discovering how little money Carole had been bringing in—nowhere close to making a profit—Bernadette had to call her twice to the conference room. Instead of prepping for the interview while she waited, Stan had been going through the profit and loss statement and quarterly reports Carole had neatly packaged for the accountant. She learned the first half of the year had left Carole with a net loss of $2,894. Not terrible, but it told the beginnings of a story.

The woman interviewing her finally showed up. Stan found her unimpressive. A beige person. She wasn't even wearing a power suit. Stan turned her corporate face on and answered the questions in her corporate voice, using all the buzzwords and smiling at the appropriate times. But the whole time her mind was on Carole's file, wondering what else she might find.

They had her set up to talk with three other people over the next two-plus hours before they had Bernadette see her out, practically promising her an offer within the week, after they cleared the usual red tape. Stan assured them she'd be eagerly awaiting and hurried out to her car.

Instead of hitting the highway back to Frog Ledge, Stan drove to her favorite coffee shop near her old place. She stuck the folder she'd removed back into the briefcase and hauled it inside. She ordered a latte with a double shot and sat down with the goods. An hour and a half later, she had a good financial picture of Carole's clinic. And it was dreary. Her father had paid the mortgage off years ago, and all she had to do was keep up with operating expenses. She hadn't been doing that well. Hence, a proposal Amara Leonard and Vincent DiMauro had written to buy the business. The transaction Amy had mentioned. If Carole accepted, she wouldn't have to ever worry about working again. It was a generous offer that likely would have put Amara and Vincent in debt for a long time.

But Carole had turned them down. *No* had

been scrawled in vehement red pen across the formal paperwork, and it had been folded into thirds and stuck in the back of the file labeled as ACCOUNTANT. Clipped to it were a number of e-mail exchanges between the two parties. They started out polite; but by the time Stan got to the bottom of the pile of twenty or so, the tone had changed. Vincent DiMauro had been angry at the rejection and had repeatedly asked for the opportunity to meet again in person. His last e-mail, dated three days before Carole's death, ended on an ominous note: I'm just going to show up, and then you'll have to talk to me.

Stan gasped; then she glanced around to see if anyone had noticed. If Vincent DiMauro had gone to see Carole, and the meeting hadn't gone as planned, who knew what he would have done? He could've stabbed her in a fit of anger, not re-alizing it would kill her. Maybe he knew that she'd kept these e-mails and he figured he'd burn the place down to get rid of any evidence, including her hard drive.

Amy said she hadn't told the cops about this proposed transaction. Well, it was time they heard about it. Stan shoved the rest of the papers back into the briefcase and hurried to the car, a danger-ous trick on four-inch heels. She cursed the con-straints of corporate wardrobe. Between her favorite suit, which didn't feel quite right on her anymore, and the shoes, she wished she'd brought clothes to change into. She had to call Lou.

Part of her was relieved—this meant Nikki was off the hook. Although her actions were still a mystery, Stan could deal with that later. As long as her lifelong friend wasn't a killer, she didn't care what else she was doing in her spare time.

Once she was on the road, Stan plugged in her headset and called Lou's number at Troop L. Voice mail. She pounded the steering wheel in frustration.

"Trooper Sturgis, this is Stan Connor from Frog Ledge. I need you to check out a man named Vincent DiMauro in regard to Carole Morgan-wick's murder. I'll explain later, but I have some potential evidence. Call me." She recited her cell number, disconnected and hit the gas.

She was entering the Frog Ledge town limits when her cell rang. She snatched it up, hoping for a return call from Lou or someone at the barracks. Instead, a vaguely familiar voice said, "Stan, it's Sheldon Allyn. I needed to follow up with you on our discussion."

"Hi, Sheldon. What can I do for you?"

He didn't seem eager for small talk. "I'm afraid I was a tad hasty in my offer. I won't be needing a pet chef, after all. We hadn't agreed on a contract, of course, so this is merely a courtesy call, but I wanted to let you know posthaste."

"Posthaste"? Do people still talk like that? Apparently, Sheldon Allyn did. And he was canning her before he'd even hired her. "May I ask why?"

"I've simply decided to go in a different direction," he said. "But thank you for your time, it's been lovely."

And he hung up. Gone. Another door closed. There was some saying about windows opening when doors closed, but Stan felt like she was seeing an awful lot of doors slamming. Any windows in the vicinity were cloudy. Or stuck shut.

She didn't realize tears were brimming until her vision blurred and she almost missed her street. Her phone rang again, but she didn't even bother to pick it up. She'd left Lou enough information on his voice mail. They could figure it out and arrest Vincent, or not. She didn't much care at this point. Maybe she should put her house back on the market. Sell it and try California. Her dad had loved it out there. Plus, the weather was nicer. Or maybe she could rent her house out and leave tomorrow.

By the time she pulled into her driveway, she'd almost made up her mind. Her resolve strengthened even more when she got to her front door and saw the *Frog Ledge Holler*—another special edition—on her porch. Cyril Pierce really needed a vacation.

The headline, of course, was the "rash" of animal poisonings in the area. Now the tally had reached three dogs who had allegedly become ill, and the common ground among all three was Stan, as the article so objectively pointed out. Duncan had been on her porch when he'd been found ill, and the other two dogs had eaten her treats at the farmers' market this weekend. Luckily, the animals only reportedly had stomach problems. Nothing more serious than that, with the exception of Duncan, who had been hospitalized.

Stan ripped the paper in half, then tore it in half again. She didn't even want to bring it into her house to throw it away. Instead, she left it in a pile on her porch. No wonder Sheldon had reneged on his offer. He'd heard about this. Or maybe Cyril Pierce had called him for a comment, if word had gotten out about his offer. If he had been serious about wanting her, he probably had her name plugged into his Google search and got updates daily. And that was the end of that.

Time to accept her life for what it was. A failure. All the hard work she'd put into everything had been destroyed in a mere week. She'd even lost a dog who didn't belong to her. She'd better do something quick before Nutty jumped ship, too.

Her phone rang again. It was a number she didn't recognize. She let it go to voice mail before she picked it up to listen.

"Stan Connor. This is Diane. The ACO. Your dog is here. I picked her up earlier today. Please come get her before seven."

Thank goodness! She immediately started to cry again. What a dripping mess she'd turned into. She couldn't remember the last time she'd cried before moving here, unless you counted "The Elimination," and now it seemed to be one of her daily activities. At least these were good tears.

She grabbed her car keys again, still in her interview attire, and rushed to the car. She didn't have much time, and she doubted Diane would wait for her. Speeding past the town center, Stan navigated the back roads to the out-of-the-way dog pound. She hated the thought of that sweet little dog sitting in that damp, unfriendly building. Probably scared to death and surrounded by big dogs barking and growling at her. She hit the gas harder and turned onto the street leading to the park.

Quiet had settled over the wooded area. Even though dusk had barely fallen, the hush of the trees and the thick greenery gave everything a closed-in feeling. The park was supposed to close at dusk, but the gate was still open. Diane must be responsible for that, since she likely was in and out at all hours.

Stan followed the winding roads, noting the few stragglers unwilling to end their late-day summer fun. A couple of exhausted parents dragged their kids off play equipment. Farther down near the lake, a family packed up the remains of a picnic. Dinner. She was starving. She bet Scruffy was, too. She would make her a special meal when they got home. She had organic turkey in the refrigerator, and some ground beef from the co-op she had planned to cook for Nutty later in the week. But this was a special occasion.

She pulled into the pound parking lot. Diane's white truck was outside and the building was lit up. It was five to seven. She'd just made it. But Scruffy was coming home! Grinning for the first time in days, Stan grabbed her keys and jumped out. She hurried precariously across the gravel, regretting not changing her shoes. Not really the place for stilettos. Faint barking sounded from behind the building. The dogs must be out for their last playtime of the night. She shoved the heavy door open and barreled inside, calling out.

"Hey, Diane? I'm here for Scruffy."

And then she tripped, pitching forward over Diane, who was sprawled to the left of the door.

Stan's breath left her in a *whoosh*, hands automatically out to break her fall. They scraped the cement floor. One of her shoes slipped off. She twisted around; the horror of what she was seeing was dawning on her. A scream worked its way up her throat; but when her mouth opened, nothing came out.

It was happening again. Diane was dead. She looked dead, anyway. And the murderer might still be here. She had to run. But she crawled over and felt Diane's neck for a pulse, praying she'd feel something. If Diane was dead, she would get blamed. Stan would be tossed in jail without a second thought.

Then . . . a soft moan. And a faint pulse under her fingers. Thank God. But she needed help.

"Diane?"

Nothing. Stan searched frantically in her pocket for her phone. She remembered leaving it in the car and nearly screeched in frustration. "I'll be right back," she promised, not caring if Diane could hear her. "I'm calling for help." Vaulting to her feet again, she took a step out the door . . . and slammed into a body blocking her way.

She gasped and jerked back. This time she tripped over the shoe she'd lost and landed on her butt. Pain shot through her tailbone. She ignored it and scrabbled backward with her hands and feet, crablike, kicking her other shoe off so she would be balanced when she got up. Whoever blocked her way lurched inside, almost losing his own footing.

Once he stepped under the light, she realized it was Russ, Gene's apprentice. What was the strange boy doing here? Regardless, help was help. "Something's happened," she said. "Diane needs help. Will you stay with her while I get my phone?"

The kid didn't respond, much like when she'd tried to speak to him while he mowed her lawn. Well, she didn't have time for this. She tried to push past him, but he stayed where he was, blocking her way.

"Can you let me out?" she asked, but fear started to prick her throat. He held a hand out to halt her, still not speaking.

"Get out of my way!" she shouted.

A shock of white hair appeared over his left shoulder. Gene. Thank God! He would collect his disturbed charge. "Gene! Can you please do something about him? Diane's hurt!"

Gene put his hand on the kid's shoulder and observed Stan with those watery eyes.

"Sorry," he said. "You're not goin' anywhere."

Chapter 28

Gene and Stan stared at each other over the kid's head for seconds, which seemed like hours.

"What—what are you talking about?" Her voice came out more like a croak, and she struggled to command authority. She didn't have to sound like a scared schoolgirl. "What's going on, Gene?"

Gene stepped in, lightly pushing the boy ahead of him and out of Stan's way, his limp apparent by his heavy left step on the cement floor.

"Just what I said. You ain't leaving."

He'd lost his mind. Clearly. Her legs shook, but she stepped forward. "What's wrong with you? This woman needs help. Did you do something to her?"

Stan gauged the space between Gene's body and the door. She had just decided to chance a run for it, when Gene looked down at Diane, who had started to stir. He delivered a vicious kick to her head with his heavy work boot, the one worn on his good leg. Diane immediately stilled. Gene brought his other hand up from behind him. A wood-carving knife, its grooves as razor sharp as a shark's teeth, was clenched in it.

Stan stared at him as the reality of her situation dawned on her. She took a step back, hands up in front of her in a defensive pose, and she drew on every ounce of her spin doctor skills. "Gene, this looks bad, but we can turn this into a good story. Let's stop this right now so we can all walk away from here."

He turned on her, his face full of hate. "You shoulda left it alone. What happened with me and Carole was between me an' Carole." He advanced on her, the knife pointed accusingly.

Stan took a step back, her mind racing. She had nowhere to go but the back of the building, where there was no exit. Except maybe through a dog run. She'd been wrong about Vincent and Amara. The killers were right in front of her, and she was screwed.

Gene pulled the heavy door shut behind him and turned to Russ, still standing frozen where Gene had shoved him. The young man's eyes were glued to the floor; his hands were clenched in front of him. If the kid had a weapon, he wasn't ready to draw it yet.

"Drag that one to the back," Gene said, waving his knife at Diane's still body. At Gene's command the boy sprang into action, shoving his hair back. Stan got her first glimpse of his eyes. They were terrified. Which was a lot better than maniacal. Finally something that could work out to her advantage, if she played it right.

Russ grabbed Diane by the armpits and dragged her across the floor, the strain showing in his biceps. He wasn't a large boy, and Diane had to be 140 or 150 pounds.

"Gene. Tell me you didn't . . . . you killed Carole."

Gene refocused on her. "You stupid city girl. Don't know how it works round here, do you? They woulda let it be after too long. Nobody cared about her, anyway, really. Nobody but me, an' she was too stupid ta see it all this time. Her boy here finally could see what she was about, too. Knew he could count on me, instead."

"Her . . ." The light went on in Stan's brain, and she didn't like the view. "You're Carole's son," she said to Russ. If he really was Carole's son, his name would be Adam. Had Gene given him an alias?

No response from him, but Gene shook his head vehemently. "He's *my* son. He had no use for her. She sent him away! Sent him away and I never even knew he existed."

His son? The last piece clicked into place. Maybe too late. His hatred for Carole was so apparent that Stan felt it spilling over to encompass her.

"So that's your son and Carole never told you? Adam. Is his real name Adam?" Out of the corner of her eye she saw the kid react to his real name. She was right. The validation filled her with dread.

"That's what *she* named him. Course I couldn't call him that 'round here, what with everything going on. People would be thinking the wrong thing. Buncha busybodies. How'd you know that, anyway?" He moved forward, faster than she thought he was able.

Stan shrank back, held up her hands in what

she hoped was a soothing gesture. "You haven't seen him in a long time, your son. You must have missed at least twenty, twenty-two years? I can see how that would make you mad." She held up her hands and spoke soothingly as her eyes darted around, looking for something, anything, to help her. "No one would blame you for that."

He frowned at her and motioned to the back of the room. "Twenty-three years, you want the real number. And he needed me. He . . . he's been sick. I coulda helped him." Gene looked at him again. His son didn't seem to hear him. Gene shook his head and turned back to Stan. "Over there. Sit. At the desk."

Diane's desk, in the back of the room against the cement wall. That little alcove was as good as putting herself in a grave. She needed to stay out here, where she could make a break for the door or window. As it was, she was nearly backed against the wall. She reached in her pocket to feel for her keys. Still in there.

Her brain kicked into action. This was, on some level, like the CEO problem she'd faced at Warner. Like her former president, Gene had done a bad thing and she had to make up a good story out of it. If she could get him to believe her, she might be able to get out of this.

She didn't want to think about how she'd gotten fired for failing last time. Hands in front of her, she stood firm. "Carole took advantage of you, didn't she, Gene? What happened that day? Tell me so I can help you tell your story."

"'Help'? What help? I don't need no story. They're gonna say what they're gonna say anyway.

Won't matter that I didn't mean ta do it. She just made me so mad, and that damn needle was in her hand . . . . how was I s'posed ta know what was in it would kill her?" Gene's eyes flared at the memory, and he refocused on Stan. "It don't matter. We just gotta get you outta the way, then me and my boy'll be fine. We'll get outta this town and go live the life we never got to live." Adoration filled his gaze as he watched the boy, still struggling with Diane's weight.

"What kind of life were you supposed to live, Gene?" Stan glanced at the boy, who took great care to tuck Diane's legs and arms in the right position. Almost like she was being laid out for a viewing. Out of the corner of her eye, she saw a dog leash hanging from one of the chain-link runs behind her. She inched back, half a step at a time. The kid was the wild card, but she'd have to take her chances.

"We never got the chance to find out! That rotten mother of his kept him from me! His whole life. I missed everything." Hysteria blurred the edges of his voice. His hands shook as he tried to wipe his eyes. "Until now."

She moved fast. Took two steps left, grabbed the leash, wrapped it around her hand. Made sure the metal piece that clipped on the collar was at the other end. She leaped forward, using the leash like a whip, hearing a satisfying *clang* as it connected with the knife. Gene bellowed as his knife clattered to the cement floor. She dove for it, praying the kid wasn't diving for her. Her hand closed around the blade itself and she felt it slice into her palm, but she hung on and bolted for the door. Cursing the gravel that cut her feet, she yanked her keys out of her pocket. And stopped in front of her car.

The driver's-side front and back tires were slashed, leaving her car at a lopsided angle. With no means of escape.

"Run somewhere!" the voice in her head screamed.

But where? The park was just as scary, and Gene had the home court advantage. She may have gotten his knife, but he probably had others.

His truck. If the universe was on her side, it would be open and the keys would be in it. She whirled and ran to it, yanked the door handle. Locked. She slammed her hand against the door, spattering blood. Cursed at the pain that shot through her hand. Now what?

The barking increased as the dogs out back worked themselves into a frenzy. And then she remembered. The boy was afraid of dogs. Even Gene's mild-mannered pooch, he'd told her once. If her pursuers came face-to-face with a yard filled with pit bulls . . .

Gene appeared on the step, shouting something she couldn't make out. Stan dropped against the side of the truck and peered around. When he turned to shout something else to the boy, she made her move.

Stan sprinted back to the building and pressed flat against the concrete, inching around to the gate leading to the dog area. She heard Gene's awkward shuffle as he pursued her, dragging his bad leg. She hoped the boy was with him. As she got closer, the dogs got louder. She unlocked the gate and dove in. Hit the ground and rolled into a crouch. A stampede of rushing paws came at her. She braced herself, channeling her grandmother with all the strength she had. If there was ever a time she needed the abilities of an animal whisperer, it was now. The dogs' breath grew hotter as they approached, panting, excited, finally getting to be part of whatever action they had been hearing.

Then Stan felt a sloppy tongue on her face. Not teeth. She opened her eyes to see a massive pit bull face in front of hers. The brown dog. The leader. Henry. He remembered her, or maybe it was her treats. Whatever the reason, the dog kissed her again and charged out of the gate, his pals all behind him. A canine SWAT team. Her heart swelled with gratitude. Now she could get to her phone and call for help.

"Go get 'em, guys," she whispered, and ran to the gate. They followed her as if they had understood and took off around the corner, right into the building, their barking a cacophony of reproach.

Stan raced out of the pen to her car. She fumbled her way inside, dug around in her purse and found her phone. Called 911 and relayed as much of the story as she could; then she ran back inside, stopping short in amazement.

Her friends had done their job. Gene and Russ/Adam were in one of the empty dog runs; the boy was crying and shaking. Gene attempted to quiet him. The dogs waited in a semicircle around the door, barking and growling like any good watchdog would do. In the corner Diane had struggled to a sitting position, holding her head. Stan ran to her.

"Are you okay? I called for help. You should stay there. You might have a concussion."

Diane looked at Stan. Her face was pale, her eyes black. She took in the dogs and their captives. Stan's torn suit, her bare feet and bloody hand. She slumped back and shook her head, wincing. "You get here and this town goes straight to hell," she muttered.

Two state police cars blared into the parking lot, lights flashing. Stan ran outside and threw up her arms, waving frantically as they rushed in. Lou led the pack.

"Wait! Don't scare the dogs. Everything's under control," she called.

Lou drew up short at the maniacal barking coming from behind her. "Doesn't sound like it's under control!" But he held up a hand behind him, warning his fellow officers to hang back.

"Carole's killer is in here. The dogs have him cornered," she said. "Cover the back end of the dog run. I'll put the dogs back in their pens."

"You will?" Lou looked doubtful, peering over her shoulder.

"Yes. Just get ready to arrest them, will you? And take this."

She handed Gene's knife to Lou, still covered in her blood from the cut on her hand.

"Are you hurt?"

"I'm fine."

Lou looked like he didn't believe her, but he used a napkin from his pocket to pick up the weapon. Stan heard him tell one of the other troopers to call an ambulance.

She used the treats Diane kept on her desk to tear the dogs away from their prey and get them into their runs. They weren't as effective as Stan's treats, but the dogs were more than willing to eat them, anyway. Once they were safely locked up, Lou and his sidekicks swarmed in and pulled Gene and Russ out of the dog run. Lou handed them off to his fellow officers and turned to Stan.

"Your hand is bleeding. You should go to the hospital."

Stan looked down at her hand. It was a superficial slice. She hoped. She took off her suit jacket and tied one arm around her hand.

Lou gaped at her. "You're gonna ruin that."

"It's fine. Take care of Diane first."

"The EMTs are here," Lou said. Two guys came in with a stretcher and went to Diane.

"Wait!" Stan said, remembering why she'd come to the pound in the first place. She went over to where they were loading Diane onto the stretcher. "Where's Scruffy?"

Diane looked pained. "He made me call and leave you that message, before he bashed me over the head. I don't have her. I'm sorry."

That was enough to take the elation out of knowing the murderer was behind bars. Stan blinked back tears and turned away. Then she felt a hand on her shoulder.

"You all right?" Lou asked. "Other than that hand?"

She shrugged.

"You lose your shoes?"

Stan had almost forgotten about her bare feet. "I think it's safe to say this whole outfit is a loss. I can't wait to throw it away."

Lou shook his head. "C'mon, I'll drive you to the hospital. We'll get that hand stitched up."

Chapter 29

"I had to keep it quiet. Otherwise, the whole thing would've been blown."

Nikki and Stan sat in Izzy Sweet's Sweets drinking iced lattes. Scruffy was curled up at Stan's feet. The dog rarely left her side after Lou rescued her from Gene's house after his arrest and Stan had officially adopted her. It was two weeks to the day after Carole's murder, less than a week since Stan's escapades at the Frog Ledge Dog Pound. The shop was filled with people. More locals, Stan noticed. Maybe the good word was spreading.

"A puppy mill sting operation. Who would've guessed?" Stan shook her head. Nikki's silence and suspicious actions hadn't had anything to do with Carole Morganwick. Instead, Nikki, Diane Kirschbaum and Perri Galveston had been working to take down a horrible puppy mill right here in Frog Ledge. The owners were breeding pit bulls and selling them to known dogfighting offenders. It still bothered Stan that Nikki had been so secretive with her, but at least it had been a noble cause.

"So you knew the woman we busted?" Nikki asked.

"Mrs. Graham." Stan shook her head. "I met her at the farmers' market. I should've known from her winning personality."

"And her stinkin' son," Izzy said, slapping a tray of pastries in front of them. Junior, Gene's dog, followed at her heels. He'd gone to live with Izzy, Bax and Elvira while his owner awaited his fate. "Boy, do they steam my broccoli."

"'Steam my broccoli'?" Stan giggled. "I've never heard that. Sorry." She sobered at Izzy's dirty look. "Come sit, Izzy."

"Her son—Thurman, how's that for a pretentious piece of scum?—was the ringleader, but she happily took the profits. It was an awful place. A couple of those dogs in the pound were hers. Amazing how friendly, right? The big brown one Diane saved by having a kid pretend to buy him for fighting, so we could be sure." Nikki picked up a warm chocolate chip cookie and took a bite. "This is amazing."

"Those dogs were awesome. I was thinking of adopting Henry, the brown one. I swear he saved my life."

"You should adopt him. Scruffy needs a playmate." Izzy reached down and ruffled Scruffy's curly hair, earning a lick on the hand from the schnoodle. "Those people are scum. They should rot in jail. Thank you for stopping them, Nikki. Free coffee forever!" Izzy pushed the plate over. "And cookies, of course."

"We'll have to see what happens. They seized

the rest of the dogs and filed charges. That's all we can do right now." Nikki licked her fingers. "I can't believe you thought I was a killer, Stan. Jeez! It's kind of flattering, though."

"'Flattering'? You idiot. What was I supposed to think? You were acting weird. And plotting with Diane. I was just wrong on what you were plotting."

"So it was Carole's scorned lover. What a shocker!" Nikki shook her head. "These guys are such clichés."

"Yeah, but what he did to that child." Izzy shook her head. "Tragic. And the boy was already a mess. He built that explosive, you know. The one that destroyed Carole's clinic and hurt Trooper Pasquale. Some kind of homemade bomb that worked pretty well, I'd say."

Stan nodded. Cyril had been putting out daily editions of the *Holler* as the story unraveled. He'd gotten a lot of the details from Carole's brother. "That's why Carole had left town. She knew her son had problems, even when he was a kid. And Gene was married, so she'd never told him about the baby."

Stan tried to remember all the details that had broken loose like a tidal wave after Gene's arrest. Carole's brother had actively tried to get help for his nephew in the early days. But the boy's mental illness had been a constant struggle, until he couldn't keep up with it anymore. Eventually Carole shut him out and disappeared with the boy. She'd kept her married name, Cross, until returning to Frog Ledge a few years ago.

"So he got in trouble and she figured his real

father was her last hope to get him some help?"
Izzy sighed when Stan nodded.

"But he didn't take the news so well."

"What happened to the kid, now that he's in
jail?" Nikki asked.

"Hospitalized while they figure out what's
wrong with him and what to do about it."

The three women were silent, pondering that.
Through the window Stan saw Jake outside.
Duncan was on a leash today, sitting on the sidewalk while Jake talked with someone. She was
happy to see both of them, even if it was through
a window. She had some meals for Duncan in her
bag. When she was done with her friends, she'd
go see them.

"Well, at least you're off the hook for the
murder," Nikki said. "And you're really over corporate America? I'm still reeling from that."

"I told you, I turned the job down." Stan
smiled. Bernadette had been shocked.

"Get out," Izzy said.

"Never thought I'd see the day," Nikki said.

"I expected that from Nikki, not you," Stan said
to Izzy. "Why are you so surprised? You barely
know me."

"Honey, I'm observant. You seemed lost when
you got here."

Izzy was right. It had been just over two weeks
since Stan showed up in town. She had been
adrift and trying to hide it until she could get
back what she thought was her identity. Today she
felt like a different person—a person who didn't
belong in corporate America. She would stop
groveling at their feet for them to take her back.

She was ready for a new identity.

"Well, congratulations. About time. And you got rid of the corporate jerk of a boyfriend, too. That's even better." Nikki high-fived her.

Stan hadn't talked to Richard since the ill-fated night she'd caught him with Michelle. He hadn't called, either, which she found telling. And sad. But liberating, too. It was truly a new day. Theme song: *"We Are Never Getting Back Together."*

"Guess what else I did." Stan leaned forward, elbows on the table, and grinned. She felt light, free, like a kid telling secrets with her friends. "I told Sheldon Allyn to stuff it."

"You what!" Nikki squealed.

"I did." Stan sat back, proud of herself. "He heard about Cyril's story about the poisoned dogs and took his offer back. Then he changed his mind back when everyone realized no one was poisoning dogs, least of all me. But it's too little, too late, in my mind."

Izzy dropped her head into her palm. Nikki looked devastated.

"What was the real story about the dogs?" Izzy asked. "I'm still afraid to put Bax and Elvira out in the backyard."

"Didn't you read Cyril's story?" Stan pulled it out of her bag. She'd been keeping it with her as proof since he'd printed it three days ago, exonerating her of the alleged poisonings. Duncan had literally eaten himself sick when he'd discovered a truck-load of rotting food a local cafe had thrown out during his trip to Stan's house that morning. And Mrs. Graham had lied about one of her dogs being sick after hearing about Duncan, mostly to

divert the heat coming down on her own head.
Phineas Dobbins' mother had panicked when she'd
put the rumors together with a tummy ache the dog
was suffering from. He'd since gotten the all clear
from the emergency vet. No conspiracy theory. And
no dog murderer. All was well in Frog Ledge again.

"Do you have any idea the PR ops for Pets' Last
Chance you just destroyed by turning down Sheldon Allyn?" Nikki demanded, but she smiled.

Stan spread her hands. "Sorry, but I don't care.
I'm done working for other people."

"So what's the plan, Stan?" Nikki grinned. "I
love when I get to say that."

"I'll cook for animals, but I'll do it my way." She
already had a name for her new business: Pawsitively Organic Gourmet Pet Food. And one recur-
ring customer: Char and Ray's dog, Savannah.
They had never wavered in their support of Stan,
despite the ugly rumors, and Stan had no doubt
they'd have other customers flocking to her door
in no time.

Izzy looked impressed. "So tell us about it. And
sign me up for weekly treats!"

"You're already on the list. I haven't nailed
down exactly what the business will look like yet,
but I'll figure it out." She smiled. "I've got time."

Kneading to Die Recipes

Stan's Apple-Cinnamon Appetizers for Dogs and Cats

1 large Macintosh apple
1/4 cup organic raw honey
1/2 cup of water
1/2 teaspoon cinnamon
1 cup organic rolled oats
1-1/2 cups spelt flour
1/8 cup spelt flour

Directions:
Preheat oven to 350° F (180° C).

Core, slice and mince the apple (or use a food processor). In a large bowl, combine the apple bits, honey, water, cinnamon, and oats. Gradually blend in the 1-1/2 cups flour, adding enough to form a stiff dough.

In a small bowl, add the 1/8 cup flour. Spoon the dough by rounded teaspoon onto ungreased baking sheets, spacing about 2 inches (5 cm) apart. Using the bottom of a glass dipped in flour (to prevent sticking), flatten each spoonful of dough into a circle—or make them into your pet's favorite shape. Make them as large or small as you choose.

Bake for 30 minutes. Remove from the oven and flip each cookie to brown evenly on both sides. Reduce oven temperature to 325° F (180° C). Return to the oven and bake for an additional 30 minutes. Cool before serving.

Makes about 3 dozen. Freeze a portion for later.

Nutty's Cheese-y Treats

3/4 cup shredded or grated cheddar cheese
3/4 cup organic spelt flour
1/4 cup plain Greek yogurt
1/4 cup organic polenta
5 tbsp. grated parmesan cheese or parmesan-flavored
  rice topping

Preheat oven to 350 and prepare a cookie sheet with organic cooking spray. Combine all ingredients in a bowl and add water if too dry. Knead the dough into a ball, roll it out to 1/4 inch. Cut into 1-2 inch pieces and bake for 25 minutes.

Scruffy's Comfort Cookies (adapted from a vegetarian, IBD-safe recipe)

1 cup organic spelt flour
3/4 cup oat bran
1 cup rolled oat
2 tsp baking soda
1-1/2 tsp ground cinnamon
1 tsp ground nutmeg
1 tsp ground allspice
1 cup organic butter
1/4 cup brown sugar
3/4 cup cane sugar
2 tblsp molasses
1 egg
1 tsp organic vanilla

Preheat oven to 300. Mix flour, oat bran, rolled oats, baking soda, cinnamon, nutmeg and allspice in bowl. Set aside. In a larger bowl, beat butter and sugars until smooth. Add molasses, egg, vanilla and blend. Add flour mixture. Use cookie scooper or spoon to transfer to ungreased cookie sheet. Bake for 15 minutes or until brown.

**Here's an exciting sneak peek of
Liz Mugavero's next
Pawsitively Organic Mystery!**

The chain saw appeared out of nowhere, its wide arc narrowly missing the top of her head.

The revving sound filled Stan Connor's ears, loud as a swarm of attack bees surrounding her. She caught a flash of the blade, sharp and silver in the moonlight as it swung. She thought she may have screamed, but she couldn't be sure. She dove for the grass, still clutching her Pyrex containers of bat- and pumpkin-shaped doggie treats she'd spent the last two weeks baking. A fleeting thought ran through her brain: *Does it hurt to be decapitated?*

Then the buzzing noise ceased abruptly. Behind her, Brenna McGee, her new assistant, burst out laughing. Stan risked a glance behind her. Brenna was bent over at the waist, covering her mouth with her hand, silent laughter rocking her body. The chain saw hung at the side of a figure dressed completely in black, save for the grotesque mask of a face twisted into a scream. A rubber knife protruded from its head. The figure pulled up the mask.

"Thanks for blowing my cover, McGee." The high-pitched voice didn't fit the costume. Stan took a closer look. The boy under the mask couldn't be more than fifteen. He seemed annoyed that he couldn't actually hack someone up in his role.

Brenna wiped her eyes. "Really, Danny? You couldn't scare a pack of kindergartners." Both their eyes turned to Stan. Brenna reconsidered. "Well, she's not in kindergarten. And does your mother know you're out here with that thing? Bet she doesn't."

Brenna reached for the containers of treats and Stan's bag of party goods. Luckily, everything had survived the fall miraculously unscathed. If they hadn't, she may have had to use the chain saw on him, since she'd spent the last two weeks baking the darn things.

The boy hung his head, the chain saw drooping by his leg. "I was just playin' around. Trying to get people amped for the maze. Don't tell my mom, please? She gets, like, mad about stuff like that." Danny shifted from foot to foot. The mask slid halfway down over his face again. "You okay, miss?" he asked Stan, still sprawled in the dirt listening to the exchange.

Stan got to her feet, brushing her jeans off with her free hand. Despite the fact that seconds ago she'd thought she was going to lose her head, she had to hand it to the kid. Once upon a time, Stan had been queen of Halloween pranks, and she couldn't help but admire a good one. Waiting at the dairy farm gate—when people weren't expecting to be scared—was clever. "I'm fine. But aren't the Halloween props supposed to be *in* the corn maze?"

In addition to their dairy farm duties, the Happy Cow owners also had acres of corn, which they turned into a maze at the end of the season. Some people around town whispered they were doing it for the money, that things had been tough for the Hoffman family in recent years. Stan was still too new to Frog Ledge to know if that was true or not.

"Danny was never good at following directions." Brenna winked at him. "I used to babysit him."

Danny rolled his eyes. "Like, a million years ago. Want me to take you guys—uh, ladies—inside?" Now that he'd stepped out of character, he'd reverted back to being gentlemanly.

"I think we're okay." Stan glanced at Brenna for confirmation. Brenna nodded. Stan turned back to Danny. "I wouldn't want to take you away from your post. I bet people won't be expecting you. Or your chain saw," she added, eyeing the machine dubiously. "You should at least remove the chain first."

"So you gonna tell Mom?" He jumped from foot to foot, teenage adrenaline raging.

"Just go put it away before you actually slice someone up by mistake." Brenna shook her head. "We'll go find your mother. We have to set up for the doggie party." She looked at Stan.

"She's in the house." He pointed. "And thanks!" He took off running, the weight of the chain saw dragging one side of him down, giving him a monster-like moonlit shadow.

Stan looked at Brenna, who shrugged. "The Hoffmans have always been a little crazy. Emmalee's sweet, though. It's Hal and the kids you have to worry about, clearly. We should get set up. The maze opens soon. Wait till you see it. It's getting way better every year."

From her house, two doors away from the farm, Stan had watched the transformation with the same excitement she'd had as a kid heading to the scariest haunted house. The Happy Cow Dairy Farm's innocent-by-day atmosphere had been transformed into a Halloween junkie's dream. Illuminated figures lit up the yard every few feet, from witches to ghosts to scary scarecrows to arched-back black cats. Even the roof of the barn, where the dairy cows stayed, had been draped with glittering cobwebs and enormous spiders.

Off to the right, the Hoffmans' farmhouse was strung with purple and orange lights, more cobwebs and evil-looking pumpkin faces, which flashed eerily in the dusk. She loved Halloween. In a family of people who were Christmas types, she'd always been the odd one who adored getting scared senseless. Aside from the ad hoc chain saw at the entrance, of course.

It was the height of the Halloween season—two weeks before the main event. The crisp fall air had settled over their small Connecticut town, and the leaves were brilliant with color. *It's true. Nothing compares to fall in New England*, Stan thought.

"You're gonna go through the maze later, right?" Brenna was clearly itching to partake in the festivities.

"I'd love to. We'll have to see how the party goes first." Stan checked her watch as they made their way to the farmhouse. "Is this really the town's first Halloween costume doggie party?"

Brenna turned back to Stan and arched an eyebrow. Before she could respond, a ghost popped up off the grass and screamed at her. She and Stan both jumped.

"Oh, cool! I haven't seen those since I was a kid." Stan stopped to admire the ghost, which immediately dropped to the ground in preparation for the next unsuspecting soul who stepped on the booby trap.

"They're really going all out this year. Anyway, you think people had doggie parties around here before?" Brenna's tone indicated Stan would be a fool if she replied affirmatively.

"Well, why this year?"

"Because every dog around here loves your treats, and Emmalee has a fenced-in area that's perfect for a doggie party." Brenna waved in the general direction of the house. "Benny is psyched, I'm sure."

Benny was the fox terrier guest of honor. His parents, Nancy and Jim, had contacted Stan a few weeks ago, doing serious due diligence on the prospective costume party. Emmalee had offered her fenced-in yard for a nominal fee, and they had asked Stan to cater.

Stan was thrilled to oblige. She'd just started getting her new business, Pawsitively Organic Gourmet Pet Food, off the ground. A party was a great way to get exposure, and it gave her a chance to get Brenna involved. Aside from working nights and weekends at her brother Jake's bar, Brenna studied political science by day and harbored a secret interest in animal nutrition, which she satisfied in any spare free time she had.

"Plus, I think it really is true . . . that Em needs cash." Brenna lowered her voice as they neared the house. "Hal's at the bar almost every night. Jake had to shut him off a couple of times, and I think he just goes somewhere else after that. He's really giving Em a run for her money."

"That's too bad." Stan had never met Hal. She'd seen him around town here and there. Emmalee worked at the farm pretty much nonstop. She also took their goods to the farmers' market, did home deliveries of their milk and kept an eye on the other local farms that operated under the Happy Cow name. Now she was renting out her yard, too. If the stories were true, Stan felt sorry for her.

She followed Brenna up the porch steps. The old Lab, who always hung out on the porch, barked halfheartedly from inside. A minute later, Emmalee yanked open the door. Describing her appearance as "frazzled" would be putting it mildly. Her brown hair seemed even more shot through with gray than the last time Stan had seen her. The long hours of physical labor the farm demanded of her had caused Emmalee to lose weight—but not in a muscle-gaining good way. The sound of a crying child wafted out at them from another room.

"Hi, ladies, come on in." Despite whatever was going on, Emmalee managed a smile. "I had Danny set up some tables for you out back for the party. Nancy and Benny are out back. Jim went to get some pooper-scooper bags."

"Ah, can't run out of those." Stan smiled. "How are you, Emmalee?"

Emmalee shrugged. Behind her, the shrieking child got louder. "Doing fine, doing fine. Have you seen Danny, by the way? He told me he'd do tickets for the maze, and it's darn near opening time."

Stan and Brenna glanced at each other. Brenna cleared her throat. "He, uh, went to the barn for a minute. He said he'd be right back. Do you need help with Chris?"

Emmalee glanced behind her, toward the sound of the child, fatigue slipping into her eyes. "I suppose so. Hal was supposed to take him out, all dressed up, to scare people in the maze. All the actors should be in their places by now. We have some scary things in there this year, we do. But Hal hasn't come home yet." She sighed. "So, yes, if you want to entertain Chris for a while, I'd sure appreciate it. I have a couple things left to do before I shut the barn down for the night."

"I'll do that and meet you outside," Brenna told Stan.

"Come on, I'll take you out." Emmalee led Stan out back. Inside, the child finally stopped crying. Emmalee looked up and crossed herself. Stan could see the lights from the corn maze ahead. She wondered if Danny had put the chain saw away before manning the ticket booth.

"Benny is dressed up like a bumblebee. He's none too happy about it, either," Emmalee confided. "But the other dog owners promised they'd dress up their dogs, too."

"I'll make sure Benny gets special treatment as the host," Stan said as Emmalee unlatched the gate and they stepped into the yard. Benny, a chunky black-and-white dog crammed into a hideous black-and-yellow-striped ensemble, lumbered over to them. The headpiece with the antennas was sliding forward.

"Benny! Your antennas!" Benny's owner, Nancy, equally crammed into her jeans and knitted pumpkin sweater, chased him and stooped to right his headpiece. "He's having trouble keeping it on," she said, standing up and thrusting a hand at Stan. "So nice to meet you finally. Benny is so excited!"

"I'm so glad," Stan said. "I'll set up the treats and the prizes I brought for the games. You can pick out Benny's first, since he's the host."

Nancy beamed. "Let's do it. Before Nyla gets here." She wrinkled her nose.

"Nyla?" Stan asked.

"The poodle from down the road. She competes with Benny for everything." Nancy rolled her eyes.

A bark sounded from the front, followed by a ringing doorbell. "Excuse me, I'll go let the guests in," Emmalee said. "Stan, set up however you want." She hurried back inside.

"Okay, so here's what we have. Benny, you want to see?" Stan set her bag on the table and began unloading. "These are some new chews that I picked up. All natural, from a local farm." She held one out for inspection. Benny immediately snatched it and dashed under the table.

"Ben-Ben! Manners!" Nancy sighed. "What kind of chew? He likes it."

Stan hesitated. Some people got freaked out

when she told them it was a cow trachea. But the reality was, it was the best treat for a dog. Rawhide was junk in comparison. Before she could answer Nancy, she heard shouts from out by the corn maze. Both women turned in that direction. Benny continued to eat his treat. Emmalee returned with a man holding a boxer on a leash. They both paused when they heard the shouting, now joined by screams.

"What's all that ruckus about?" Emmalee asked, shaking her head. "If that boy is up to something again—"

"Mrs. Hoffman!" A girl dressed as a sexy vampire with a stake in her heart ran up to the fence. "You've gotta come right now. To the maze. Something's happened to Mr. Hoffman."